Escape to Redemption

Escape to Redemption

Peter M. Parr

Winchester, UK
Washington, USA

First published by Roundfire Books, 2016
Roundfire Books is an imprint of John Hunt Publishing Ltd., Laurel House, Station Approach,
Alresford, Hants, SO24 9JH, UK
office1@jhpbooks.net
www.johnhuntpublishing.com
www.roundfire-books.com

For distributor details and how to order please visit the 'Ordering' section on our website.

Text copyright: Peter M. Parr 2015

Quotations used in Chapter 21

The quotations on Kogut's study wall, "Nothing real can be threatened" and "Nothing unreal
exists" are from the Introduction to A Course in Miracles (Text, Introduction 2:2-3). All quotes
from A Course in Miracles are from the Second Edition, 1996, © Foundation for Inner Peace, P.O.
Box 598, Mill Valley, 94942-0598, www.acim.org and info@acim.org.

ISBN: 978 1 78535 227 0
Library of Congress Control Number: 2015958689

A CIP catalogue record for this book is available from the British Library.

Design: Stuart Davies

Printed in the USA by Edwards Brothers Malloy

We operate a distinctive and ethical publishing philosophy in all
areas of our business, from our global network of authors to
production and worldwide distribution.

Acknowledgements

To my mum, Eva, for her insights which proved so valuable to me in developing my characters and for her support throughout the many years I worked on this book.

To members of the Tonbridge writers' group, Westminster Quakers writing group, and all those who offered comments and suggestions on earlier drafts.

Chapter 1

The man with the orange face

December 2003

Josie runs out to the road. The street is spinning and with each step her knees feel like they'll give way. She reaches the BMW. Freezes. Snaz has the key and he's still inside the house.

A light goes on in an upstairs window. A neighbour might have heard. Josie's hand trembles as she crouches by the car, trying to steady herself on the ground. She's wearing black, but someone might see her face, her hair. She tries the car door, forgetting it's locked. All she can do is wait for Snaz, but there's nowhere for her to hide.

She can't go back to the house for him. When she ran from the living room, Rook was on his knees, crouched beside the young man. 'He's dead. You've killed my boy.' And everywhere there's blood. The moment she fired reverberates in her mind.

She hears a clattering sound – a can rolling on the pavement – and, in the shadows, makes out someone coming. She stiffens upright, her brain says run, but panic keeps her rooted to the ground. This pure fear she's known once before.

It's too late, the man's seen her. His dog strains at its leash and jumps at her, makes her stumble against the car. 'He won't hurt you,' the man says. 'Don't be frightened. He's a big softy like me.' He's smiling. His face is orange. They're standing under a light.

Josie raises her hand to hide her face, but he's already seen her. 'Nice motor,' he says as the foul-smelling beast climbs her legs. She tries to push it off her and fumbles in her bag, pretending to search for the key.

'Come on, boy.' The man yanks his dog's lead. 'The pretty lass doesn't want to talk to us.' At last he's going, still watching her over his shoulder. She's clutching her phone, but there's no one she can ring for help. And her boyfriend is still in there with Rook. He should have followed her. Why is he still in the house?

A new dread engulfs her. Rook saw her shoot his son. He's going to go to the police. To stop him, she approaches the house again, scared even more than the first time and wishing she still has the gun. Her steps become shorter, more hesitant, on the gravel path that splits his weed-ravaged lawn.

Rook's front door is wide open. Did she leave it like that? Paralysed, Josie stands outside the porch, too frightened to go further, but unable to turn back. The police might already be coming. *Or what if…?* The thought sends cold lightning through her body. When she dropped the gun, did Snaz pick it up or did *Rook* get to it first? She peers into the hall and calls to Snaz, but her voice is a whisper, she barely hears herself. And then comes the shot – like a firecracker exploding inside her head. Snaz is tearing towards her and before she can think or move he seizes her arm and they're running, she's too scared to check if they're being chased. He aims the key at the car, but the locks don't release. Again he presses it – she wants to grab the key from him and try it herself – until at last, the click. She heaves the door open, crashes into the passenger seat and the car's already moving as she pulls the door shut. At the street corner by the pillar-box is the man with the orange face. He's seen her. He knows.

The glare of the headlamps reflects in the wet tarmac. They pass Kilburn tube station, an off-licence, a fish-and-chip shop being locked up. Josie can hear her heartbeat above the engine.

How can it be so easy to kill someone? One startled reflex, that was all. Her eyes fix on her hands and she tugs at the fingers of her gloves, at the white cuffs of fur, but the leather seems glued to her skin. She rips them off inside out and tramples them under her feet.

'Is Rook dead?' she asks Snaz.

He doesn't answer though, and when they come to red traffic

lights he doesn't slow down.

'Stop,' Josie manages. 'The cameras!'

From the top deck of a night bus a man looks down at them, and she shields herself from his stare. The signals take forever to change.

She notices a mark on Snaz's jacket. 'Your arm.' She points. Not one stain, but many, spattered all down his sleeve.

Snaz follows her eyes and studies the leather. 'I can't see anything.' He flicks the light switch. 'Where, Josie, where?'

'I thought I saw blood. Turn the light off.'

Finally he accelerates and the spots move, shadows cast by drops of water on the windscreen. Outside, a supermarket trolley lies abandoned by the roadside, and signposts point to Hampstead, Finchley Road and the West End.

By a bus shelter Snaz slams on the brakes. Josie pitches forward and catches the dashboard. She isn't wearing her belt. He launches himself from the car, and for a second she doesn't know what's going on until he hunches by the post and is sick.

She leans over to beg him to hurry up and, in the door pocket, spies the gun. Hide it. But where? She glances about the car, opens the glove compartment and remembers too late not to touch the weapon with her hands. There's nothing to wipe it with. Snaz keeps the BMW like a shrine. She pulls off her scarf and rubs it clean. Holding it, even through the material, makes her whole body crawl. They have to get rid of the gun.

When Snaz sits next to her, his face is alien. Beads of sweat glaze his dark olive skin. 'I had no other choice,' he says, in a voice that isn't his. 'He saw you kill his son.'

She stutters. 'No one else was meant to be there. You told me Rook lived alone.'

'I said we shouldn't go there, but you didn't listen to me.'

She has no answer and then he turns away. It's the worst silence she's endured since she was three years old, hiding under her bed from the man who was hurting Mummy, and no longer hearing her screams.

Perhaps a minute later, or it may be only seconds, two women step into the street. Arm-in-arm, they cut across the road. One wears a loop of tinsel like a garland round her neck. Josie watches through her fingers, hears the click-clack of their heels as they pass. The sound of their laughter makes her shrink.

When they've gone, Snaz touches her arm. 'It'll be okay, yeah?'

How can she tell him she's been seen?

'If we stick together,' he adds. She feels his hand shaking and he returns it to the wheel.

Josie watches the drops on the windscreen, the shops lining the street, and all the time knows the man will remember her. He spoke to her right outside the house. All she can think is that she has to get away, immediately, before he goes to the police. 'Drive,' she says. 'Take me home.'

Chapter 2

Josie

August 1998

Snaz stopped by the iron gates, twice his height and coated with anti-climb paint. Trafalgar Lodge. With its four-columned porch and circular drive, the house could have been transported there from Hollywood. It didn't surprise him to find the side gate locked. He pressed the button on the intercom and waited for a response, beginning to doubt why he'd come. He had no chance with a girl like Josie. Except, she'd phoned him and invited him here. She wouldn't have asked him round if she had no interest in him at all.

A crackle, then Josie's voice: 'Hello. Yes?'

'It's Snaz.'

'Oh, hi.' He heard a buzzer and the side gate glided open.

Snaz checked his reflection in the polished plaque that had the house name embossed on it. He did up the top button of his shirt, then undid it again...it looked stupid done up without a tie. *This feels like going for a job interview,* he thought as he walked up the drive.

The door opened and there stood Josie in tight jeans and a white silk blouse, dressed down but even more achingly gorgeous than he remembered from the club.

'Thanks for coming.' She gave him a peck on the cheek, ducking away before he could kiss her back. 'Did you find it easily?'

'Yeah.'

'I expected you to be driving.'

Snaz had parked round the corner when he'd first seen the house. He hadn't wanted Josie to see his cheap old Ford. 'I fancied a walk,' he said. 'It's good to get some sunshine after all the rain.' Here he was on Josie's doorstep, talking about the weather, nervous like some spotty kid on a first date.

'Are you going to come in?' she asked.

'Sure. Nice car.' He nodded towards the Mercedes.

'My mum's. Speak of the devil,' she whispered.

A woman bore down on them. 'Who are you? Have you come to read the meters?'

'His name's Snaz,' Josie introduced him. 'We met at a club.'

Snaz held out his hand, but Josie's mum didn't take it. She merely frowned.

'Come on,' Josie said to him, starting up the stairs.

'Excuse me!' Her mum's tone reminded Snaz of his English teacher at school. 'Where exactly do you think you are going?'

'Up to my room.'

'To your bedroom? With a man?'

'I'm eighteen now, Mummy. I can do what I like.'

'Not while you live under this roof, young lady.'

'Maybe it'd be better if we went out?' Snaz suggested to Josie. He didn't feel comfortable here, never mind Josie's mum.

'Why? This is my house as much as hers. If I want to have a guest round, it's none of her business.'

'Wait until your father hears you brought home a man.'

By now Josie was halfway up the stairs and all Snaz could see of her were the frayed legs of her jeans. 'Yes, you tell him. What's he going to do?'

He found himself left in the hallway, alone with Josie's mum. Pale and brittle like a figurine, one gentle push and she'd topple over and crack.

'I hope you know what you're letting yourself in for,' she said to him, before flicking her head and beating a retreat down the hall.

Snaz caught up with Josie at the top of the staircase.

'Sorry for my mum's comment about reading the meters. She's a bit of a racist, I'm afraid.'

'Is that what it is?'

'My mum and I share a mutual antipathy. When I go up to Oxford next month I'll be out of her hair and she won't need to worry. You look shocked, Snaz. I bet you're really sweet to your mother.'

'I never see her,' he said.

'Really?'

'She... It's a long story. My aunt brought me up.'

Josie looked like she might say something, but didn't. After a pause she went into her bedroom. 'Make yourself at home,' she told him, closing the door and then perching on the chair by her dressing table. He marvelled at the clutter of perfumes and make-up bottles.

Snaz saw no chair to sit on, only her single bed. He meandered to the window and looked out onto the back garden. 'You've got a tennis court!'

'Do you play?' she asked.

'Never have.'

'Pity. I'd have given you a game.'

Snaz kicked himself for missing out on a chance to see her in a skimpy tennis outfit. 'I play football,' he said, the first thing that came to him. When she showed no interest, he changed the subject. 'Is that photo of your dad?'

Josie nodded.

'You get on better with him than with your mum?'

'He's alright, when he's actually here. He's always off on business trips. The States, usually. I think he's in Poland this time.'

'What does he do?'

'He runs his own business putting buyers in touch with sellers. Sometimes it's property. Sometimes it's art. I don't think he cares too much if there's money in it. One day he might stop and enjoy what he has.'

Snaz groped for something else to say. He noticed a higgledy-piggledy stack of CDs on the chest of drawers and was about to ask her what music she liked.

'I wanted to thank you again for what you did,' she said.

'That's okay. Anyone would have done the same.'

'Not anyone would have seen that man spike my drink. I'm lucky you were watching me so closely. I saw you.' She smiled.

Snaz felt himself blush. 'You've got to be careful in clubs. Some blokes try anything.'

'It's my friend's fault for dragging me there, then leaving with the first man she set eyes on.'

'Did you get home okay?' Snaz asked.

'You saw me into a cab.'

'I mean, you felt alright, did you? You weren't shaken up?'

A lock of her hair fell across her face and she brushed it to one side. You couldn't call her a redhead, but her hair was redder than blonde. *There must be a word for hair that colour,* Snaz thought.

'Is it true what you told him, about being a boxer?'

Snaz smiled. 'I've boxed as many times as I've played tennis. He didn't know that though. But I can handle myself. I could've dealt with him.'

'Why don't you sit down? I want to ask you something. It's kind of a favour.'

He sat on the edge of her bed.

Josie picked up a birthday card from her dressing table and held it out to him. She had tiny dainty hands. 'What do you make of this?'

He pulled his eyes away from her to the picture of a kitten, all fluffy fur and ribbons. Sickeningly cute.

'Read inside.'

Happy birthday. From Erin, a friend. Call me if you want to know the truth. And underneath, the sender had written a phone number. 'Who's Erin?' he asked.

'That's the thing. I haven't a clue. I rang her, and she wants to meet me. She says there's something I ought to know, but she can't tell me over the phone. Her accent is ghastly, like she finds it too much of an effort to pronounce her t's.'

'It sounds dodgy. What'll you do?'

'*Dodgy*,' Josie repeated, and Snaz wondered if she considered his way of speaking ghastly as well. 'That's what I thought. Will you come with me, to go to meet her? I'm going on Saturday.'

'Sure. I mean, if you want me to.' It sounded odd; not exactly a date, but at least he'd see her again.

* * *

They had a job to find the cafe, off the main road between a halal take-away and a laundrette. A woman in her forties stood up, gaping at Josie. *Mutton dressed as lamb* was the first thought that came to Snaz's mind.

'Are you Erin?' Josie asked.

The woman kept on staring. 'You're such a likeness.'

'Are you going to tell me who you are?'

'Won't you sit down?' asked Erin. 'I have to sit – my legs have gone all like blancmange. I can't get over it, to finally see you. I've been working out what I'd say. And now you're here I don't know how to start.'

The waitress came over.

'Have something to drink, Josie. My treat. What can I get you?' Erin asked.

'Espresso.'

'We don't do espresso,' said the waitress. 'I can do you black coffee or white.'

'Black,' said Josie. 'Actually, whatever. I'm not staying.'

For a moment, Erin glanced at Snaz. Prior to that, she hadn't acknowledged his existence. 'Can I get you something too?'

'I'm alright, thanks.' He sat back from the table and wondered where to suggest to Josie they go next. The cinema? Hardly original, and he wanted to look at *her* and not a film. For a meal?

He doubted she'd be impressed by any place he knew or could afford. Camden Market? What could interest her there? Maybe if they simply went for a walk in Finsbury Park he could see if she'd let him put his arm around her. Start slow and romantic.

'I bought you a birthday present. I'm sorry it's two weeks late.' Erin fumbled in her tiger-skin patterned handbag, pulled out a Spice Girls CD, and left it on the table when Josie didn't take it. Snaz stopped himself laughing. 'You don't like it.' Erin's rasping voice faltered. 'I'm not sure what kind of music you're into.'

'How did you know it was my birthday?' Josie asked her. 'Who are you anyway? Why did you write to me? And why are you giving me a birthday present when I've never met you before?'

'Josie, you don't remember me, but we have met. Your mum and me were best mates.'

Josie stared at her gaudy make-up, at her suit a size too small. 'Mum and *you*?'

The woman reached into her furry bag again and took out a see-through plastic wallet with a newspaper cutting folded inside it. Snaz wondered at her claw-like pink nails as she pointed to a picture on the yellowed page.

Josie shrugged, but not before Snaz saw her flinch. 'So you've got a picture of some woman who looks a bit like me,' she said. 'So what?'

Snaz leaned forward to see. At first he thought it *was* Josie's picture: the pout, the raised cheekbones, most of all her eyes. He found it creepy. 'More than a bit,' he said.

Josie cast him a look.

'Read what it says,' Erin begged her. 'Read the article, please.'

Snaz watched Josie scan the cutting. Her lips parted. Then she put the paper down. 'Why are you showing me this?' she asked Erin. 'What's it got to do with me?'

'Lucy was your mum, Josie. Your real mum.'

. Josie looked at the photograph. Then at Erin. Then at the

photo again.

'You don't remember, do you? You were barely three when she died.'

'You're lying.'

Snaz picked up the cutting. *Girl, 3, hides as mum is stabbed… PM speaks of shock… Police were called to the prostitute's Finchley flat by a neighbour who heard shouts… …arrived to find the victim dead… …multiple stab wounds to her body and…*

Josie snatched the article, tried to rip it up, but the plastic wouldn't tear. 'I've got a mum. She may not be much but at least she isn't a whore.' She spat the last word and stood up. 'We're going. I don't have to listen to these lies. Are you coming?' Then, a split second later: 'Fine, don't,' she said before Snaz could reply.

The slamming door rattled Erin's empty cup and saucer on the table.

Snaz studied the photo. It could have been Josie's eyes staring back at him, and he knew Erin wasn't lying. *Murdered: Lucy Snowball, 23.*

Erin's eye make-up had started to run. She struggled to pluck a paper napkin from the rack on the table and ended up pulling out three. 'Are you Josie's boyfriend?'

The question caught Snaz off guard. 'Sort of.'

'Go after her... Wait.' Erin touched his hand. 'I didn't mean to upset her. But don't you think she has a right to know?'

Chapter 3

A bad day

Breakfast in the morning room at Trafalgar Lodge. The first time since her birthday that the four of them had sat round a table. Josie stabbed her grapefruit. She'd never really belonged here.

The man who she'd thought was her dad sat hidden behind the business section of *The Telegraph*. Joseph Davenport. She'd have to get used to calling him Joseph. If she listened carefully, she could hear his lungs expand and contract.

The woman she'd thought was her mum dissected a croissant. Beatrice had never shown her any love, and now she understood why.

Nathan stirred his coffee. She did still think of him as her brother. After the initial shell-shock, she'd wondered if they could have had the same parents, a fleeting hope among the thousand thoughts swirling in her mind. But there'd been no mention of a baby brother in the newspaper cutting Erin had shown her. It didn't mean they hadn't adopted him too though. And if they had, he had a right to be told, just as she did. Better it all came out.

'A bad day for the dollar,' said Joseph.

Covering his mouth, Nathan yawned.

Beatrice nodded to him for the marmalade. 'I think this week I might go to Fortnums,' she said.

Her husband turned the page of his paper.

'I know your secret,' Josie said.

Nathan put down his coffee cup.

Beatrice stared at her.

Joseph folded down his *Telegraph*.

Josie looked from one pair of eyes to the next. She took a sip from her orange juice. Finally, she said it: 'Who were my real parents?'

'What do you mean?' said Joseph. She could tell he knew it sounded pathetic. 'Who have you been speaking to?'

'I know about Lucy.' Josie gave Beatrice a sideways glance. 'My *real* mum. What about my real dad?'

'I am your dad, Princess,' he said.

'Don't lie to me. I'm adopted. I want to know the truth.'

'What about me?' Nathan asked. 'Am I adopted too?'

Beatrice rushed to comfort him. 'No, darling, of course not. You're our son, our natural son.' She turned for a second to Josie. 'I'm sorry you had to find out from someone else, but they obviously haven't told you everything. You're not adopted, not technically. Joseph, it's time you told her the whole story. You've left it far too long.'

Joseph stood and approached Josie. He crouched besides her, looking into her eyes, and tried to put his arm around her. He smelled stale. She'd never noticed that before.

'Come now, Princess. Come with me.' He took her to the next room, half carrying her, sweeping her along in his arms. Then he closed the door and came to sit next to her on the couch. 'Josie, listen to me. I promise you, I won't lie. I am your father. Beatrice isn't your mother, you're right about that. But I am your natural father.'

'How can you be?'

He sighed. 'I had an affair...with Lucy. You're mine, Josie. I've had the tests done. You're my daughter and I love you and what you've found out doesn't have to change a thing.'

He leaned to put his arm around her but she raised a hand, stopped him coming nearer. 'It said in the paper... It said she was a prostitute.'

'She was your mum, Josie.'

'How *could* she be a prostitute? If I'm your daughter, how could you *let* her? After I was born.'

She wanted him to explain, to tell her that the truth she was piecing together wasn't true at all; that she'd got it wrong; that he'd loved her mum; and that the stupid newspaper article had it wrong too. 'Oh, Josie,' was all he said.

'Why did she need to do that? Didn't you give her money to support me? You let my mum sleep with other men. You let that happen. With me in the same flat.'

He shut his eyes for a long moment. 'How can I explain to you? I gave her... I *offered* her... I didn't know she was doing that. That's the honest-to-God truth.'

'Don't touch me.' Josie stood up, away from him. 'Don't even come near me. You let my mum become a whore.'

'It's not so simple.' His voice sounded higher, pleading. 'There's more...'

Josie shook her head. 'You've lost any right.' She felt she'd faint or throw up if she stayed in the same room with him any longer. 'You *aren't* my dad.'

* * *

'I had to tell someone,' Josie said, when she'd finished telling Snaz. 'Both your parents left you, didn't they? How can parents leave their kids? He said Mum had been too proud to accept money from him, but he should have made her. And if he'd cared about me at all he'd have known what she was doing and stopped it.'

'I'm sorry,' Snaz said.

'Don't tell me you're sorry. I'm sick of hearing *sorry. He* said he was sorry. Like *sorry* makes it better. My mum *died* because of him.'

'I don't know what else to say,' said Snaz. 'I can get why you hate him.'

'I want to kill him,' she said. 'If he died, I wouldn't care.'

Snaz took her hand. It felt good, him gripping it. She felt wanted. Safe.

'So what happened after that?' Snaz said. 'After he admitted it?'

'I packed some stuff. I'm staying with my friend. I'm meant to be going up to Oxford in a couple of weeks, but I don't think I can. *He* wants me to go. I feel so flat.'

'Can I help? Can I do anything?'

'You're doing enough by just being here. Listening and not...'

'Not what?'

'Taking advantage.' She forced a smile. 'Just...be my friend.'

Chapter 4

The test

September 2003

Snaz lay back, head on his pillow, basking in the warm afterglow of ecstasy. Josie's head rested on his chest, her breathing in time with his. He loved these moments, probably as much as the sex. They stayed like this for only a minute, even less. But then she rolled off him and got out of the bed.

She always did this. Upped and left straight away. And every time he said nothing. But today he felt braver, brave enough to challenge her. She couldn't simply leave when it'd been so perfect; when being together felt so right. 'The world won't end if you stay the night with me,' he said.

She scooped her knickers from the floor and slipped them on, then scanned the room for her bra.

'I said the world won't end if you stay the night.'

She found it on the other side of the room, caught in a clinch with his T-shirt. 'I can't,' she said.

'You mean you don't want to.'

'I prefer to sleep in my own bed.'

'Is it the bed, or is it me?'

'It's *me*,' she said, meeting his eyes for a moment as she grappled with her bra strap.

'Do you love me, Josie? You never say you do.'

A pout, no smile. 'We've just made love.'

'That's not what I asked.'

'People use that word all the time without knowing what it means. Someone told me only four percent of people even know what real love is.'

Snaz propped himself up on his arms. 'Four percent? They have a statistic for love? Who told you that? I bet it was

Henderson! And I suppose he claims to be one of that exclusive four percent. I suppose he knows the secret?'

'It doesn't matter, Snaz. Forget I said it.'

'Pete bloody Henderson. Love guru! So what did he say?'

'He said a couple of things.'

'Like?'

'He said to love someone means to care about them so much that you value their happiness as much as your own.'

'I do,' Snaz cut in. '*More* than my own happiness. Value yours.'

She stopped in the middle of zipping up her skirt.

'Why do you think I don't complain when you go off with Henderson?'

Josie went over to the mirror and brushed her hair into place with her fingers. Snaz gazed at her as though for the first time: the small of her back, the perfect curves of her bottom, her delicate size three and a half feet. She had her gold anklet on today, her latest new favourite piece. Why did she even need jewellery? There wasn't an inch of her he would change.

Men would kill to be her boyfriend, Snaz thought. He should be content. And yet it wasn't enough for him any more, to play a bit-part in her life.

'There's another thing,' she said, still with her back to him. 'It's the test for whether you love someone...'

'*His* test.'

'You'd be prepared to let them go and wish them well if they'd be happier with someone else.'

Snaz regretted starting this conversation. If he pushed her too much he risked her leaving for good. But he had to know where he stood. 'Would you? Be happier with someone else? Would you be happier with *him*?'

She came and perched on the side of the bed. 'Honey. Darling.' She stroked his hair. 'I care about you. We have fun together, don't we? But I want to be free and not tied down.'

He turned his head away from her.

'What do you want from me, baby?' she asked.

'Five years we've been seeing each other. It was five years last month. I want you to commit to me. We don't have to get married. But I want us to be together – to live together. And I wish you'd stop seeing Henderson.'

'You're jealous?'

He couldn't believe she sounded surprised. 'Of course I'm jealous. When you spend half your time with him.'

'We've been through this. I thought you were cool about it.' She moved her hands to her lap. 'He's a friend, nothing else. I don't sleep with him.'

'You don't *sleep* with me. Not literally.'

'I told you before. He can't do it. And even if he could have sex, I don't like him in that way.'

The problem with dating an actress was he could never tell if she was lying. 'So what do you see in him? If you don't fancy him, and you don't have sex?'

'I told you, he's a friend.'

'There must be more to it.'

'He listens to me. He makes me feel good. It's difficult to put into words. He accepts me and doesn't try to change me. He doesn't mind that I'm with you.'

'I can't help being jealous. I'm a normal man, not some holier-than-thou yoga instructor who reads *The Guardian* and drinks green tea. But I do love you. I don't care what Henderson says. And I'd do anything for you.' He thought about what he'd just said. 'That's a better definition than anything he can come up with.'

Josie stood up and grabbed her blouse which had landed on the arm of the chair. 'You wouldn't though. Do anything for me. I asked you to help me and you wouldn't do it.'

Snaz's heart plummeted. Now he *really* wished he hadn't said anything. A month had gone by and he'd started believing –

hoping – that what she'd asked had only been a drunken whim. 'Josie, that's not fair. That wasn't a reasonable request.'

'Why not reasonable? You have contacts. You'd know who to ask.'

'I *used to* have contacts. I don't want to go back to having anything to do with those people.' *I ended up in prison last time,* he almost said.

'All I'm saying is if you wanted to, you could.'

'But the whole idea is crazy.'

'No, Snaz. Crazy is me knowing what happened to my mum, and Curtis Rook's part in it, and doing nothing. I'm not asking *you* to do anything. I'm only asking you to help me get a gun.'

Chapter 5

Escape

December 2003

Josie shut her eyes, but when she opened them she was still with Snaz in the car, the smell of his puke in the air, her gloves on the floor by her feet.

Finally they reached her apartment. Snaz pulled up next to her Mini, startling her when he turned off the engine and took the key from the ignition. If he came up to her flat, he wouldn't leave, and he'd ask her questions she couldn't answer. Besides, she had no time, she had to get away. 'I'll call you tomorrow,' she said.

Before she could get out of the car, Snaz opened the driver's-side door, and the icy air hit her like a slap. 'We *killed* two people.'

In her mind, Josie saw an image of Rook's son lying on his side, no longer moving. He had a child's face, the fine shadow of a moustache. How old could he have been? Seventeen? Maybe younger. A nauseous feeling rose inside her, and she thought she might throw up. 'I need time on my own to think.'

'Are you saying you want me to go?' Snaz said.

She almost told him about the man with the dog, but stopped herself. If Snaz knew someone had seen her, he'd panic and he might do anything. 'The gun. You need to get rid of the gun.'

'I can do it tomorrow.'

'You can't leave it in the car. What if someone finds it? Please, Snaz, get rid of it now. Somewhere far away.'

At last he nodded.

'I'll phone you,' she promised, pushing open the car door.

He leaned across, seized her wrist and clenched it so tight it hurt her. 'If I hadn't shot him…' He said nothing more, but she got his message: *I did it for you.*

By the door to her apartment block, Josie checked over her shoulder. *Please don't let him come after me.* She dropped her key as she hurried to fit it in the lock.

Inside, Josie went straight to the bathroom to wash her hands. For a minute or more she held them under hot water, scrubbed them with soap and brush until they felt raw. Then she tore off her coat, her black roll-neck top and trousers, bundled them all into the washing machine and set the programme to the highest temperature, not caring if the clothes ended up ruined. She'd never wear those clothes again.

She desperately wanted to shower, but she hadn't time. Going to her bedroom, she scrambled into the first warm clothes she laid her hands on – a cashmere sweater, jeans – then dragged a suitcase from beneath her boots and ski gear in the wardrobe and lifted it onto her unmade bed.

Her head swirled with one desperate thought after another. She had to leave the country, but where to go? She had no plane ticket. Could she simply turn up at the airport and get a flight? There'd be none, anyway, not until the morning. But if she waited until then, it might be too late to escape. She had no real friends left who she could go to for help, nobody she could rely on. And she had no intention of calling her dad.

Maybe if she drove to Dover and caught a ferry, it'd be safer, faster, than getting a flight. But what then? Stay in France? She knew no one there and didn't speak any French. Head for Spain? If the witness identified her – and by the way he'd stared at her she had no doubt he remembered her face – even that wouldn't be far enough away.

Josie realised that she might be leaving for ever. She became still, took in the room: her own modelling photos on the wall, the clothes in her cupboard, far too many to take with her. This was her home.

Feeling faint, Josie resumed packing. Her black velvet dress she couldn't part with, her silk *Dolce and Gabbana* blouse she had to take too. As she folded it in the suitcase, it suddenly struck her as ridiculous to be worrying about clothes. She'd killed someone, someone barely older than a child. Maybe she deserved to be caught. Maybe she should hand herself in? Josie dismissed the thought. He'd run at her with a knife. If she hadn't shot him, he would have killed her.

She pulled a fleece from off its hanger, the mauve one she'd worn last spring the day she'd climbed Snowdon with Pete. She paused, thinking of how Pete *had* been a real friend. How different things would be if she hadn't split up with him. Josie realised in that moment she'd made a huge mistake.

* * *

The guard at the border crossing studied Josie's passport photo, then fixed his eyes on her. She'd grown her hair longer since her year at drama school when she'd had the picture taken, reverted to her natural copper blonde. Another soldier paused in front of her Mini and she flinched when she noticed the gun hanging from his belt.

The barrier rose and Josie put her foot down. *Too fast.* She eased off the gas pedal, certain the guards must be watching her. Even when she could no longer see the border point, she continued to glance in the mirror, terrified by a vision of flashing blue lights, not yet daring to believe she was safe. She cursed each lorry that slowed her down. Overtaking one, she cut back into her lane with a second to spare to a blaring cacophony of horns. The speedo showed over eighty. *Cool it,* she told herself as her car pitched about on the uneven road.

Half an hour from the border, Josie began to feel less tense. When a sign showed another four hundred kilometres to Warsaw, she resigned herself to stopping somewhere for the night.

The highway kept on straight and unrelenting, hemmed on

either side by louring forests of pine. Josie started to doubt if she should be running to a foreign country she'd never been to and leaving Snaz to cope on his own. But she had no alternative. The man with the dog might already have gone to the police. She imagined detectives at this very moment ringing the bell at her flat.

A shining halo appeared from out of the mist... A petrol station. Exhausted, Josie turned into the forecourt, stopped the car and closed her aching eyes.

The cashier observed her through thick-rimmed glasses as she set the red plastic basket in front of him.

He transferred his gaze to her shopping and in slow motion passed the packet of chocolate coated currants over the scanner, and the *Diet Coke,* and the bacon baguette. He yawned, covering his mouth with her street map of Warsaw still in his hand. 'Which number petrol please?'

Josie hadn't noted the pump number when she'd filled her car. 'It's the red Mini.'

In Polish, he read out the total, then yawned again as if he was the one who'd driven across three countries in a day.

She took a fifty-euro note from her purse, hoping that would cover it, but the cashier shook his head.

'No take euros,' he said.

Josie felt helpless. She'd forgotten to get any money on the Polish side of the border. After seeing the guard with the handgun, she'd been so anxious to get away.

'Zlotys only,' he repeated. 'Or you can use card.'

If she used a card to pay, the police would be able to trace her. She saw the man behind her in the queue growing impatient, a CCTV camera blinking above the door. She couldn't leave without paying.

Josie scrawled her signature and waited an eternity for him to process the payment.

As she slunk to the door, she smelled the aroma of coffee and noticed a man by the magazine stand, drinking from a Styrofoam cup. She approached the drinks machine, tried to work out which of its buttons to press. *Herbata. Cacao. Kawa z mlekiem* must be coffee with milk. She pressed the button marked simply *kawa*, but the machine returned her two-euro coin.

Outside, her eyes welled as she returned to her car. She hated Poland, she'd already made up her mind. She grasped the cold metal of the door handle and sat shivering inside.

A tap on the glass made her jump and she saw the man who'd been drinking a coffee, holding out a cup.

His stubbled face looked coarse, but not threatening. He gestured to her to lower the window.

She did, only a fraction.

'You want coffee?' he said, holding out a cup.

Her mind told her to be careful, not to take the risk. But the pull of the coffee won out. With one hand on the key, she lowered the window further, enough to take the drink.

'You need zlotys?' he asked. 'You want sell euros? Or Great Britain pounds? I give you good rate.'

She rested the cup between her legs. She was still holding the fifty-euro note, scrunched in her hand. She passed it through the window and he unfurled it and held it up to the light.

'Only fifty? You don't want change more?'

Josie stayed silent, scared that if she gave him more money he'd make off with it and give her nothing back, or cheat her with the rate – she had no idea how much a zloty was worth.

He filed the money in his wallet and counted out four banknotes. Then he reached into his pocket and she heard the rattle of change.

'Why you come to Poland?' he asked, giving her the zlotys, standing back from her car.

Josie readied herself to drive off. 'I'm visiting my boyfriend in Warsaw.'

The man's smile returned. 'It's long way to Warsaw. You want stay in hotel? Come, I show you good place.'

Chapter 6

Flat 418

The border guard ordered Josie from her car. Inside the boot, he found a bulging bin liner. When he made her open it, Rook's son's arm slumped out and brushed against her leg.

Josie jolted awake, her heart pummelling her rib cage. A nightmare. Only a nightmare. But as her eyes adjusted to the dark motel room, it began to sink in. Apart from the ending, the rest of it was real. She had killed someone. A person was dead because of her.

By five AM she'd had enough of tossing and turning on the mattress. She pulled off her sweat-drenched nightdress, gathered the few things she'd unpacked. In the lobby, the receptionist was snoring at his desk. Josie had to cough to wake him to pay for her room.

It took her six more hours to reach Warsaw and another of driving around in circles to find the address where Pete was staying. She knew his aunt, Dorota, lived in a flat, but she hadn't pictured a twelve-storey-high concrete tower block, the lift out of order with a handwritten note taped to its door.

Josie heard footsteps on the stairs below and glanced over the banister to see a gangly man in a bearskin hat bounding up the steps two at a time. Resting her suitcase on the grimy landing floor, she stepped aside for him to pass.

He said something and before Josie could stop him, he seized her case.

'What are you doing?' she protested when he began to make off with it. All the things she needed were inside that case.

'Ah, English.' The man turned round, smiling through his bushy moustache. 'I have sister in England, in Swindon. Do you know town Swindon? Beautiful place. Which floor you go to? I hope not all the way to top!'

'I think it's this floor, thanks.' Josie caught up with him, reclaimed her luggage.

As he held the hallway door open for her, she had the thought that he wouldn't be so willing to help if he knew what she had done.

A real Christmas tree leaned against the wall outside flat 418, its branches tied up with string. Josie had forgotten it was that hypocritical time of year.

The doorbell gave a shrill sound. A dog barked in the opposite flat, and at the far end of the dimly-lit corridor, another yelped in support. Josie put her ear to the door – could she hear people talking? Perhaps Pete had noticed her car parked outside or spied her through the peephole. She'd been kidding herself, thinking she could turn up here and Pete would take her in as though they'd never broken up. She remembered what she'd said to him – over three months ago now – when he'd rung her, wanting still to be friends: 'I don't think so, Pete. I believe in clean breaks.' She hadn't meant to sound mean, but Snaz had been with her, listening in.

She jabbed the bell again, wondering what she'd do if he didn't let her in. She dreaded another night alone in a hotel. She'd almost given up hope when the door opened.

The young man who stared at her had to be Pete's cousin. He had a chubbier face than her ex-boyfriend's and wiry hair – dark the way she liked it, but the family resemblance was clear.

'Hi.' Josie mustered the airline-stewardess smile she'd perfected at drama school. 'Is Pete in?'

He stood with his mouth ajar, as if he had a cold.

Perhaps he didn't speak English. 'Peter Henderson?' Josie asked again, peering around his shoulder.

'He's out.'

She spotted Pete's favourite moss-green sweater on the coat

rack. 'I'm Josie. Are you Adam?' Pete had mentioned a cousin Adam: "If we ever get married," he'd said once, testing her reaction, "I'm going to ask Adam to be my best man."

'Marcin,' said the boy. The younger cousin, then. She detected resentment in his voice.

He had one hand in the pocket of his tatty jeans, the other wrapped round the door.

'Marcin, would it be alright if...? Can I wait here for Pete until he's back? I've driven from London and I'm shattered. I need to talk to him, to apologise,' she added, speaking up so Pete would hear her if he was only pretending to be out.

'Moment,' he said, disappearing inside behind another door.

The dogs kept barking, aggravating her headache. She wished someone would make them shut up. Josie hauled her cappuccino *Prada* suitcase into the hall, left it beneath the coat rack and closed the front door.

She found Marcin standing by the television, speaking to an older man who she presumed must be his dad. No sign of Pete.

The man rose from his armchair and his newspaper fell disordered on the worn parquet floor. 'Hello,' he said, coming over. 'I'm Grzegorz. It's the same like Greg in English.'

'Josie.' She accepted his hand. 'I'm... I'm a friend of Pete's.'

'How do you do, Josie. I'm pleased to meet you. My goodness, you're shivering. Will you drink a tea?'

'I'd love a coffee, please,' she replied, surprised by his good English. She'd have to be careful what she said. She held her hands together to stop them shaking, conscious of Marcin watching too.

'Put the kettle on,' Greg instructed the boy. 'Do please sit,' he said, removing a pile of newspapers to make space for her on the orange-brown patterned sofa, a relic from the seventies with sponge showing through its threadbare arms.

After so many hours of driving, Josie had no desire to sit, but she feared he might think her rude.

'Josie is short for Josephine, yes? Like the wife of Napoleon.' Greg took one of the chairs from the table and sat facing her, tapping his bony fingers on his knees. He wore a grey tracksuit top and shiny trousers; sandals and no socks. She cringed at his scaly milky-yellow toenails. 'So what are you doing in Warsaw? Do you have family here too?'

'Um, no. I've come to see Pete.'

Greg stared at her wide-eyed, like his son had done when he opened the door.

She regretted not inventing a better story. She'd come all this way simply to see Pete? 'We used to be more than friends,' she said. 'I've always wanted to visit Poland. It sounded so nice when he spoke about it.'

'Peter didn't tell us you were coming.'

'He doesn't know. I wanted it to be a surprise.'

'He doesn't expect you?'

'I'm crazy like that. Impulsive.' Crazy was right. She realised how mad an idea it'd been.

Greg brought his chair up closer to her. 'So, are you planning the long stay in Warsaw?'

'I guess that depends on Pete.' All she wanted was to lie down, to close her eyes, and for her throbbing headache to go away.

But Greg kept talking. 'My wife makes pizza for dinner. Will you stay to eat with us?'

'I'd love to, if it's okay.'

'Dorota makes good pizza,' he said, as though he'd misunderstood. 'I'm sure they be back soon. Peter is helping her to carry the shopping.' He gazed at her the way men of a certain age often did: with that look of forlorn admiration. 'I didn't realise he had such good taste.'

She smiled for a second, before dreadful reality seized her again.

'Is something the matter?'

'I'm hot. It's too hot in here.' She scrambled out of her leather coat.

'Oh, let me take that for you.' He went to the hall and hung it on the rack over Pete's sweater. Spotting her suitcase, he asked, 'Where are you staying?'

'I don't know yet. Is there a hotel nearby?'

Greg didn't hesitate. 'Hotel? Don't be silly. You can stay here with us.'

'Really, can I?'

'You're Peter's friend.' He sat next to her on the couch this time. He didn't move the TV guide and it crumpled under his weight.

She edged along the seat to make more space for him and tried to keep from looking at his toenails. Cobwebs covered the lampshade. A rubber plant on the windowsill cried out for water. In silence, they stared at the TV... The news, Josie shuddered when she realised. What if they reported about her? Showed her photograph? 'Can I use your bathroom?' she asked, her heart setting off yet again.

'Of course. It's at end of the corridor.' Greg called after her, 'Pull the light above the basin. The main light doesn't work.'

Josie found the bathroom engaged. She could hear water guzzling down a plughole and made out Marcin's silhouette through the frosted glass.

Not wanting to return to Greg in the sitting room, she stepped into the kitchen. She saw cups and plates stacked in the sink and next to it, a slab of half-rolled dough on the worktop.

A photo stood on the windowsill: Marcin as a child with a striking boy several years older than him, whose deep brown eyes drew her in. Josie picked up the frame.

A footstep on the sticky floor made her start and she turned to see Marcin behind her, his hair combed back and glossy. He hadn't been wearing aftershave when he'd opened the front door.

His eyes fell on the picture in her hand.

She put it back on the shelf where a faint line in the dust marked its place. 'Who's the guy with you?' she asked.

'My brother Adam,' he said.

So that was Adam. If he'd been in his late teens in the picture, it'd make him about twenty-five now, going by Marcin – a couple of years older than her.

Marcin opened a cupboard, took out a glass, then put it back and picked a less cloudy one instead. He dropped in a teabag and filled the glass from the kettle before she could stop him to say she wanted coffee. 'You have it with milk or with lemon?' he asked.

'Milk.'

She moved out of his way so he could get to the fridge.

'Sorry,' he said. '*Nie ma.* Mama gone to buy some.'

He opened the cupboard again and she pressed herself back against the worktop. He put a sugar bowl next to the tea and rinsed a dirty spoon.

Josie was about to escape to the bathroom when the dog started barking again. She heard people outside the flat: a woman, and Pete's familiar voice, and braced herself as the front door opened.

'Hello, Pete,' she began.

Chapter 7

Deserted

'Hi, it's Josie. I can't speak to you now, so leave a message after the tone and if I like you, maybe I'll call you back. Ciao.'

Snaz clenched his phone. Why wasn't she answering? He'd lost count of the messages he'd left on her mobile, on her landline, and of all the texts he'd sent. 'Where the hell are you? You can't expect me to handle this alone.'

A teenage couple walked by, wrapped in each other's arms. Snaz needed Josie with him. He wanted to hold her and to have her hold him and tell him it would be okay; that they'd help each other through this, and no one would find out what they'd done. He knew he had to act as normal, but how, when he couldn't eat a sandwich without throwing up, when his body felt like he'd drunk poison? And Josie had gone away.

His head would explode if he didn't talk to her. It'd been her plan to go to Rook's house, her idea to take a gun. Now he wanted her to tell him where to dump it. Surely it must be safer to throw it off the pier here in Southend than to leave it in a bin where someone might find it. But he wanted to check with Josie first, so they could decide together what to do. She shouldn't be leaving it all to him.

Snaz passed Adventure Island, completely deserted and all its rides still. He looked at the pier, his gaze following its long promenade. He could barely make out the end of it in the mist, a mile from the shore, where the sky became one with the sea.

The young woman at the pier kiosk called after him, 'Wait, you've forgotten your change. It might never happen,' she said, giving him some coins. He stared back at her and the smile went from her face.

The walkway looked even longer than it had from the shore. He remembered the excitement of coming here as a boy, walking on the longest pier in the world. It'd always been sunny when Grace brought him here. Grace! She'd been more like a mum to him than an aunt. He shuddered at the thought of her finding out he'd killed a man.

Him, a murderer. He'd stood next to his own friend's dad and fired a bullet into his chest.

He should never have gone with Josie to Rook's house, or even got her a gun. He'd tried to talk her out of going through with her plan. Couldn't she see it was crazy?

But she'd shone her cobalt eyes at him. 'My mum would be alive if it wasn't for Rook.'

'But Josie, Rook couldn't have known that man would attack her.'

'Are you serious? How can you defend him? He took her money. He had a duty to protect her. He's no less guilty than if he'd killed her himself.'

'Perhaps we should wait though. I'm not sure he trusts me yet.'

'What do you mean, he doesn't trust you?'

'I've got a bad feeling about this. I don't understand why it has to be tomorrow.' He wanted more time to convince her to see sense.

'It has to be. If you won't help me, I'll do it myself.'

She meant it too, he could tell from her face. If he let her go to Rook's house on her own and something happened to her… His eyes traced the veins on her delicate hand. 'Okay, we'll go there together, but why do we need a gun?'

'I want him to admit he was responsible.'

'And then what?' Snaz asked her.

The boiler clicked in the kitchen as the central heating fired up. 'I want him to feel the same fear my mum felt.'

Snaz saw two figures ahead of him on the pier, like apparitions, mere outlines of an adult and child. He stopped as the mist closed around them. He didn't believe in ghosts.

He transferred his sports bag to his other hand, feeling sick again at the thought of the weapon inside it. Behind him, he saw no one. Perhaps he could throw the gun over the side from here. He went up to the railings, but realised he was still too close to the shore, not half a mile from the beach. When the tide went out, you could even walk this far.

They had only meant to frighten Rook, nothing more. Josie had promised him. But despite that, she'd made him load the bullets in the weapon. 'What if Rook turns violent?' she'd said. 'If it's not loaded, I won't feel safe.' But he was there to protect her; and Rook had MS and needed a stick to walk. Snaz's heart sank lower. He knew Josie had hated Rook enough to want him dead.

The cold reached right into Snaz's bones. He'd thrown his jacket in a rubbish bin, along with all the other clothes he'd been wearing that night. Josie had bought the jacket for him, and not only the jacket. A week after he'd agreed to get hold of a handgun, she'd left car keys under his pillow: *'A present. A surprise.'* When she'd taken him outside and he saw the silver BMW, ten years old but gleaming like something fresh out of the showroom, he thought he was living a dream.

Perhaps it'd been a bribe and she'd been using him all along. 'That girl is interested only in herself,' his aunt had warned him.

To escape his thoughts, he started to run from the shore.

Snaz heard a coin fall from his pocket onto the deck and froze for a second before continuing, reminded of the moment when Josie dropped the gun. She ran from the house, while he could only stand there paralyzed and watch Rook holding his dead son. Then Rook looked across the room and saw the gun on the floor. His movement towards it jolted Snaz – made him rush to pick it up. Now Snaz wondered if it would have been better if Rook had beaten him to the gun.

Snaz wished he'd done the sensible thing and gone straight to the police. Josie hadn't meant to shoot Dean – Dean ran at her with a knife and she had no time to think. But the police wouldn't believe it'd been an accident, not when they'd gone there with a loaded weapon. If he'd gone to the police, they'd have locked Josie up, and probably him as well. And what about Rook? Maybe he would have come after them, made them pay for killing his son. Ill he might be, but Rook still had a reputation for violence. Hadn't he broken someone's nose once, simply for parking too close?

The man ahead on the pier turned around. Snaz slowed down, took another few steps and stopped cold. The man pointed at him. Or was he only pointing out the fairground to his boy? Snaz held the railing, his hands swollen from the cold. How eerily calm the sea looked, almost like a lake.

Why had no one heard from Josie? He'd tried ringing her brother Nathan and everyone who he could think of. He saw Josie's face in the water and recoiled, stepped away from the edge. She'd promised they'd be together. Nothing else mattered without her.

Remembering something made Snaz calmer: when he'd gone to Josie's flat to look for her, the woman across the corridor heard him banging on the door, and said she'd seen Josie leaving with a case. But if Josie had gone somewhere, why hadn't she called to tell him where?

Crab shells and seagull droppings littered the planks of the pier. Snaz passed under a sign that marked a mile from the shore and ran the last few metres to the shelter. As he reached the wooden hut, a gull flew from the roof, beating its wings.

Snaz watched the bird until he lost sight of it against the shoreline. The buildings on the seafront appeared tiny, the theme park like a model village. No one would find the gun here.

Chapter 8

Pete

Pete walked back out the door without saying a word.

Josie put her tea on the edge of the kitchen work surface. Her instinct told her to go after him, but Marcin and Pete's aunt Dorota formed a barrier in her way. The woman had brought the frost in with her.

'I'm Josie,' she ventured, holding out a hand.

'*Wiem,*' she said, her reply too curt to be a greeting. She passed her basket full of shopping to Marcin and whispered in his ear. Josie sensed she must be telling him about her, warning him off. She obviously knew about her break-up with Pete.

Marcin found a space beside the fridge to put the basket, then left the kitchen, stealing a final furtive glance.

Dorota was short like Josie, but hardly petite. Her nose and cheeks glowed crimson, her eyes cut like emeralds. She levered off her gloves, watching Josie all the while.

'Do you speak English?' Josie asked. 'I want to talk to Pete. To make up with him.'

Pete's aunt took a step forward, making Josie flinch. She picked her glass from the worktop and set it down again further from the edge.

Stealing past Dorota, escaping from the kitchen, Josie found Pete in the corridor outside the flat. He'd taken her suitcase and it stood next to the bare Christmas tree. Even though he had his coat on, she could see he'd lost weight.

'What are you doing here?' he demanded, his voice as stony as his expression.

'I'm sorry.'

'Answer my question!' he shouted above the barking dogs.

In eight months of going out with Pete, Josie had never heard him raise his voice. 'I want to be with you.'

Pete eyed her long enough to make her blink. 'I don't love you. I love someone else.'

She shuddered, but then realised he'd merely repeated what she'd said when she left him. A hollow feeling grew inside her. 'Darling, I didn't mean it.' She reached out to touch his arm but he backed away and stumbled against her case.

'Has he dumped you, your other man? Is that why you've come back?'

'There was no one else.'

'You can't help lying, can you? I'm surprised you never made it as an actress.' The light flickered and they both glanced up at it together. The ceiling had patches where the paint was peeling off. 'You're a fake.'

'Would I be here? Would I have driven from England if I didn't want to be with you?'

'You *drove* here?' His eyebrows rose.

'Two days it's taken me.'

The light flickered again.

'Well, now you can drive back.'

The way he said it, in triumph, stung her as much as the words. He sounded so unlike the Pete she knew. 'I can't go back. I'm in trouble.'

'Trouble? What kind of trouble?'

How could she tell him? She imagined his reaction… He'd be shocked, disgusted. He'd go to the police.

'More lies,' he said. 'You've still got my house keys. I want them back.'

Josie bowed her head. She couldn't think how to convince him to let her stay. 'Your keys are in my case,' she said to buy time.

'Get them.' He nudged the suitcase with his foot. It teetered, then crashed onto its side, sending the Christmas tree toppling to the floor. They stared at the dense tangle of branches.

The fresh pine fragrance filled Josie's lungs as she crouched down, the needles felt prickly in her hands. She struggled to stand the tree upright, hoping Pete would come to her aid, but he folded his arms.

The dogs in neighbours' flats kept barking, the light blinking off and on. 'Let's go somewhere we can talk. We could book a hotel room. The two of us, you and me.'

'I've nothing to say to you,' he said. 'Give me my keys and go.'

Josie didn't have his keys with her but she grappled with her case to get it the right way up, undid the buckles and the zip. If he wouldn't let her stay with him, she had no idea where she'd go.

'Please, Pete, I'm sorry. There were things I wasn't telling you, serious things. I didn't want you to get caught up in them.' When she'd left him, she'd done it for his own good.

'What sort of things?' He uncrossed his arms, shifted on his feet. 'Why didn't you talk to me?'

She noticed Pete's eyes were glazed. 'I'm so sorry,' was all she could say.

'You know what really hurt? Not just you leaving me, but when you said you didn't want to be friends.'

'Let me stay with you. I'll explain.'

His face dropped to her open case, her clothes jumbled inside it. 'You can't stay here.'

'For one night? Your uncle said there's room.'

He shook his head.

'Tomorrow I'll go if you still want me to, and you'll never see me again.'

'Your problem, Josie, is you're so out of touch with your own feelings you don't realise you're hurting someone else.'

'Because when I show my feelings, I'm always rejected. Like now.'

'You could have told me it was over face to face.' He choked. 'I had the hotel booked in Rome, everything. Two hours I waited at the airport. When I couldn't get you on your phone, I was frightened you'd been in a crash. Then I get home and find your message on my answer machine, *dumping me.*'

She'd rung his landline on purpose when she knew he'd be out, scared that if they talked, he'd have asked her questions and made it even harder for them both. 'It doesn't have to be over.'

'After all that?'

Josie shrunk from his unforgiving stare. Nothing she could say would make a difference. She had nothing left to try but walk away. 'You're right,' she sniffed. 'I've no right to ask you for help.' She avoided looking at him, crouched to shut her suitcase. She had to lean on top of it to get the zip to close.

'Good luck, Pete. You're a good man,' she said, wiping her eyes with the back of her wrist. 'I hope you find the woman you deserve.' She began towards the staircase. Two steps. Three. The suitcase jarred against her ankle. She limped on past the flat with the dog. If she reached the stairs and Pete didn't call after her...

'Josie,' she heard him say her name.

Chapter 9

Fourteen years

Herbes de bloody Provence. Snaz walked around the packed super-market, picking up things he didn't want and replacing them on the shelf. His aunt had asked him to buy Herbes de Provence, but how could he when Erin Reason was standing and chatting right in front of the spices.

This is ridiculous, Snaz thought. *Erin won't recognise me after five years.* And even if she did, so what? Doing shopping for his aunt wasn't a crime. He edged towards her, dodging the trolleys and evading the shoppers' eyes. What if she talked to him? If she mentioned Curtis Rook, what would he say?

'You won't guess who else I saw at the reception.' He heard Erin's loud rasping voice. 'Debs! She still works at Preston's, can you believe it? Fourteen years in that job. I think I'd go mad.'

'Fourteen years?' the other woman repeated, shaking her head. 'You wouldn't get that for killing someone.'

Snaz balked.

Erin noticed him. Her eyes were electric blue.

He lowered his head and hurried to the checkouts, not daring to look back. She'd suspect, from the way he flinched. He should have spoken to her, but what could he have said? He clenched his shopping basket with both hands.

The queues at the checkouts stretched all the way into the aisles. Snaz chose one far away from Erin and checked over his shoulder, scanning the crowds in case she was coming his way.

The lady in front of him touched his arm. A black woman, elegant and tall, she drew her trolley back. 'Here, go ahead of me,' she offered. She studied his face as black people often did, confused by Caucasian features that contradicted his dark skin.

'You were here first,' he said.

'Oh, go on. I've got a whole Christmas shop. You only have a couple of things.'

'Thanks.' He moved ahead of her, again glancing round.

'I know,' the woman said.

Stunned, he looked at her.

'Quite ridiculous, isn't it? The week before Christmas and half the tills are closed.'

In the next queue, two children chased each other between the lines of brimful carts, gurgling with laughter like drunken pixies. A man frowned at their mum, who had her face buried in the *TV Times*.

Snaz couldn't figure out why Erin would be shopping here. Didn't she live in Manor House? And why had she stopped in that very spot, by the one thing he needed to buy? *Fourteen years for killing someone*. The words echoed in his mind.

He heard his phone ring above the piped festive music. His aunt again, no doubt. He'd promised to be with her by four.

'Snaz?'

The sound of Josie's voice made him grip the phone tight to his ear.

'Snaz,' she repeated. 'Is it safe to talk?'

'Josie!' He squeezed past the overweight couple at the checkout, abandoned his basket when the cashier shouted after him. 'I left messages. Why didn't you call me back?'

'Sh,' she whispered. 'I put my phone on the kitchen worktop and forgot to take it when I left.'

'Left for where? Where are you?' He bustled his way to the exit, fighting his way through the horde of shoppers. 'I rang your brother, I tried everywhere…'

'It's okay, we're talking now.'

'Speak up.' He could barely hear her. He had the feeling she must be far away.

'I can't talk any louder. People are in the next room.'

'What people?'

'The people I'm staying with,' she said.

'Where are you?' he asked again. Crowds blocked the doorway: people opening umbrellas, carol singers outside. '… Walsall? Who do you know there?'

'Warsaw.'

'But that's…' He stopped. 'That's in Poland! I don't understand. I thought we—' *I thought we'd be together,* he'd have said if she let him finish.

'What did you do with the gun?'

He turned round when she said the word, but no one else could hear. Everyone busy in their own worlds. 'I got rid of it.'

'Where?'

'Southend pier.' Icy raindrops pricked his face. He couldn't remember where he'd parked.

'Did anyone see you?'

'No. Josie—'

'And my gloves? I left them in your car.'

He wanted to say things to her, but she kept on asking questions. 'Everything,' he lied.

'Have the police talked to you?'

'The police?'

'You might have to give a statement, if the police find out you knew Rook.'

'What do you mean, a statement?'

'It doesn't mean they suspect you, but you need to be prepared.'

Someone would tell the police he did jobs for Rook. They'd come for him.

'Are you clear what you're going to say?'

'No, what should I tell them?'

'Think, Snaz! They'll ask when you last saw him. You say – when was it, two weeks ago, Tuesday? – the last time you went to his house on your own.'

His phone bleeped. 'I want to see you,' he said.

'Snaz, listen to me. You've got to stay calm. When the police interview you—'

'Interview?'

'Take a statement. If you're nervous, they'll think you've got something to hide.'

'What if they ask me where I was on Wednesday night?'

'You haven't sorted out your alibi? For heaven's sake! Get one of your mates to say you were with them. Or two people – two is better. What about the friends you go to watch football with?'

'I can't. I go with Matt Rook.'

'Oh, I forgot.' For a moment, Josie fell silent. 'Someone else, then. You have to sort it out before the police speak to you.'

'Can't I tell them we were together at your flat?'

'No!' she snapped. 'You mustn't mention me! We don't know each other – the police mustn't find out about us.'

'Why not? What difference does it make?'

'If you mention me they'll straight away think we did it.'

'I don't get it. Why?'

'It gives you a motive. You worked for Rook, right? And you know what Rook did to my mum. If they find out we're together, you might as well admit we did it.'

The warning tone again: his battery! And then a car honked behind him and he had to jump out of its way – he'd been walking in the middle of the lane.

'Are you in your car?' Josie asked.

'I'm going back to it.' He couldn't remember where he'd parked: he'd driven this way, but there hadn't been any spaces. He walked back the way he'd come. 'Josie, I have to tell you something. Just now in the shop, I saw Erin.'

'Erin Reason?'

'Why today? In my local shop! It's a bad omen.'

'What did you say to her?'

'Nothing, I didn't say anything. But she saw me. I think she knows.'

'Knows Rook's dead, you mean?' she whispered after a pause. 'Is it on the news? It must be. Do the police have any leads?'

'I'm not sure. I haven't watched TV.'

'The papers?'

'I haven't— She'll guess it was us!'

'How? If you didn't—' Josie broke off. 'If you said something to her you must tell me.'

'I didn't.'

'Then how the... How *on earth* can Erin know?'

'I think you should call her,' he said.

'Are you crazy? Call and say what?'

'Check if she... If you were there, you'd understand. Her being in the shop: it's a sign.'

'A sign of what? Snaz, it's a coincidence. Okay, if it makes you happy, I'll ring her.'

'Today?'

'Fine, tonight,' she said.

'What will you say to her?' He stepped in a puddle and cursed as cold water went straight through into his trainer.

She exhaled. 'Don't worry, I'll handle it. You've got to stay calm.'

'After what we did! You talk like nothing's happened.'

She didn't answer.

'Josie, say something. Why are you in Poland? Why have you gone there and left me?'

She didn't reply.

'Are you still there?'

'It's okay,' she said finally. 'Nobody's left anyone. Listen to me. Rook was an evil man.'

Snaz remembered chats he'd had with Rook, about Arsenal, about *Top Gear*. 'He was my mate's dad. I can't sleep, I can't think straight. Every time I close my eyes, I see his face.'

'I can't sleep either,' Josie said.

'You can't?' Hearing her say that made him feel less inadequate.

'Honey, we'll get through this. You had to do what you did, we both did, and now we need to stay strong.'

The warning tone bleeped. The last bar flashed on his phone. 'My phone's about to die. It's beeping. The battery's about to run out.'

She swore under her breath.

'How do I get hold of you? Josie, tell me, quick.'

'I'm thinking. Use this number I'm calling you from. Save it in your memory. No, wait, it's best if I call you. We've got to be careful. I'm using Pete's phone.'

'Pete? You can't mean you're with Henderson?'

'… It's not what you think. I'll explain.'

'I don't believe this. You said, if I helped you, we'd be together. You and me.'

'We will be.'

'Then why are you with Henderson? I need to see you. I can't do this alone… I'll come to Poland.'

'No, don't. It'd be suspicious. You have to act like everything's normal. Stay where you are. Give me two or three days and I'll work something out.'

He was back near the entrance to the shop. The choir was singing "Silent Night". 'Did you plan to kill Rook all along? Would you have killed him, if Dean hadn't come in? Josie, I need to know.'

The tone sounded and the line went dead, and then the screen on his phone cut out too. Snaz shivered in the rain.

Chapter 10

Grace

'For what we are about to receive, may the Lord make us truly thankful. Amen.'

While his aunt prayed aloud, Snaz eyed the chicken casserole with trepidation. He worried about eating for fear of being sick. He wished he'd rung and told his aunt he felt unwell and couldn't visit her. He'd thought about it but, knowing Grace, she'd have insisted on coming to *his* flat and playing nursemaid. Better to visit her, stay for dinner and then make his excuses and leave.

'So, how has your week been, Simon?' she asked, offering him a bowl of boiled carrots.

'Fine.' He helped himself to just a spoonful, then to another when she continued to hold out the bowl.

'Are you busy at work?'

Snaz nodded. He'd been due back in this morning and had forgotten to ring in sick.

'Are you taking time off for Christmas? Surely there can't be anyone who wants their car repaired between Christmas and the New Year? I hope that boss of yours isn't making you work.'

'Someone has to cover.'

'But why you, Simon? You need to stand up for yourself. You always put other people's needs before your own and they take advantage. Like with that Josephine.'

Snaz flinched when Grace said her name. She always said it with a sneer of contempt. *Josephine.* Like a rotten nut had got into her chocolate.

He recalled the one occasion Grace and Josie had met, when he'd had his appendix out and they'd both turned up at the hospital to visit him at the same time.

Josie had made an effort. 'Mrs Freedman? Oh, what a…

surprise. I'm Josie.'

Grace had stared for a moment. '*You're* Josephine?'

'I didn't realise who you were just now...'

'Evidently,' said Grace.

'You've met?' Snaz asked.

'Just now, in the Ladies,' Grace said. 'Josephine was having a conversation on her mobile phone.'

'My friend rang.' Josie sounded nervous, like she needed to explain. 'More an acquaintance really. She can go on and on and sometimes I have to say what she wants to hear, otherwise I'd never get her off the phone.'

How awkward he'd felt when Josie asked him a question – how was he feeling after the op? – and Grace simply sat with her arms crossed and her lips curled around her teeth. Snaz wondered if it might be Josie's clothes that his aunt objected to, although she'd dressed quite modestly that day.

When Josie got up to leave after a few minutes, Snaz didn't blame her. 'I'd better be going,' she said.

'Yes,' said Grace. 'I'm sure you have other people to see.'

Josie frowned. 'I'll speak to you later,' she said to him, kissing him only on the cheek. 'I'll come again tomorrow, later in the evening maybe. Let me know if there's anything you want me to bring. Mrs Freedman.' She'd acknowledged Grace.

That night, he'd rung Josie to apologise for his aunt. 'She's never normally like that. I don't understand it.'

'Maybe she sees me as a threat. Thinks I'm going to steal her little boy from her.'

'I wish you would,' Snaz remembered saying.

Josie had changed the subject then.

Grace cleared away Snaz's plate. 'Are you all right, Simon? You've hardly touched a thing. I thought you liked my chicken.'

'It was good, Auntie, but I'm not hungry.' He shrank from her touch when she placed her hand on his forehead.

'Your temperature's normal, but you don't look well at all.'

'I think I might have flu.'

'Oh, Simon, the bug going around is nasty. On the news, they say it's an epidemic.'

'You've seen the news?'

'Yes, and half of my church house group have it too.'

Snaz breathed out. In the framed print on the wall an elderly couple cuddled together on a bench, watching a Caribbean sunset. He'd wanted to spend his life with Josie and to grow old with her. Instead she'd run away to Pete Henderson, her yoga instructor. Would Henderson have killed a man for her? Snaz scrunched the corner of the tablecloth in his fist and stood up.

'That's right,' his aunt said. 'Go and check if there's anything nice on the television. Maybe there's a film. I'll do the washing-up and join you. Can I bring you a tea?'

'No, I have to go.'

'Go where?' She left the plates on the worktop and came over to him. 'You only got here an hour ago. Why must you leave so soon?'

He coughed. 'I don't want you to catch my flu.'

She shook her head. 'No, it's more than a cold. I know you too well. For a month you haven't been yourself. Is it something to do with that Josephine?'

Snaz froze. 'Why should it be?'

'When you answered the phone this morning, you thought it was her calling. You called me by her name. Are you still dating her, Simon? It's difficult, I realise. But you're a good young man, far too good for her. She may have a pretty face and a trim figure – but who wouldn't look like a stick insect if they didn't have to work and could spend all day at the gym? There are more important things. One day you will meet the woman who is right for you.' She reached to put her arm around him, but he backed away.

'I'm sorry, I really need to go.'

Grace followed him to the corridor, where he sat on the bottom stair to put on his trainers. They were still soaked through from the puddle he'd stepped in.

'You are coming to spend Christmas here, though?'

'I haven't thought about it yet.'

'Well you need to think soon. Christmas is next week.'

Snaz made a mess of tying his shoelace and had to start over again. 'I don't know. Maybe.'

'If you don't get a better offer, is what you mean. Well, you need to make up your mind so I know what food to buy.'

Great, Snaz thought. He'd upset her now. 'I'll ring you,' he said.

'Yes, do that.' She retreated to the living room and left him on his own in the hall.

He could hardly leave her like this. If he went abroad, it could be months before he saw her again. Josie had told him to stay put in England, but the further away from London he could get himself the better as far as he was concerned. Easy for Josie to tell him to stay here when she'd already fled.

With his laces still undone, Snaz slunk back to the living room and found his aunt sitting in the same spot where he'd found her crying five years ago because her operation had been postponed.

'I'm sorry,' he said, aware of how lame it sounded.

'No, I'm sorry. You have your own life. Of course you have better things to do than spend Christmas with your old aunt.'

'I've… I've let you down.'

'No you haven't. You're a fine young man. I'm proud of how you've turned out.'

'Don't say that.' For an awful moment it crossed his mind to tell her what he'd done. 'I should have stayed with you, Auntie, the day your operation got postponed. I went to meet Josie. I wish I'd stayed with you.'

Chapter 11

Alive

Josie sat on the bed, watching Pete put on his scarf and tuck it inside his jacket. 'Are you sure you won't come with us to church?' he asked her.

She had her excuse prepared. 'The service will be in Polish. There's no point in me going when I won't understand a word.'

'Who ever understood Catholic mass? They held it in Latin until the sixties.' He picked up his mobile from the table.

'Don't take your phone.' Josie tried to sound casual. 'I mean, you won't need it. You'll have to switch it off inside the church.'

Pete hesitated before putting it down again. 'If you're not coming, maybe I should stay here with you.'

'Why? Dorota wants you to go. Really, I'll be okay. I think I'll go back to bed and see if I can sleep.'

'Good idea, you need to rest if you're unwell.' In the hall he did an about turn, and she thought he'd changed his mind yet again. 'You meant what you said about wanting to be with me?'

'Yes, of course.'

He gave her a kiss. 'Let's put the last three months behind us. If we talk to one another, if we're open and honest, there's nothing we can't work out.'

Josie bit her lip and nodded.

Clutching her locket, winding its broken chain around her fingers, Josie stood by the window until she saw Pete and his aunt and uncle emerge from the building. In single file they walked past the cars parked on the pavement, Dorota leading the way, checking her watch.

Collapsing onto the futon, on the scrambled blanket and sheets, Josie psyched herself up to ring Snaz. She couldn't decide whether it'd be safer if he stayed in London or went abroad. If he left the country suddenly, it might make the police suspicious. But she worried about Snaz on his own in England: he hadn't even sorted out his alibi. She knew if the police arrested him he'd crumble and give her away too.

Not for the first time, Josie thought about calling her dad. He'd know what to do, and could get her what she needed: money, a lawyer. But her dad was the last person she wanted to ask for help. Besides, what would she say to him? "Dad, I killed someone"? Rook's son had attacked her, but she still had to explain going to Rook's house with a loaded gun. The enormity of what she'd done hit her with fresh force.

A cigarette, she decided. To think straight, she needed a cigarette.

Josie wandered into the living room in search of an ashtray and found Marcin slumped in Greg's armchair, munching a wafer the size of his face. He gazed up at her. 'Mama not like you smoking in the house.'

'Flat,' she corrected him. 'It's a flat, not a house.'

'She still not be happy. She be able to smell the smoke.'

Josie could do without upsetting Dorota. She had no option but to stay here for the time being and she wanted Dorota on her side. With an effort, she heaved open the stiff balcony door.

A gang of youths in hooded tracksuits loitered by the opposite block. A woman with a pug on a lead kept her head down as she marched past them. Josie rested her arms on the guardrail and drew on her cigarette.

If only that man hadn't seen her outside Rook's house. The police might identify her from the description he gave them, especially if they found out about her relationship with Snaz. She had to come up with a reason for being there in that quiet residential road.

Josie heard a wolf-whistle and took a second to notice the

youths watching her from across the courtyard. One of them called to her. She stubbed the remains of her cigarette on the barren earth in the flower box and went back inside.

Only a large crumb remained of Marcin's wafer. He plucked it from his sweater and popped it in his mouth.

Josie stopped by the TV. 'Can you get English channels?'

'Just Polish,' he replied.

'Oh. Is there a shop nearby where I can buy English papers?'

'For foreign newspapers, best is *Empik*.'

'Is it open on Sundays?'

'To four o'clock I think. Bus five hundred three goes there or you can walk to metro station. Metro is faster.'

'I've got my car,' Josie said.

'I forget you drive here. What car you have?'

'A Mini.'

Marcin sat up. 'Is it Mini Cooper?'

When she nodded, he sprang from his chair and went out onto the balcony, returning with a grin. 'Red one with the white roof!'

'Can you tell me how to drive to this *Empik* place?'

'Go out of *podworko*, turn right on Jastrzebowskiego...'

'*Where?*'

'Jastrzebowskiego. When you are at second lights, turn left on...' He mentioned another unpronounceable name.

Josie gave up. 'If you come with me you can show me the way.'

'You mean you want me go with you in your Mini? Are you wanting go now?'

Marcin's smile turned to a grimace as he lifted the half-eaten baguette from the passenger seat.

'Oh, throw it away,' Josie said to him. 'It's stale.'

She started up the engine and he lowered the electric window and chucked out the rotten sandwich. 'Did you see *Italian Job*?' he asked. 'Cool film.'

Josie remembered watching it with Snaz in Leicester Square, his kind of movie more than hers. It'd been three or four months ago, but it felt like another lifetime. For a moment she didn't make the connection between the guy she'd gone out with that night and the Snaz who'd shot Rook. He'd killed Rook to protect her, why else? And she'd left him back in London on his own.

The car jolted over a crater in the road. 'Don't they ever do repairs in this country? Which way do I turn?' Josie asked Marcin.

'Go right here.'

She took a packet of *Marlboro Lights* from the door bin, but found it empty and crushed it in her hand.

'Adam smokes,' Marcin said, his eyes fixed on her legs.

'Adam? So what's the story with your brother? Is that his girlfriend with him in the photo in your living room?' Josie already knew the answer: why else would Adam be holding hands with her? Next to Adam, the girl struck Josie as very plain. No wonder she'd been smiling like the cat that got the cream.

'They were getting married,' said Marcin.

They *are* getting married, he must mean. Josie didn't bother to correct his English this time.

'At next lights you must go left.'

Pete's mobile ring tone made her jump. She scrambled the phone out from her coat pocket, recognised Snaz's number on the display and regretted not ringing him back at the flat. What to do? Answer it? She could hardly talk to Snaz with Marcin sitting next to her.

Before Josie could make up her mind, the phone cut to voicemail. Would he leave a message? Maybe the witness had gone to the police and they'd identified her. The thought sent a shudder through her body. But surely the witness's description alone wouldn't be enough for the police to identify her – not unless they had a reason to suspect her. They could only connect her to Rook through Snaz.

Last night, before his phone battery died, Snaz had asked if she'd have killed Rook if Dean hadn't come in. Did he think she would have done? She felt an urgent need to speak with Snaz, to set him straight: she'd wanted Rook to admit responsibility, to apologise. If she saw he regretted what he'd done, she'd have walked away.

She felt Marcin touch her arm. 'You go the wrong way.'

Josie cursed, pulled up, the car's tyres scrubbing against the kerb. She waited for a gap in the traffic so she could do a U-turn.

'Twice I say to you go left.'

What must Marcin think of her? 'I'm tired, I didn't sleep last night.' He continued to stare at her, making her uncomfortable. She pointed to the shelf below the glove box. 'Why don't you put on a CD?'

He picked one and studied the back of its case. Dire Straits.

'Not that one, it's Snaz's.'

'Who's Snaz?'

What the hell was the matter with her? Every time she opened her mouth, she said something she shouldn't. 'He's a friend, an acquaintance. But the CD's scratched.'

The instant the phone rang again Josie grabbed it from her lap. Snaz again! He must have news. If he couldn't reach her, he might panic and give himself up to the police. She pictured him outside a police station, trying one last time to reach her. Her hand shook as she pressed the button to answer, held the phone to her ear.

'Josie? It's me.'

'Hi, I'm with someone.'

'I need to talk.' He sounded desperate.

'I'll ring you back, okay.'

'Josie!'

'Give me half an hour. I was going to call you.'

'Josie, he's alive.'

'What?'

'It's in the paper. He's alive.'

'Rook? He can't be.'

'Not Rook. His son, Dean. The paper says he's in intensive care.'

Alive. How? 'He can't be alive. You saw all the blood.' The phone slipped in her hand and she grabbed it, stopped it falling.

'You didn't kill him, Josie. He survived.'

Snaz's words sounded loud. Too loud. Josie realised the phone had switched on to loudspeaker. She saw Marcin staring at her, his eyes wide, his smile vanished. Josie withered; covered her mouth. He'd heard every word.

Marcin stared at the door.

She had to tell him something, but what? How to explain? *Think, Josie, think.* Before she could find words he said to her, 'Stop car'.

'Why?'

'Stop car now.'

Josie pulled up and straight away Marcin opened the door.

'Where are you going?'

He didn't answer as he got out. He set off on the pavement, looking back at her over his shoulder.

Josie opened her door and tried getting out but realised she had her seatbelt on. She scrambled free, ran after him still with no idea what to say. 'Marcin, what we said... What you heard...'

He held a hand up, stopping her. Stopping her getting close. Frightened. He was frightened of her. 'I have go somewhere,' he said. 'I forget I have go.'

'You don't think...?' She broke off. 'Please, Marcin. Please don't tell anyone what you heard.'

But he wasn't listening. He was walking away, almost running. Glancing back at her, he walked straight into a man.

Behind her, Josie heard an angry drawn-out blast of a horn. She saw her car with both its doors open, blocking a lane of the road. She'd left the keys in too. People on the opposite pavement had stopped to watch: an elderly couple; a woman with a pram.

Looking back the other way, she could no longer see Marcin. If he spoke to anyone, it'd be the end for her. He would, of course he would. First he'd tell his parents, then they'd tell Pete, and then one of them – maybe Pete himself – would go to the police.

Her legs buckling at the knees, she teetered back to her car, conscious of everyone watching her: pedestrians, drivers in the cars queuing up to get past. A man in a battered pick-up truck wound down his window and shouted, pointing at his forehead. It felt like a thousand eyes staring at her, condemning her. Josie felt like giving up.

Only when she saw the phone on the car seat did she remember what Snaz told her. She wasn't a killer. Rook's son was still alive!

Chapter 12

Henry's goal

Each time Snaz rang Josie, the line cut to voicemail. Ten minutes he waited for her to call him back. 'Josie, what happened? Where did you go?'

'I told you, I was with someone. How, Snaz? How can he be alive?'

'I don't know. His brother found him. It says in the paper he's stable. The bullet punctured the top of his lung.'

'*Stable* means he isn't going to die.'

'Josie, he knows we shot his dad. I think we should go to the police, both of us together. We can explain that Dean ran at you with a knife… We can tell them about your mum too. They'll take it into account.' He could hear Josie breathing, gasping almost. 'They might be more lenient if we give ourselves up.'

'I'm not going to prison,' she said, finally. 'I can't.'

'So what *do* we do?'

'I need to think.'

'We have to do something. Dean saw us. He definitely saw you. We should've gone straight to the police,' he said.

'Sh, let me think!'

'I kept telling you your plan was crazy.'

'Rook stole my mum from me.'

'And ever since Erin told you, you've been obsessed with paying him back.'

'What are you saying, Snaz? You think I planned to shoot Rook's son? I didn't expect him to be there. If you'd checked the other rooms…'

'So it's my fault?'

'No, it's no one's fault.'

'Aren't you even sorry?' Snaz said.

'What, for defending myself? What was I supposed to do, let him stab me?'

'But that's my whole point. If we hand ourselves in…'

'You need to leave the country,' she said. 'Get away while you can.'

'I don't want to run. I want it to be over.'

Josie spoke over him. 'Go to Guyana, you've family there.'

'I don't know them. What would I do there? I'm not going anywhere if I can't be with you.'

'Poland isn't safe. I can't stay here. I have to go somewhere else.'

Snaz didn't know if she was even listening to him. 'Well, where are you going?'

'I need to think. If you get yourself out of England, anywhere, it doesn't matter, I'll get a flight there and we'll meet up.'

'You mean it? We'll be together?'

'Just get yourself on a flight. Today. I'm serious, don't wait or it'll be too late.'

'So you'll join me and we'll be together?'

'Yes. One step at a time.'

Snaz fell onto his sofa. Glancing up, he saw Josie's photo on the wall. 'What are you wearing?' he asked her.

'Wearing? What kind of a question…? A black sweater. A leather skirt and coat.'

'If I hadn't shot Rook, he might have come after you.'

'You had to shoot him.' After a long silence she added, 'It's going to be okay, we'll get through this.' But her voice sounded shaky, uncertain. 'Snaz, what did we do?'

Suddenly, his doorbell rang. He bolted upright. He didn't expect anyone.

'What? What is it?' Josie asked.

'Someone's here.'

'Who?'

He dashed to the window and swore out loud. 'There's a

police car outside.'

'Shit,' said Josie. 'Don't let them in.'

Snaz heard a man's voice outside: 'Simon Aziz?'

'They know I'm in here,' he whispered to Josie. 'They've come for me.'

'Listen, Snaz, don't tell them anything. Don't panic. Act like you've nothing to hide. Whatever you do, for both our sakes, don't mention me.'

* * *

Snaz undid the brass door chain. It was over, he realised. No point in putting up a fight.

'Simon Aziz?'

Seeing a woman in the doorway took him by surprise.

'DS Orchard, Willesden police.' She held up an ID card. 'This is PC Eales.'

Only two of them. He'd expected a mob. Perhaps he could make a run for it.

'May we come in?'

Snaz glanced over his shoulder into the room at his car keys and passport on the coffee table. If he could grab them...

The uniformed male cop picked the junk mail from the mat as he came in and put it on the table by the door, next to Josie's gloves.

'We understand you knew Curtis Rook,' the woman said, standing between Snaz and the table. 'He's been murdered. But you know that already, I see.'

Snaz shuddered, but then glimpsed Friday's *Standard* still open on the settee. 'Yeah, I read about it,' he managed to say.

'You worked for him, right?'

He nodded. 'Sometimes. I mean kind of. I mean I did jobs for him from time to time.'

'You might be able to help us with a few things. Why don't

you sit down?'

Snaz perched on the end of the couch. He felt his heart galloping, his body all set to run. But if they were here simply to ask questions… *Don't panic*, he told himself. *Play it cool.*

Orchard took a chair from by the table and set herself in front of him. 'How long have you known Mr Rook?' she asked, her tone brusque.

'About a year, but his son I've known for longer.'

'His son Dean?'

'No, Matt, Dean's brother. I hadn't seen Dean before.'

The detective's eyes sharpened on him. 'Before what, Simon?'

'I saw his photo in the paper.' Had there been a photo? He only remembered the picture of Rook, his victim, his own friend's dad.

'What kind of work did you do for Mr Rook?'

'I collected cars for him. He bought and sold cars. I didn't know him well.'

Orchard leaned forward and Snaz shifted in his seat. 'Where were you on Wednesday night at ten o'clock?'

'At ten? With a mate. Watching football at his place.'

'Name?'

'You want his name?'

'Yes, please,' she said.

'Dave Turner.'

'And after the match?' the man chipped in, replacing Snaz's running trophy on the wrong shelf. 'The game finished before ten.'

'I stayed and had a drink. A couple of drinks.'

'What time did you leave?'

Snaz's gaze fell to the policeman's polished shoes. 'About eleven. No, later. It must've been nearly twelve.'

'And Mr Turner can corroborate this?' the woman took over again.

'Yes.'

'Address?'

'His address? Finsbury Park. Flat 3, Cornwallis Mansions.'

Eales scribbled in his notebook. Handcuffs hung from his belt.

'You understand we need to ask everyone?' Orchard explained. She had a broad face, cheeks puffed out like a hamster's. 'Can you think of anyone who might have borne a grudge against Curtis Rook?'

Snaz shook his head.

'Mr Aziz, your boss was shot, his son left for dead. Perhaps Mr Rook had crossed someone? Did you meet anyone while running your errands for him?'

PC Eales stared at Josie's portrait above the hi-fi.

'No, no one,' Snaz said loud enough to divert his attention from the photo.

'You sound very convinced,' said Orchard.

'I can't think of anyone.'

'Someone wanted him dead.' Her eyes stayed fixed on him.

The silence drew out and he felt he needed to say something. 'You haven't spoken to Dean?'

'We will do soon. Once he's well enough.'

'He'll survive then?'

'Survive, probably. Make a full recovery? It's too early to say.'

Dread rose in Snaz as he listened to the sergeant. Dean would describe him. They'd find out he'd been in the house.

If he confessed now, he could at least explain: after Josie shot Dean, he'd panicked. He'd never wanted to take her to Rook's place. None of this had been his idea.

Eales had his eyes fixed on the picture again: Josie straddling a chair like Christine Keeler in that pose. Snaz could still be with her. If he flew to Poland, he could be with her tonight, hold her again.

'Who's the model?' the PC asked.

'No one. I mean no one I've met. I downloaded the picture

from a website.'

Orchard frowned and rose from the chair. 'Thank you for your time.'

Were they leaving? Was that it? His heart hung in the air. He followed them to the door and the sergeant handed him her card. 'Here's my direct line. Call me if you think of anything.'

They went out into the corridor and Snaz started to close the door, but Eales raised an arm, stopping him. 'So you're a Gooner then?'

'What?'

'I noticed your Arsenal mug.'

'Oh, yeah.'

'Me too. Was it a good game on Wednesday night? I had to work, but I heard we played them off the park.'

'Oh, yes.' Snaz didn't even know the result. If the cop asked him the score…

'Did you see Henry's goal?'

'Yes. Great.'

Eales' face grew a smile. 'Who've we got today?'

'Is it Blackburn?' Snaz remembered Matt calling him last weekend, asking if he wanted to go to the game. He'd made an excuse about being away with Josie.

'I think we'll get a result,' the cop said, maintaining eye contact as he followed Orchard towards the lift.

When the cops left, Snaz slumped against the door. 'Soon,' they'd said, 'we'll talk to Dean soon.' He rushed to the cupboard in his bedroom, hauled his rucksack out from under the box of vinyl records he kept meaning to give to a charity shop and ripped clothes off their hangers: sweatshirt, tracksuit, running top. He grabbed three or four shirts – a black silk one Josie had got him – threw them all at once with their hangers onto the pile. Crouching among the scattered clothes, stuffing them into his bag, he heard the unmistakable rattle of the lift and stopped, paralyzed. The police coming back? He sprang to the window, knocked his knee against the chair Orchard had left in the middle of the room. If they found him packing to escape... He breathed again when he saw them by the patrol car, talking over the roof. Orchard looked up towards him. Snaz let go of the curtain, clutching his knee, praying she hadn't noticed him. What were they saying? They must suspect him. They couldn't arrest him without proof, but they'd have it once they talked to Dean.

Eales got in the driver's side and the car moved off. Snaz watched until it turned the corner.

His bag was already bulging. What else did he need? His passport – thank God they hadn't spotted it. Underwear. He pulled the drawer, but found only three odd socks. Everything else in the wash. He went to the laundry basket and realised as he lifted the lid that he needed to book a flight.

He crashed on the bed and tore through the pages of the newspaper a handful at a time, reached the sport and shuffled back. Travel. *Flight Line. Cheap flights to Europe and US.* He found his phone under the paper and dialled 0845... Then cancelled the call and searched the memory for Dave T's number. His alibi! The police would be checking it now!

Ring tone.

His heart beat like waiting for the start of a race.

Ring tone.

Pick up, Dave.

Ring tone.

Answer the phone!

Snaz was on his knees when he heard his friend's voice.

'I need a favour.'

'Snaz? What's up, man?'

'Wednesday night. You have to tell them I was with you.'

'Tell who? I thought you went to the game?'

He clambered to his feet. 'I'm in trouble. I need an alibi. Please.'

'What kind of trouble?' asked Dave.

'You need to tell them we watched the match at your place. They're coming to question you.'

'Who, mate? Not the police?'

Snaz went to the window. A boy kicked a football and it bounced on someone's car.

'Whoa, man,' said Dave, 'you want me to lie to the police?'

'I'm asking for your help.'

'What's it worth?'

'You want money? Take the BMW. It's yours.'

'You're serious, ain't you? I don't want your car! I'm ribbing you, man. What is it? What you done?'

'I'm in trouble. I need time to get away. Wednesday night. I got to you at seven and we watched the whole match.'

'Okay, man. But I don't get it. If I lie for you, you gonna tell me what's up?'

'I didn't want... I only went there to help her out.' He stopped himself. Mustn't say too much. 'They showed the match on TV, right?'

'Yeah.' Dave's voice became quiet.

'I left at eleven. No, wait.' He tried to think what he'd told Eales. 'Half past eleven. We had a few drinks.'

'Half eleven. I got it. You can count on me.'

'I'm sorry. There's no one else I can ask.'

'Hey, we're mates.'

'I owe you, Dave.'

'You do know the score?'

'What?'

'The match! Man, you don't even know the result?'

'I haven't checked it.'

'It must be *serious*, if you haven't checked the score. Man, if you're a suspect and they think you did whatever this thing is and you say, "I was at Dave's, watching Arsene's boys", they might ask you about the game.'

'We won, yes?'

'Easy, man. Two-nil. Pires... Freddie Ljungberg... Arsenal topped the group.'

'What about Henry?'

'Yeah, Thierry played okay, not one of his best games though. Had a free-kick, but their keeper got to it. Chance before half time, but he scuffed it wide.'

'What about his goal? Henry's goal?'

'What goal, man? Henry never scored.'

Chapter 13

Santas and angels

It had begun to snow. Wet snowflakes landed on Josie's car windscreen and melted within seconds. A few metres in front of where she'd parked, a man dressed as Father Christmas, complete with white beard, got into a taxi. Josie dug her finger-nails into her palms until they hurt. No, this wasn't a dream.

Okay get a grip, she said to herself. *Deep breath.* Clenching the steering wheel, she inhaled like Pete had taught her to in yoga class, but couldn't hold the breath inside her for more than a second before it came bursting from her lungs. Marcin would go to the police. They'd already caught up with Snaz. Another deep breath. *Got to stay calm.* Josie recognised she had no option left but to ask her dad for help.

She keyed in her old home phone number on Pete's mobile, mistyped it and had to begin again. Taking another rushed intake of breath, she waited for her dad to answer. *Please don't be out.* But the phone just rang and rang.

Sunday, Josie realised. Sunday morning. He'd be out on the golf course and not back for hours. And Josie didn't have his mobile number. 'Why are you never there for me?' she cried into the phone.

The lift was still broken, so Josie had to climb eight flights of stairs to the flat. It had been half an hour since Marcin ran off, long enough for him to have got back and told Pete and his family what he'd overheard. If he had, she'd act bewildered and claim Marcin was making it up. But, "You didn't kill him. He survived."? No one would invent a story like that.

She rang the doorbell and Pete himself opened the door. 'Where did you sneak off to?' he asked, half smiling. 'I thought you were going to try to get some sleep?'

'I went to buy migraine tablets. Is Marcin back?' She scanned the coat rack but couldn't see the anorak he'd been wearing.

'No, I assumed you were with him.'

'He... He went off somewhere on his own.' Josie realised it'd be wise to get her explanation in first, before Marcin blabbed, but she couldn't think of anything plausible and having Dorota frowning at her from the kitchen didn't help. It occurred to her to grab her stuff and leave, before Marcin got back. But where would she go? No, she had to try explaining things to Pete. She scrambled out of her coat and escaped to the bedroom, out of Dorota's glare.

Pete followed her and perched himself on the sofa.

'I need to tell you something,' she said, still out of breath from climbing the stairs.

'Actually I wanted to talk to you too. But you go first.'

'No,' Josie said, 'after you.'

He patted a hand next to him, and when she sat down he shuffled up close and reached for her hand. 'I've been offered a lecturing job in London. It's only for a few hours a week and the money's not great, but it's what I enjoy doing.'

'You're going back to London?'

'I couldn't decide whether to take it, but if we're back together, if we're going to try to make a go of things...'

'When? When are you going back to England?'

'The job's as maternity cover for someone. It starts in February.'

'But...' Josie didn't know how to tell him she couldn't go back.

'I missed you, Josie,' he said. 'The few months we had together – I've never felt so alive. I had a thought this morning. If things go well, maybe in spring, perhaps we could think about living together.'

'Living together?'

'Renting a place. I could move in to yours, or we could get a flat between us, maybe somewhere out of town. Hey, when you go back to England, I could come with you in your car,' he said. 'We could share the driving.' He let go of her hand and started to stroke a finger along the hem of her skirt.

Josie couldn't concentrate. Snaz might have told the police it'd been her idea to threaten Rook and that she'd persuaded him to load the gun.

'So what do you say?' Pete asked, and Josie realised she hadn't been listening. 'Will you think about it?'

'Yes, I'll think about it,' she said. 'I'm sorry. I'm not myself with this headache.' She stumbled to her feet. 'I need to get some air.'

They'd brought the Christmas tree into the flat and it stood bare and desolate in the corner of the sitting room. Josie grabbed her cigarettes and lighter from the table and yanked the balcony door open.

It dawned on her that she might never be able to go back home. All the things she'd enjoyed: the nightlife, the parties; mornings working out at the fitness club; hailing a taxi to Piccadilly and wandering round the Bond Street boutiques. She lived for the buzz of London. If she had to stay in hiding in a backwater like Warsaw or who knows where next. But if the alternative was prison...

'I thought you'd given up smoking.' Pete startled her. She hadn't heard him join her outside on the balcony.

They stood alongside one another, taking in the same skyline, the pregnant clouds beyond the tower blocks. His thoughts must have been a world away from hers. 'They reckon it's going to get colder,' he said eventually. 'We might get a few centimetres of snow. Oh, what did you want to tell me?'

'It's about Marcin.'

'Really? What about him?'

'I don't know how to say this. When you were out at church, I asked him where I could buy headache pills and he said he'd show me if I took him for a ride in my car.'

'But there's a box of aspirin in the bathroom. He could have given you that.'

'Pete, you're not listening to me. In the car, when I was driving, he put his hand on my leg.'

'What?' Pete sounded incredulous. 'Marcin? What do you mean, your leg?'

'Sh… Someone might hear you. Above my knee where my skirt ends. I had to push him off me.'

Pete's forehead crinkled. 'I can't believe he'd do that. Wait 'til I tell Dorota.'

'No, I don't want to get him into trouble. Nothing happened, not really. It was more embarrassing than anything else.'

'I'll talk to him.'

'No, don't,' she pleaded. 'I'm sure he didn't mean any harm.'

'But what the hell was he thinking?' Pete tutted. 'You're here for two days and this happens.'

'I'm sure he feels bad enough. Please let's forget about it. He's not going to do it again.'

Pete huffed. 'Well, if you're sure.' After an uncomfortable silence, he changed the subject. 'Do you fancy decorating the Christmas tree with me? It might help to take your mind off your headache.'

Pete began by winding the fairy lights in a helter-skelter around the tree. 'Are you going to help me or only stand and watch?'

Josie prised open a box of baubles, getting her fingertips covered with coarse dust which she rubbed off on her skirt.

'No, not those. Start with the larger ones.'

'Does it matter?'

'Always begin at the bottom and work up. Those glittery ones are light, so they go near the top.'

She hung an ornament from the nearest branch, catching a

glimpse of her distorted reflection in the red glass.

'This is what Christmas is all about,' said Pete. 'Family, snow, being with someone who...' He stopped in mid-sentence. 'Being with you.'

She showed him a teardrop-shaped bauble. 'What about this one?'

'Anywhere near the bottom. No, it's too close there to the other blue one.'

'I've never dressed a tree.'

'What, not when you were little?' Pete sounded amazed.

Josie remembered one Christmas long ago – she must have been about six – she'd asked if she could help with the tree. Beatrice had promised, 'Tomorrow, if you're a good girl.' When she'd run downstairs the next morning, she found the tree almost finished and Beatrice lifting up her younger brother so he could put the star on the top.

'… Are there any gold bulbs left?'

Josie caught the end of what Pete was saying and checked in the tray. 'This one doesn't have string.'

'Leave it on the table for Dorota to mend. Okay, where's the other box?'

They covered the tree until trinkets weighed down every branch. Greg wandered into the room and nodded his approval.

Josie found a bulging envelope filled with homemade decorations, faded felt-tip drawings of Santas and angels mounted on coloured cards. 'Should we put these up too?'

'I'm not sure there's room for them.' Pete took the envelope from her and left it on the table next to the broken bulb. 'Where's the star?'

Josie found it lying on the sofa and offered it to him.

'You do it,' he said.

'Me?'

'Go on,' he encouraged.

Josie realised she still had her boots on. She unzipped them and took them off, then climbed up on the chair.

As she set the silver foil star at the top of the tree she heard Pete's phone ring in the room next door. Josie froze, convinced it must be Snaz. Maybe the police hadn't arrested him?

'It's probably my mum,' said Pete, heading for the bedroom.

The ringing stopped and Josie heard Pete's voice, but not loud enough to make out his words. She stepped down off the chair and went to the corridor to listen.

'We're back together,' she heard Pete say. 'And we're thinking of getting a place together... Yes, that's right. Isn't it good news?'

Josie began to back away. It must have been his mum after all, though she doubted Pete's mum would see them being back together as good news.

She'd only taken a couple of steps when Pete called to her, 'Darling, it's for you. It's your friend, Snaz. Oh, hang on, the line's gone dead, blasted thing. Why don't you ring him back?'

Chapter 14

A normal family

Within minutes, Pete had fallen asleep. He lay on his side, curled up towards her, his head half on her pillow. Josie listened to his steady breathing and imagined how he'd react when he found out. Pete even refused to watch violent films. The mere thought of her going with a gun to someone's house would repulse him. He wouldn't believe she'd only taken the gun with her to scare Rook, and neither would the police.

Josie shivered at the idea of them searching for her, hunting her down. How stupid she'd been to use her credit card. It wouldn't take the police long to work out she'd come to Poland. They'd put her in prison. She'd be in her forties, Erin's age, before she got out.

Beneath the door, a narrow shaft of light filtered into the bedroom from the corridor. Josie strained her eyes to read her watch and saw the hands together at the top. The sofa bed creaked when she peeled back the quilt, stood and took Pete's phone from the table. As she tiptoed to get her handbag, Pete groaned and rolled over onto his back. Josie held her breath, but he slept on.

In the hall, Josie slid into her ankle boots, trying not to make a sound as she zipped them up. She slipped her coat on over her nightshirt and groped among the tiddlywink coins in Pete's jacket pocket for the key so she'd be able to let herself back into the flat.

She jumped when Greg appeared in the sitting-room doorway dressed in a vest and pyjama bottoms.

'I have to fetch something from my car,' she told him in a whisper. 'I won't be long.'

'Josephine, I must ask you something.'

She braced herself.

'This morning, you were out with Marcin, yes, and then he went off on his own? Are you sure he didn't say where he was going?'

Josie felt her cheeks redden.

'Dorota is… We both are worried. Marcin has never been out this late without saying to us first.'

'I'm sure he'll be okay,' Josie said. She left Greg in the hall and slunk out of the flat.

Halfway down the stairwell she had the horrible thought: *Marcin might be at a police station.* She hesitated, half expecting to find police waiting by her car.

The cold hit Josie's cheeks when she stepped outside the lobby of the apartment block. No sign of anyone. Frost covered the pavement and the car windows glistened as though dusted with diamonds. Josie walked on the crisp grass so she wouldn't slip. When she reached her Mini she sat inside it and started up the engine, turned down the fan to stop it blowing icy air into her face.

She checked Pete's phone for a signal: not great, but enough. Fingers shaking, she keyed in her dad's number on the mobile. Three times during the day she'd attempted to call him. She prayed that this time he'd be in, but her hope drained away with every unanswered ring.

She'd almost given up when Beatrice, her stepmother, answered. 'Who is this?'

'It's me, Josie.'

'Josephine?' For a moment her stepmum was quiet. 'Have you any idea what the time is?'

'I want to speak to my dad.'

'He isn't home. And even if he was, it's ten past…it's the middle of the night.'

'But I need to talk to him.'

'He's in Boston, so you'll have to wait until next weekend

when he gets back. And if it's money you're after you can come here to see your father and ask him face to face.' She paused. 'He misses you. Though the way you behave towards him I can't for the life of me understand why.'

'It isn't money. Can you give me his mobile number? I need his help.'

'For months on end you haven't been in touch. And now you ring up at past eleven o'clock and you tell me you need his help.' She mimicked Josie's last words. 'And you're rude, too. You haven't asked me yet how I am. Well, I'm sorry, Josephine. You cannot cut yourself off from him and then come running when it suits you and expect him to be at your beck and call.'

'Please.'

'No, Josephine. Whatever it is can wait until your father gets back.'

'It can't wait, you bitch! I need to talk to him.'

Beatrice gasped. 'How dare you speak to me like that!'

Josie ended the call so as not to give Beatrice the satisfaction, then punched the steering wheel. She couldn't wait a week for her dad to get back from the States. If she waited even one day to get his help the police might find her.

The only other way she could get in touch with him was through her brother, but she didn't have Nathan's number either except stored on her own mobile phone. She'd got as far as Dover when she realised she'd forgotten it, and by then she hadn't dared to turn back.

She sat in her car, its frosted-up windows making it like a cocoon. Her lips quavered and she felt tears come. *Why me? Why do things always happen to me?* If her mum hadn't been murdered... If her dad had stayed with her mum instead of marrying Beatrice, and she'd had a normal family... Josie reached into her handbag for a tissue and spotted her passport. Suddenly it came to her: she'd written Nathan's number as next of kin in the back of her passport. She kicked herself for not thinking of it before.

* * *

'What do you want, Josie?'

She and Nathan had grown apart since he found out she was only his half-sister, and the episode with Clara hadn't helped, but his unfriendly tone still took Josie aback. 'I'm trying to get hold of Dad.'

'Oh?'

'Is he in the States?'

'That's right.'

'Have you got his mobile number?'

'Why your sudden interest? It was his birthday three weeks ago. Where were you then? Did you even send him a card?'

She pleaded, 'You must have his mobile number. I need to talk to him. I'm in trouble.'

'Trouble? Why am I not surprised?'

Something wrenched in Josie's chest. 'You still haven't forgiven me, have you? I've said I'm sorry. It was over a year ago. You're happy with Clara now.'

'No thanks to you.'

'I'm still your sister, Nat.'

'And this isn't the time to talk about it. It's late and I've got work in the morning.'

'Then just give me Dad's number. That's all I want... The police are after me. I need his help,' she added when he didn't reply.

'What do you mean, the police?'

'I...' Josie realised she had no choice but to tell him more. 'Someone attacked me. He attacked me and I...' No, she couldn't say it. 'I need Dad's number, Nat.'

'Attacked you? What happened? Are you okay?'

'I had to defend myself. I had to. If I hadn't shot him, he'd have killed me.' Saying it, telling someone, felt like jumping off a cliff into the sea. An earthquake tremored inside her. 'Say something, Nat.'

'I don't have time for this, Josie, if it's one of your attention-seeking games.'

'Do I sound like I'm making it up?'

A crack formed in the frost on the car windscreen as the ice began to melt.

'You can't have shot anyone,' Nathan said. 'Why would you have a gun?'

Josie felt a sickly swooning sensation. 'We only meant to frighten him, but his son ran at me with a knife.'

'Who are you talking about? And who's *we*?'

'Me and Snaz. They've arrested him and they're after me.'

'No,' he said. 'If you want to talk, come round tomorrow evening and let's talk. But don't make up these stories...'

Josie held the phone away from her head. *I'm your sister,* she wanted to say. *I'm two years older than you and you treat me like a child.* She composed herself. 'I'm not lying this time. All I'm asking you for is Dad's mobile. You won't give it to me? Well, when you speak to him, at least tell him I phoned. Tell him I'm in Poland, in Warsaw. And when I end up going to prison, remember I asked you for help.'

Chapter 15

Justice

Snaz entered the police-station waiting room, but stopped when he saw the cop behind the counter, a bulldog of a man with a rough-cut face.

The policeman looked up at him. 'Can I help?'

'I've...' Snaz took a step closer. 'I've come to see DS Orchard.'

'What's it regarding?'

'I talked to her yesterday and she gave me her card.' He fumbled for it in his pockets.

'And your name is...?'

'Snaz. Simon Aziz.'

'I'll check if she's around.' The cop went into the office behind the partition and Snaz watched him speaking on a phone. Soon he returned. 'DS Orchard isn't in, but if you tell me what it's about there might be someone else who can help.'

'I spoke to her yesterday,' Snaz said again. 'It's about Rook, Curtis Rook, the man who was shot.'

'Oh.' The cop eyed Snaz more keenly. 'Grab a pew, sir. I think DCI Mercer's about.'

Snaz took the seat nearest the exit. A yellow notice stood out among the posters on the wall: *CCTV in operation. Your actions are being recorded.* He saw the camera in the corner, over the counter, aimed squarely at him. Snaz crossed his arms and observed his own wet footprints on the floor tiles. From the chair, he traced them to the door.

It suddenly struck him as mad to have come here when he still had a chance to leave the country and get away.

The cop must have read his mind. 'Bear with us. The DCI will be with you in a tick.'

Snaz's gaze returned to the posters. *As a witness the evidence you give is vital to help defend justice.* Where was the justice in Josie escaping and him going to jail? She'd lied and used him to get back at Rook; promised that if he helped her, things would change. Oh, they'd changed all right. She'd shacked up with her yoga instructor. Every time Snaz thought of her with that creep Pete Henderson, he wanted to grab her by the throat.

The door swung open and a blast of fresh air hit Snaz as a man came in from the street. Middle-Eastern-looking, in a scruffy jacket, he started gabbling to the cop in a heavy accent. Snaz could barely make out a word he said.

'Slow down,' the cop said. 'Who's Nassar? Start again.'

Snaz shut his eyes, trying to concentrate on what he'd tell the police. Perhaps they'd talked to Dean since yesterday. He dismissed the idea. If so, they'd have arrested him. Yet he'd come to the station himself and they were making him wait. They mustn't suspect him at all.

He pictured the red blotch, small at first, spreading on Dean's shirt. If Dean died, the cops might never find out he'd been involved. He'd have given himself up for nothing.

The policeman was preoccupied with the foreigner. The door remained open. Seizing his chance, Snaz lurched for the exit.

Pressing into the wind, the cold rain blowing into his face, he hurried back to the road where he'd parked. How stupid to have gone to the police station. He'd wanted to get back at Josie, but what had he been thinking? They'd send him to prison too, for being there and helping her. Or they might not believe what he told them. With his criminal record, why would they believe his story over hers?

Snaz had the corner in sight when he heard a man shout behind him, 'Wait up!', and then the words he dreaded: 'Simon Aziz!' He kept on walking, pretending he hadn't heard, praying the man wouldn't chase after him. But then he heard someone running. He turned in horror and a man in a suit caught up with him. 'Simon Aziz? I'm DCI Mercer, I'm leading the Curtis Rook murder investigation. Sorry to keep you waiting back there. I understand you've some information for us. Will you come back inside?'

* * *

Uniformed officers stepped aside as the detective led Snaz through a labyrinth of corridors. He marched too fast for Snaz's liking, and with his shaven head raised high.

Mercer opened a door and pointed Snaz to one of the chairs. Going to the cupboard, he took out three cassettes. 'Rotten weather today, isn't it? I hate this time of year, Christmas and all that malarkey.' He cut the wrapping with his teeth and slotted the tapes into the machine, then sat at the table facing Snaz. 'Where are you from?' he asked.

'Edmonton.'

'I meant originally. Your folks?'

'Guyana. My granddad went there from India,' Snaz replied.

A leggy WPC walked past before another plain-clothes cop, older than Mercer and weary-looking, joined them in the room and shut the door. Acknowledging Snaz, he handed Mercer a file, then started the tape machine.

'Interview commencing...' Mercer checked his watch. 'One-thirty-three PM. Present: DCI Mercer, DS Turvey, Simon Aziz. Mr Aziz is here of his own accord and isn't under arrest.' He paused. 'You don't mind if we record this?'

Snaz didn't want them thinking he had anything to hide. 'No.'

'You spoke to DS Orchard yesterday. Have you thought of something more?' Mercer began.

'Is Dean going to recover?' Snaz asked.

'It's a life-threatening injury, but we expect he'll pull through.'

Snaz hoped they didn't notice him shudder. He might as well admit to being there if they'd find out anyway from Dean.

'So what is it you have to tell us?' the DCI asked again.

How to say it? How to convince them it hadn't been his idea?

Mercer flicked through the folder. 'Four years ago you were done for stealing a car. "First offence, completely out of character", it says in your file. What happened, did you fall in with the wrong crowd?'

'I guess.'

'You worked for the victim, right?'

'I told the woman cop yesterday.'

Mercer laid the folder on the desk. 'Listen, Simon. I don't give a monkey's about hot motors or anything else you might be involved with. My sole interest is in finding the murderer. Whoever shot Mr Rook is an extremely dangerous man. He killed in cold blood.'

The words stung him. 'It isn't like that,' Snaz said.

'What isn't?'

The other officer coughed.

For a second Mercer transferred his glare to his colleague. Snaz looked away. He breathed in the vague smell of disinfectant and began to feel sick.

'You were saying, Simon?' Mercer pressed. 'It's not like we think?'

This is it, Snaz thought. *No way to backtrack now.* Better to get his story in before Josie went to them herself. They'd never believe him if she spoke to them first. 'No one was supposed to get hurt.'

'What are you saying? Do you know what happened?'

He whispered, 'Yes'.

'Do you know who shot Curtis Rook?'

Snaz bowed his head.

'Were you at Rook's house when he was shot?'

'Yes.'

The detective clenched a fist. 'Simon Aziz, I need to caution you that you do not have to say anything further, but it may harm your defence if you fail to mention when questioned something you later rely on in court. Anything you do say will be given in evidence. You are entitled to see a solicitor, free legal advice is available. Do you want to speak with a brief?'

Snaz wanted it to be over. 'I don't need a brief.'

'Did you kill Curtis Rook?'

The direct question stunned him. 'No, wait, I didn't say that. We weren't going to use the gun. We took it to frighten Rook. That's what she told me.'

'Who told you?'

'Josie Davenport.'

Mercer glanced at his colleague, who shrugged.

Snaz reached in his pocket. 'My wallet,' he said, raising his palms in alarm when the other cop jumped up and made for him. 'I'm just getting my wallet.' He took out Josie's picture and avoided looking at it as he passed it to Mercer.

'An attractive girl,' said the DCI. 'How is she involved?'

'She shot Dean,' Snaz said.

The DCI put his finger on the photo. 'This woman shot Dean?' He didn't sound like he believed it.

'Yes.'

'Josie Davenport?'

'Yes.'

'Why?'

'He ran at her with a knife.'

'Maybe he was defending himself,' DS Turvey chipped in. 'Why did you go to Rook's house with a gun?'

'Josie had the gun, not me. I thought she only wanted to frighten Rook. If I knew she wanted to kill him, I'd never have helped her.'

Mercer leaned forward. 'Let's get this straight. You went to Rook's house with this Josie?'

'Yes.'

'Was anyone else with you? For the tape, the suspect is shaking his head.'

'I tried to talk her out of it but she said if I didn't go with her she'd do it on her own.'

'Do what?'

'Go there. Threaten Rook.'

'So you went with her to Rook's house and took a gun with you?'

'I keep telling you, Josie had the gun. I gave it to her before we went in.'

'So you obtained the firearm?'

Snaz twisted his hands. Would they believe him if he denied it? Maybe he ought to speak to a brief.

The detective pressed him. 'Answer yes or no please.'

'Yes.'

'And what happened when you got to the house?'

'I went in on my own. Rook expected me because I had some money for him from a car I'd sold.'

'And Josie?'

'She waited outside. I went into the front room with Rook and he counted the cash in the envelope. He gave me back my cut and fifty quid for petrol. I didn't want to take it, but I thought unless I did he'd be suspicious.'

'Suspicious of what?' Mercer leaned across the table.

Snaz tried to move his chair backwards, but found its legs were fixed to the ground. 'That something wasn't right.'

'So you took your cut. Then what did you do?'

'Nothing. I let myself out. I hoped Josie had changed her mind, but when I opened the front door, I saw her waiting there. I tried telling her again not to go in but she pushed past me.'

'Why didn't you stop her? Surely you could have stopped her going inside.'

'I thought if I did, she'd leave me.'

'You two are an item?' Mercer asked.

Snaz's nose kept running and he didn't have a tissue. He sniffed. 'She told me we'd be together. She used me so I'd get a gun for her.'

'Josie Davenport asked you to obtain a firearm?'

'Yes.'

'Did she tell you why?'

'To frighten Rook.'

'Frighten him? Was that the word she used?'

Snaz struggled to recall. 'She said she wanted him to feel the fear her mum must have felt. Her mum was murdered,' he explained.

'Murdered? Hang on, by Curtis Rook?'

'No, but she blamed him. Rook had been her mum's pimp and one of her clients killed her.'

'Then why didn't she come to us?'

'How could she? She was three when her mum died. Check your records. Lucy Snowball was her mum's name.'

'We will check. Maybe we can help you, but you need to tell us everything.'

'I have,' Snaz said, wiping his nose on the back of his hand. 'I am.'

'If Josie simply intended to frighten Rook, why did he end up dead?'

'I thought Rook was alone in the house, but Dean was in the kitchen and he must have heard us. The door opened and the next thing he's rushing at Josie with a knife.'

Mercer stopped him. 'Back a step. Josie enters the house. Where's the gun at this point?'

'In her handbag.'

'Then what? Did you follow her inside?'

'She was speaking to Rook. Then she took out the gun.'

'And you didn't stop her?'

'She wasn't going to use it. I didn't think she'd use it. She'd told me she wanted to frighten him, but then we were going to leave.'

'But you didn't leave, did you? Rook ended up dead.'

The silence drew out longer. Snaz shrunk from Mercer's stare and his eyes fell on Josie's smiling photograph. He'd taken it at Ayia Napa. How long ago last summer seemed now.

Mercer continued, 'If you didn't intend to shoot Rook, how did it happen?'

'Dean ran at Josie with a bread knife. If she hadn't fired, he'd have killed her.'

'So what did you do after she shot Dean?' Mercer said. 'A sixteen-year-old boy is wounded. He's bleeding. Did you call an ambulance? If, like you say, she shot him in self-defence? You hadn't planned to shoot anyone. Why not phone for help?'

'I wanted to.'

'But you didn't, Simon,' the DCI said.

'We thought he was dead.'

'Dead?'

'She... Dean had blood all over him. He'd stopped moving. I would've called an ambulance if I'd known he was still alive.'

The cops were vultures. They'd probe and tear and rip away at him until they had what they wanted. But he wasn't going to break. His heart thumped, the veins throbbed in his temples. 'Josie panicked. Rook had seen her shoot Dean and she thought he'd go to the police. That's the reason she shot him too. That's why Josie killed Rook.'

Chapter 16

Nowhere else to go

The cola in the fridge had lost its fizz. Josie swallowed a mouthful, then poured the rest of her glass down the sink. The digital clock on the oven said 2:35, but no one showed any sign of making lunch. Josie eyed the two wrinkled apples in the fruit bowl. Yesterday she'd passed them over, but today she took one. As she wondered back to the bedroom, she heard keys jangling in the hallway outside, and then the door shot open. In front of her stood Marcin.

His eyes narrowed as he stared at her. Josie opened her mouth to say something, but before any words came out Dorota gusted from the sitting room, almost knocking her over. Screaming at Marcin, Dorota half hugged, half shook him, and then dragged him off to the sitting room without letting him take off his coat.

Thoughts tumbled through Josie's mind. Where would she go if they threw her out? What if they called the police?

She escaped to the bedroom, grabbed her blouse from the radiator in case she had to leave in a hurry, snatched her make-up bag from the table. Hearing Marcin's raised voice made her stop. He said a few words before Dorota interrupted and Greg joined in, shouting above them both. Josie felt certain they must be talking about her, arguing over what to do.

Josie perched on the end of the bed and, emptying the money from her purse, unfurled a flimsy banknote. Twenty measly zlotys – worth less than five pounds. She didn't have enough in cash to pay for a hotel room, not even for one night.

Pete joined her in the bedroom, put his half-drunk glass of tea next to her apple on the table and sat beside her. 'Family row,' he said. 'I thought I'd better keep out of it.'

'Has Marcin said anything yet?' Josie asked. 'About what

happened yesterday in the car?'

'No, I'd hardly expect him to admit what he did.'

'Did he say where he's been?'

'Staying with Adam, he claims, but that doesn't explain why he waited until this morning to ring home. His parents were convinced something bad had happened to him. I had to tell Greg about him coming on to you...'

Josie cut in. 'You told your uncle?'

'I had to, or otherwise they'd have called the police.'

Alarmed, Josie stared at Pete.

'Marcin might be seventeen, but he's young for his age,' Pete said. 'It's the first time he hasn't come home.'

'And what did Greg say when you told him?'

'Let's just say I wouldn't want to be in Marcin's shoes now.'

Josie heard Marcin talking again in his high-pitched whine, perhaps explaining the real reason why he hadn't come home. Pete raised his head to listen.

'Pete,' Josie touched his arm to get his attention. 'You do believe me, don't you? About what Marcin did?'

'Yes, of course. Why wouldn't I?'

'Forget I said anything. With this headache, I'm not thinking straight.'

'Are you still not feeling any better?'

'Here,' she said, pressing her forehead. 'It's a constant drilling.'

'My mum puts most headaches down to stress. Are you anxious about something? Tell you what, take off your shoes.'

'What for?'

'Take them off, go on. Rest your feet on my lap.'

'Why?'

'Mum did a course on reflexology at Islington College. They say all the nerves are connected, and if you massage someone's feet it relieves the tension and helps their headache go.' Pete clasped her foot and worked his fingers into the arch. 'Your feet are tiny,' he said with wonder. 'They're not much bigger than my hand.'

In the living room, everyone had gone quiet. Josie couldn't remember the exact words she'd used when she'd spoken to Snaz in the car, only that she'd said too much. *He can't be alive. You saw the blood.* She winced at the thought of saying those things with Marcin sitting beside her.

'What is it?' Pete asked.

'Hurts,' she said, moving her foot.

'I'm not surprised, when you're so tense. You need to relax.' He released his grip, glided his hand up her leg, above her knee. Their eyes met as he found the top of her stocking and peeled it down and off her leg. For a second, she thought of Snaz.

Pete resumed massaging her, stroking her sole more gently than before. She felt the touch of his fingers on her bare skin. One by one he tended to each of her toes.

'How does that feel?' he asked her.

'Tickles.'

He smiled and began to tickle her deliberately.

'Stop it!' She jerked her foot away. Pete switched to her other foot. 'I'm not in the mood.' Aware that she'd snapped at him, she added, 'I can't help it, can I, if I'm not feeling well?'

In the silence that followed, Josie made out Greg say her name.

She had nowhere else to go. If she used a credit card to pay for a hotel room, the police would track her down. She needed to stay in hiding until Dad returned from the States and she could get his help. Her one hope was that Greg and Dorota would believe the story she'd told Pete, rather than Marcin's.

'Why don't we go to the Old Town tomorrow?' Pete suggested. 'I can show you the marketplace and *Nowy Swiat*. Maybe we can go for a meal. It'd give us a chance to talk.'

'Talk about what?'

'Things. Me and you. I've been thinking,' he continued.

'You've met my mum and my friends from the sangha and now the rest of my family too, but I hardly know a thing about your family or friends. Apart from that Snaz chap who turned up at my yoga class once and made a fool of himself, I've never met any of them. And you don't talk about them either, your friends or your family.'

Josie resisted the urge to answer back that not everyone had the fortune to be blessed with a fairytale background like his. 'There's not much to talk about,' she said.

'What about your brother? Nathan, isn't it? What's he like?'

'He's got his job in the City and a wife who makes jam.'

Pete must have detected the resentment in her voice. 'I thought you were close?'

Josie shut her eyes a moment. 'It used to be me and him against the world.'

'Used to be?'

'He switched sides.'

'Maybe you should too,' he said. 'Switch sides. Quit fighting the world.'

It's too late for that, she thought. 'Can you...? Can you hold me?' She sat back upright and wrapped her arms round Pete, squeezed him tight the way she wanted to be held.

She was still clinging to him when the door opened and Marcin came into the room. He fixed his eyes on Josie and she noticed his clenched fists. 'I want to speak to you,' he said.

Pete let go of her and faced Marcin. 'I think you should apologise.' Pete said something in Polish before adding, 'Don't pretend you don't know what I mean.'

'Pete,' Josie said, 'let me talk to him.' She whispered in his ear, 'I think he might want to say sorry. We'll be right outside.'

Josie went to the door, pausing until Marcin followed her. She went to the end of the corridor, far enough away so no one would overhear.

'Okay,' Marcin said when they reached the stairwell. 'I worked it out what you do. You are driving in your car, you with your friend who you speak to on phone. You have accident and hit someone, but you don't stop. This is what happened, yes?'

Josie couldn't believe it.

'I am right, yes?'

Josie was about to tell him he'd got it wrong, then had a thought. Why not let him believe she'd been talking about a hit-and-run? An accident can happen to anyone. If she played along with this, at least it would buy her more time. 'A man stepped out in front of me. I had no chance to brake.'

'Why you not go to police?' he said.

'I thought I'd killed him. I panicked.'

'Were you drinking?' asked Marcin.

'Drinking?'

'When you hit him, were you drunk?'

'No. It could have been Pete driving, or anyone. It was dark and...I didn't see him. He just stepped out.'

'You've told Pete?'

'I can't. I'm scared to. If the police find out, I'll go to prison.' Josie looked at Marcin, this young man of the same age as the one she'd shot. A child. Barely more than a child. And as she looked into his eyes, she didn't want to go on lying. 'I thought I'd killed him. For four days, I thought I'd killed him. It's the worst feeling. I can't describe it to you.' She paused. 'You feel frozen, and you want to warm yourself so you stand by a fire, but however close you get to it, you can never feel warm.' Josie broke off. Marcin's expression troubled her. If anything, it had hardened. 'Are you going to tell anyone? Please, Marcin, I need more time.'

'You lied about me. You make up untrue story. Why should I help you?'

Chapter 17

Self-defence

'Look at him. Look at what you've done.'

Snaz heard Curtis Rook's voice and bolted upright, but saw nothing apart from the walls of the police-station cell. The light was on as he'd left it; the only sound, the distant murmur of a fan.

He clambered up from the mattress on the floor and pressed the call button next to the light switch, but this time had to wait longer before hearing the duty officer's footsteps coming from the end of the hall. The policeman stopped outside his cell and after a pause the shutter opened. 'What is it now?'

'Can I have a drink?' Snaz asked.

'You had one an hour ago.'

Snaz peered through the slit at the policeman's unmoved eyes. 'Some water, please.'

The metal panel slammed in his face and Snaz heard the guard walk away. As the footsteps became muffled, the realisation hit home: if they charged him with murder, he'd have fourteen years of prison to get through. Fourteen years, and this was only the first night.

He sat on the bare plastic mattress and leaned his head against the cold wall. His eyelids dropped and before long the images returned: Dean lying wounded, and Josie with the gun at her feet, her face partly hidden behind her gloves. Snaz watched her edge backwards, and then she turned and ran from the house.

Before Snaz could follow her, Rook made him stop. Crouched on the floor, holding his son, he cried out, 'Look at him. Look at what you've done.'

Blood covered Dean's shirt. So much blood. Rook's hands were red with it too.

This wasn't meant to happen, he remembered thinking. *Dean shouldn't have been here.*

Both at the same time, he and Rook noticed the gun on the carpet between them. Instinctively, Snaz rushed to seize it. A moment slower and Rook might have reached it first.

Rook clambered to his feet and backed away until he stumbled into the sofa. The gold cross around his neck caught the light.

Snaz couldn't do it. He couldn't kill someone, his mate's dad. But a voice in his head kept screaming at him: *Rook saw everything, he'll go to the police. Josie will end up in prison.* Or maybe – and this thought made Snaz shudder – Rook might *not* go to the police. He might come after them himself. He wouldn't let them get away with killing his son. Now all Snaz could think of was Rook hunting them down. *I have to kill him. It's him or us.*

Snaz aimed at Rook's chest, trying to keep his arm steady. He heard the man speaking, but blanked out the words as his finger tightened on the trigger until…a thud and a jolt up his arm. But the voice kept on talking, using his name. He felt someone shaking his shoulder and became aware of the policeman standing over him, holding out a drink.

Snaz reached for the plastic cup, but it slipped when he took hold of it and the water spilled across the mattress.

'You're not getting another,' said the officer. He moved away and was about to close the door.

'I want to speak to a lawyer,' Snaz said.

'It's three AM.'

'I'm entitled. I want to talk to a brief.'

* * *

'Rupert Francis,' the solicitor introduced himself. He couldn't be older than twenty-five. 'Sit down then,' he said as Snaz continued to stare at him. He folded *The Times* away in his satchel, took out a leaflet along with a small pink booklet and offered them to Snaz. 'These tell you about your rights. Have they let you make a phone call?'

'They said I could.'

'Is there no one you want informed of your arrest? Your parents, maybe?'

Snaz shook his head. 'I'm not in touch with them. There's my aunt, but I don't want her involved.'

'Very well.' The solicitor had downy stubble and fine blond hair, acne on his forehead. 'I've spoken to the investigating officer. They've not been able to get a statement from Dean yet. In the circumstances, I'd expect them to apply to the magistrate to keep you here for as long as they can.'

'How long?'

'In a murder case, they're allowed up to ninety-six hours. Four days.'

'Murder? But it was self-defence! Rook would have killed us if…' Snaz stopped himself. 'We didn't have any choice.'

The solicitor surveyed him. 'The difficulty is you went to Curtis Rook's house with a loaded weapon.'

'It was Josie's idea, not mine.'

'Can you prove it?'

Snaz folded the leaflet, then unfolded it again.

'You've told Mercer that Josie Davenport shot Dean because he attacked her with a knife?'

Snaz nodded.

'Assuming Dean recovers, will he corroborate what you've said?'

'Corroborate?'

'Forgive me. Will what Dean tells the police tally with your own account of the events?'

'Dean knows Josie had the gun.'

'Was he conscious when Curtis Rook was shot?'

Snaz twined his feet together beneath the seat. Dean had slumped to the floor and his arm had fallen by his side. He'd been unconscious, surely. But everything was blurred in Snaz's mind. What if Dean was still conscious when he shot Rook?

'Simon? Mr Aziz?'

'I don't think he saw.'

'Dean didn't see Josie shoot his father?'

'No.'

'Supposing she claims it was you?'

The question cut through Snaz like a blade. 'Josie's the one who wanted Rook dead. I had nothing against him. Why would I want to kill him?'

'I hear you,' said the solicitor, 'but it's your word against hers.'

'Why would I kill my mate's dad?'

'It's not for me to speculate. Perhaps to protect Josie?'

'Why should I look out for Josie? She never looks out for anyone except herself.'

Francis scribbled on his yellow pad.

Snaz couldn't read what he'd written. 'You think I murdered Rook, don't you? I didn't have to hand myself in. I could've run away like Josie did.'

'Mr Aziz…'

'I thought you were meant to be on my side.' Snaz noticed the CCTV camera fixed to the wall of the windowless room.

'It's for security only, nobody can hear us,' the solicitor assured him. 'Simon, I'm here to advise you and to help you gather your thoughts. When the police question you, you need to be clear what to say.'

'What should I say? I don't want to go to prison.'

'Say no more than you have to. They can charge you with supplying an illegal firearm and probably with conspiracy too, but as for Curtis Rook's murder, they haven't any proof.'

'Conspiracy? You mean like I planned it? I didn't plan any of this.'

After a moment, the solicitor said, 'When you went with Josie to Rook's house, did you know the weapon was loaded?'

'No, I…' Snaz realised he had to deny it. 'No.'

'So Josie loaded it herself?'

'Yes,' Snaz said. 'She must have.' Even as he answered, he imagined the next question: how would she know how to? He needed to make something up… The night before, when she'd come to his flat and he'd tried to talk her out of going to Rook's house… He could say she'd asked him how to load the gun and he'd shown her, but then he'd taken the bullets out again and left them in a jar on his table and…

'Mr Aziz?' The solicitor interrupted his thinking. 'Did you hear me? I asked who left Rook's house first, Josie or you?'

'Josie. No, me. We left at the same time.'

'While you were in the house, did you have the gun at any point?'

'No, she had it all the time.'

'And she still had it when you left?'

'Yes.'

The solicitor stared at him.

'I've told you, yes.'

Francis clicked twice on the end of his pen. 'Mr Aziz, my job is to advise you, and my advice is to play a straight bat. If you did kill Curtis Rook – *if* you did – the likelihood is they'll find out. Better to admit it and show remorse than to seek to cover it up. When it comes to sentencing, they'll bear your remorse in mind. Consider that, is all I'm saying.'

Chapter 18

Ordinary people

Josie stared open-mouthed at the fish in the bathtub. *I'm going mad,* she thought. But the huge thing was moving, wafting its fins. She gazed at its shimmering scales. Then it turned and thrashed the water, splitting her reflection into quivering shards.

She stomped back to the bedroom, where Pete had his head buried in a book.

'There's a fish in the bath,' she said to him.

'The carp,' he replied, barely looking up.

'I can see it's a carp, but what is it doing there?'

'Swimming, I expect.'

She scowled at him.

'One of Greg's friends works on a fish farm and gave it to him as a present,' Pete said. 'He shouldn't have accepted it. There's still a week to go before Christmas and he can hardly keep it in the bath until then. He'll have to kill it and put it in the freezer.'

Was everyone in Poland crazy, or only this family? 'Well he better get on with it. I need a bath.'

'You had a shower this morning.' Pete returned to his book.

'Can I borrow your phone?' she asked.

'It's out of credit,' he replied. 'Costs a fortune to call home from here. Who do you want to ring anyway?'

'My brother.' She scrambled for something more to say. 'It's his birthday and I forgot to send him a card.'

'Ouch. Why not ask Greg if you can use the landline? I'm sure he won't mind.'

Josie went straight to the lounge, but stalled when she saw Marcin reclined on the settee next to the phone. 'Can I...? Can I use your phone?' she asked. Lowering her voice to a whisper, she added, 'It's about... I want to find out if there's any news.'

Marcin put down his magazine. 'You mean about the man you hit with your car?'

Josie cringed, put a finger to her lips. 'Sh, not so loud.'

'I'm interested what you will do if he dies? Will you go to police then?'

'Please, Marcin, people will hear.'

He continued loudly, ignoring her plea. 'If what you say is true…if this accident is not your fault, why you have fear to go to police?'

'Because they'll send me to prison. They won't believe it was self-defence.'

His eyes narrowed and Josie realised what she'd said. 'Self-defence? What you talk about?'

'Nothing.' She backtracked. 'What I meant is I couldn't stop the car in time. But they won't care. They'll still lock me up.'

Marcin kept on staring at her.

Josie wanted to take back what she'd said about him, but how could she? Before she could think things through, Dorota came in with a piping bowl of soup and cast them an inquiring glance.

'Peter, *zupa gotowa!*' Dorota called in a shrill voice. She went back to the kitchen and returned with a second bowl.

Josie came to the table and chose a seat so she wouldn't be facing Marcin. The thick yellow soup had scraps of bacon in it. She had no appetite, but told herself if she could manage some it might boost her strength.

Pete passed his aunt by the doorway and sat next to Josie. He tipped the saucer of croutons and rather too many fell into his bowl.

Marcin sat opposite Pete. Josie could sense him staring at her.

Dorota returned with two more bowls on a tray and Greg followed, clutching an overfilled one in both hands. He lowered it onto his placemat, spilling a bit, licked his fingers and went to the sideboard for the wicker breadbasket. In it Josie saw the three slices they'd cut for her at breakfast which she'd left untouched on her plate.

'So, Josephine,' Greg said, 'what do you think about Warsaw? What impression our city makes for you?'

'I haven't had a chance to see much of it,' she managed to respond.

'Then Peter must show you. It would be a crime to come to Warsaw and not visit Old Town.'

Marcin sniffed.

For a while they all ate without speaking, Pete and Greg vying with one another for who could slurp their soup the loudest. Greg tutted when a car alarm went off outside. Eventually he turned to Josie again. 'Peter must show you the Opera House. Or better,' he said to Pete, 'you can invite her one evening for the opera. I have the programme somewhere. Take her to see *Halka*.' Greg smiled at Josie, revealing his several metal fillings. 'Have you bring with you a dress to wear?'

Josie wished he'd stop talking and leave her alone. She pretended to listen and nodded, but her thoughts were on what she'd do when Marcin blabbed. Maybe they wouldn't believe him. But if they did? She had to speak to her dad, and soon. The thought of having to tell him everything. She stiffened further, stung by how bad it would sound if she admitted to persuading Snaz to load the gun. When she'd first asked Snaz to get her a weapon, she hadn't believed he'd do it. They were ordinary people. He was a car mechanic and a hospital radio DJ. How on earth had he found a gun?

When he told her weeks later that he'd got one, she'd been shocked but curious to see it. The polished black weapon nestled in a shoebox was small enough for her bag, though when she picked it up, it weighed far more than she expected. She'd raised her arm, pointed the gun at the mirror and saw the void of the barrel. Only then did she wonder if she really could pay Rook back.

'Darling, would you pass me the bread, please?'

It took Josie a second to register what Pete said.

He hesitated when he saw the hard slices, took one from the basket, but set it on the side of his plate.

She'd shot Dean, but it had been Snaz's fault as much as her own. His fault, for getting the weapon. His, for not making sure Rook was alone in the house.

Josie was the last to finish her soup. Dorota took the bowls away and the rest of them waited for the main course. The car alarm kept blaring. Even Pete had lost patience and started shaking his head.

Marcin went over to the window. After a bit he looked at Josie. 'It's yours,' he said.

'What?'

'The alarm. It's your Mini.'

Josie shot up, came to the window and saw her Mini's lights flashing. The last thing she needed: to draw attention to her car. 'I have to stop it,' she said, rushing to grab her coat.

She cursed again when the dog in the end flat barked at her. The lift still had an "out of order" sign taped to its door, so she ran down the stairs two at a time until she stumbled and almost fell. A short line of beer cans stood in a row on the next-to-bottom step.

She reached the front door at the same time as a wrinkled old woman who had shopping bags weighing down both arms. Josie held the door open – *get a move on – hurry up* – then cut across the grass towards her car, icy raindrops pricking her face like needles.

Josie took out her keys and stopped the alarm. No one was around. She had no idea what had set it off. 'Bloody stupid thing.' She turned to head back to the flat.

She'd got halfway back to the lobby when a man shouted, 'Hey!' Josie carried on, but then the man called her name.

Her legs kept on walking, but inside she froze. It had to be the police. Who else would know her name? Turning round, she faced the man. He was tall, young, not in a uniform but wearing a black leather jacket. And then she recognised him: Marcin's brother, Adam. She breathed again.

He approached her. He looked rougher than in the photos she'd seen in the flat, unshaven and tired, like he'd spent the night on the town.

She tried a smile, but he didn't return it.

'We must talk,' he said, pointing to a black Mercedes parked nearby. It sounded like an order.

'What do you want to talk about?'

'Guess.'

She understood then, and a shockwave of fear passed through her body. 'Marcin must have spoken to you.'

'Not only Marcin. I know *exactly* why you come here. I know about *Curtis Rook.*'

Josie reeled. How? How could he know?

'The police are looking for you, so you come to Poland to escape.'

Josie had nothing to hold on to. Nowhere to flee.

'Tell me,' Adam said, 'does Pete know?'

She shook her head.

'I didn't think so. Okay, you come with me in the car.'

'What for? Where?'

'You will find out,' he said.

'I can't come. We're in the middle of eating. They'll wonder where I am. They'll call the police.'

He stared up at the flat. Josie looked too and noticed Marcin watching them from the balcony. Even from down here, she could make out the smirk on his face.

'Go up,' Adam said. 'Tell them you have go out. I wait here for you. Five minutes,' he added.

'What do I say to them?'

'Your problem, not mine.'

'What if I don't come down?'

'Five minutes,' he repeated. 'You don't come, I go up and I tell Pete about your secret. And then...' He took a phone from his jacket. 'Then I telephone police.'

Chapter 19

Stay calm

Snaz recoiled in his chair when he heard DCI Mercer's voice in the corridor outside. He'd been praying it would be DS Orchard who'd interview him. Anyone but Mercer.

'I want the son of a bitch nailed,' the DCI said loud enough for Snaz to hear him. 'We both know he did it. I want a confession. Remember your promotion board is coming up in the New Year.'

Snaz's solicitor put his timesheet aside. 'Don't rise to their bait. Stay calm and don't forget what we discussed.'

Snaz couldn't remember a thing, not even what he'd said in his first interview with Mercer. His mind swirled with questions the police might ask him. Questions like, why hadn't he come to them sooner? And why had he lied and given a false alibi when they'd called at his flat? Before he could ask the lawyer for advice on how to answer them, Mercer strode into the room.

'Apologies for keeping you waiting.' He set a folder on the table, along with a *Mars* bar and a watch with a broken strap.

'I hope you weren't trying to intimidate my client,' Snaz's lawyer said.

'I beg your pardon?'

'Oh, come on. I distinctly heard you outside: "I want him nailed…"'

'Mr Francis, I was referring to a sex offender, a different case.'

'My client came here of his own free will and has co-operated throughout.'

'Of course.' Smiling, Mercer turned to Snaz. 'I trust they've given you something decent to eat?'

The older detective, Turvey, joined them in the room and loaded new cassettes in the machine.

Mercer didn't wait for him to sit down. 'Interview

commencing at fourteen-thirty-three. Present are DCI Mercer, DS Turvey and Simon Aziz. Also in attendance is Mr Francis, Mr Aziz's brief.' He read Snaz his rights again and then began to thumb through his papers. 'I'd like to go over a couple of things with you, to be absolutely certain I've understood.'

Snaz had been to the toilet ten minutes ago, but he wanted to go again.

'You've admitted you obtained a revolver for Josie Davenport, with which she planned to threaten Curtis Rook. You went with her to Curtis's house and assisted her in gaining entry, though you knew she had a loaded weapon. Did you or didn't you? Please confirm for the tape.'

'Yes, but…'

'How long did all this take to arrange: your job with Curtis, gaining his trust, not to mention getting hold of the firearm? A lot of trouble to have you go to, isn't it, if she only meant to give someone a scare? Did you never wonder if she intended to do something more?'

Snaz swallowed. 'Like what?'

'Did Josie blame Curtis Rook for her mother's death?'

'He used to be a pimp. He took money from her mum, but did nothing to protect her.'

'Would it be fair to say she wanted revenge then?'

'Yes.'

'Would merely frightening Curtis have been enough for her? You've heard the expression, "an eye for an eye and a tooth for a tooth"?'

'I can't say what was going through her head.'

'Tell me about the weapon. Why did you load it?'

'I didn't want to. She told me to.'

'And why do you think she did that?'

Snaz's head dropped.

Sergeant Turvey chipped in. 'Josie asks you to obtain a firearm and you do it. She asks you to load the weapon and you do that.

What if she asked you to kill Curtis? Would you have done that for her too?'

'No.' He faced the DS down. Mercer was the one who scared him.

'Okay, Simon,' Mercer said. 'Had you any idea Dean would be there when you went to Curtis's house?'

'No, he didn't live with his dad. He'd never been there when I'd called round in the past.'

'You must have been stunned when he ran from the kitchen?'

Snaz wasn't sure what to say. Of course he'd been stunned. But Josie had fired before he could react.

'And Josie, too. She thought she'd killed him, didn't she? She must have been in a state of shock,' Mercer said. 'Am I right?'

'I suppose.'

'I'm simply attempting to build a picture. Dean runs at Josie with a bread knife and Josie shoots him. Thinking she's killed him, she drops the gun – the natural physical reaction for a person who's in shock. The revolver is lying on the floor where Curtis Rook can get to it. You don't even think. It's your self-preservation instinct that makes you pick it up.'

'I didn't pick it up.'

'So Josie did drop the gun, then?'

'I never said that. Why won't you believe me? I didn't have to come to you. I could've run away abroad like she did.'

'DCI Mercer, you're sailing very close to the wind,' Francis intervened. 'This experience has been stressful enough for my client without you putting words in his mouth.'

Mercer raised his palms. 'Then tell us what *did* happen after Dean was shot. Step by step, in your own words.'

'*Josie* shot Rook,' Snaz said again.

'Immediately after she shot Dean?'

'I guess. Yes.'

'You guess yes,' Mercer parodied. 'You've stated previously you would've called for help, but you thought Dean was dead, right?'

'Yes.'

'So then Josie couldn't have shot Rook *immediately*.'

'I don't know. It was...I don't know...a few seconds.'

'She just shot him. Bang!' said Mercer.

'She shot him, yes.'

'Dean I can understand. He ran at her with a knife – she shot him to protect herself. But to recover from the shock of what's happened and pull herself together enough to shoot Curtis Rook... That's what I'm struggling to grasp.'

'It's what happened,' Snaz said.

'You witnessed Josie shoot two people. Why did you protect her?' Mercer asked. 'Why didn't you come straight to us?'

Snaz turned to his lawyer.

'You're under no obligation to reply to any question,' Francis said.

'None whatsoever,' confirmed Mercer, his eyes fixed on Snaz. 'But it may harm your defence if you do not mention when questioned something you later rely on in court. Why not be up front, if you've nothing to hide?'

'She begged me not to hand her in. She said if I went to the police, she'd tell you it was me.'

'You who shot Curtis?' Mercer said with exaggerated disbelief. 'Why on earth would she claim that?'

Snaz wanted to run from the room. 'To save her own skin.'

'To want to save your skin is one thing, but to be prepared to see an innocent person go to jail? That's pretty base, wouldn't you agree?'

Snaz moved his hands from the table but replaced them when he spotted the film of sweat on the surface where they'd been.

Turvey joined in again. 'Where's the murder weapon?'

'Josie took it. I don't know what she did with it.'

'Josie *took* it?'

Shit, Snaz thought. 'She kept it with her. She never gave it back to me, is what I mean.'

'Okay, so Curtis has been shot and killed. What happened next?' Mercer spoke more gently now. 'Did you run from the house?'

'Yes.'

'What about Josie? Was she waiting for you in the car?'

Snaz spotted the trap. 'No, she was with me. We ran to the car together.'

'Whose car was it, yours or hers?'

'Mine.'

'So you drove, did you, and Josie sat beside you?'

He thought for a moment, wondered where this might be leading. 'Yes.'

'Where did you go?'

'I took her back to her flat.'

'And where's the revolver while you're driving? Did you give it to Josie to get rid of, or did you put it in the boot?' Mercer smiled.

'No, I...' Snaz sensed another trick. 'I told you. Josie still had the gun!'

Mercer dropped his pen and then, glancing at Turvey, leaned back in his seat. A short time passed before he resumed. 'So let's talk about Josie. How did you meet her?'

'In a club.'

'How long ago?'

'Six years. Five and a half.'

'Were you already acquainted with Curtis back then?'

'No, but I used to watch Arsenal with his son.'

'Not his son Dean?'

'Matt, Dean's brother.'

'I'd like you to think back to when Josie first asked you to obtain a firearm. When was it, roughly? How long before the shootings?'

'September maybe. I can't remember the exact date.'

'But at least a couple of months? Do you recollect what she said? It's not your ordinary run-of-the-mill favour for a girl to ask her bloke.'

'She wanted to pay Rook back.'

'Were those the precise words she used?'

'I think so, yes.'

'One more question, Simon.' Mercer scraped a fingernail between his teeth. 'If the intention was to threaten Curtis, not to kill him, why not have used a replica handgun or an air pistol? It would have been easier to obtain. Less risky too.'

'I'd no idea where to get any kind of gun. Time was running out. I spoke to someone I used to know and he put me in touch with a man.'

'What's the name of this man?' Turvey asked.

'The one I got the gun from? I don't know his name. He was Irish.'

'What do you mean by "time was running out"?' Mercer again.

'Josie said we had to go to Rook's house on the tenth of December.'

'Why then?'

'That day she was exactly the same age as her mum had been when she was killed.'

'The same age?'

'I don't just mean twenty-three. She'd worked it out to the day. You see how she planned it?'

'Where can we find Josie Davenport?' Mercer asked.

'She's staying in Poland, in Warsaw, with a bloke called Pete Henderson.'

'Is this Henderson involved?'

'He might be. I don't know.'

A knock on the door made them both look up.

Turvey went to open it and Snaz recognised DS Orchard's voice: 'Excuse me, guv,' she said to Mercer. 'Can I have a word?'

Mercer went out and closed the door behind him.

'Interview suspended at fourteen-forty-seven. DCI Mercer leaves the room.' DS Turvey stopped the tape. 'Is that a Wasps tie you're wearing?' he asked Francis, as Snaz turned towards the lawyer.

'It is,' Francis said.

'You're a club member then?'

'I am.'

'My nephew turns out for the second fifteen. Rich Cox.' Turvey took a tube of throat lozenges from his jacket.

'Oh, I think I know who you mean. Outside centre, isn't he?'

'It's where they play him, but if you ask me, his natural position is fly half. Yeah, I get along to watch them when I can. I saw the Leicester game last month. Most weekends I'm working.'

Snaz wanted to scream at them to shut up. He couldn't think straight with them talking. He had to concentrate. He'd spotted some traps already, but what if there'd been others? Perhaps without realising it, he'd given himself away.

The door opened and Mercer returned to his chair, signalled to Turvey to re-start the tapes. 'Interview recommencing fourteen-fifty.' For what felt like a minute, he stared at Snaz in silence. 'We've spoken to Dean,' he said at last.

Chapter 20

Twenty minutes

Adam was leaning against the Mercedes, not bothered by the drizzle. When he saw Josie, he made a show of checking his watch. 'I told you five minutes,' he said. 'You take twenty.'

'They had the meal on the table. I couldn't leave in the middle of it. When I said I needed to go out, Pete wanted to come with me. I had trouble convincing him to let me go on my own.'

Adam opened the rear door of the car. 'Get in.'

Josie hesitated. 'I thought you wanted to talk.'

'Yes.'

'So why do you want me in the back?'

'Just...don't argue.'

She thought it best to do what he wanted. Before she could close the door herself, he pushed it shut, then walked around the front of the car to the driver's seat.

'I told Pete I'll be back in twenty minutes,' she said when he started the engine. She'd actually said up to an hour, but she had no intention of admitting that to Adam. The sooner she got this over with, the better. 'If I'm not back at three, he'll be worried.'

Adam shrugged and she recalled what he'd said before: "Your problem, not mine." She hated it when the other person held all the cards.

They reached the main road and still he said nothing.

'So are you going to tell me what you want?' Josie heard a loud click and realised he'd locked all the doors. 'What are you doing?' she asked. He was taking her to the police, she became certain. 'I lied,' she said. 'Pete does know about Rook. He's involved in what happened. If you take me to the police, they'll come after your cousin too.'

Adam scoffed. 'I don't think so. This is Pete we talk about. I know my own cousin.'

They sped past the place where a couple of days earlier Marcin had got out of her car. Marcin must have gone to Adam and told him what he'd heard her say, and Adam had done more research. She imagined articles in the papers, her picture splashed all over news sites on the internet. He'd discovered the police were after her, and he intended to hand her over. She kicked the seat.

At the traffic lights, she expected Adam to turn right towards the city centre but he changed lanes and headed left. The windscreen wipers rasped against the glass.

'You've got it wrong,' Josie said. 'I didn't shoot anyone, why won't you believe me? Please don't hand me in.'

'I'm not.'

Yeah, right, she thought. What other possible explanation could he have for effectively kidnapping her? Unless... She sat forward. 'Do you want money from me? How much do you want?'

'Don't insult me.' Contempt in his voice. 'You dump my cousin, you tell lies about my brother. If you didn't shoot the man in London then for what reason did you run away here?'

She took a breath to compose herself. No point in denying what he already knew. 'Okay, I admit I shot Rook's son, but in self-defence. He attacked me and I...'

Adam cut her off. 'I don't want listen your explanation. Be quiet and let me drive.'

Josie let go of the front seat. She hadn't registered before how luxurious the car was: leather upholstery, wood trimming every-where and even a mini bar. It made no sense that Adam could afford such a posh car while his parents lived in a rundown tower block and slept on a sofa bed in the living room. 'You must have a good job to drive a car like this.'

'It's not my car,' he replied.

She noticed the newspaper folded in the pouch behind

Adam's seat was printed in Cyrillic. 'Whose is it then?'

'It belongs to man I work for.'

Josie looked out through the tinted glass of the window. They appeared to be leaving the city. The houses by the roadside had private yards with chickens running free, and on a muddy patch of land, she saw a lone scraggy goat.

When she caught Adam looking at her in the mirror, he averted his eyes like a startled schoolboy. He was her type: handsome but rugged, dark in more ways than one. And now he was watching her again.

The clock on the dashboard showed five past three. Twenty minutes had passed since they'd left the flat and they must have driven over ten miles. Josie believed Adam now, about not going to the police. If so, he'd have gone to the nearest station. He wouldn't be driving deep into the countryside.

The further he took her from the city, the darker it grew outside, the more Josie started to panic. She considered what other motives he could have. Maybe he wanted to frighten her, to warn her off involving Pete? Or perhaps whoever he worked for meant to hold her hostage and demand a ransom from her dad. For a second it even occurred to her Adam might be working for Rook. She had to remind herself Rook was dead. But Adam could be working for someone connected with him, like Dean's brother Matt. *Please not that.*

'Pete loves me,' she said. 'If anything happens to me, he won't forgive you.' Nothing she said prompted a reaction from Adam.

'Stop the car. I'm feeling sick.' If she could get him to stop and open the door, she could make a run for it. He'd chase her and catch her, but she'd scream and put up a struggle, use her nails to scratch his eyes. There were other cars around. She counted on another driver coming to her aid. 'Stop the car and let me out,' she repeated. 'I'm going to be sick.'

To her surprise, he did pull over. 'Are you serious?' He

lowered the electric window part of the way down. 'Listen, we almost there.'

'Where?' Josie begged. 'Where are you taking me?'

'To the house of man I work for. Pan Kogut, he is asking everyone to find you.'

'Who's Pan Kogut? Does he work for the police?'

'He doesn't work for anyone.'

'Then what does he want with me?'

'He said to bring you to his house. He didn't tell me reason. Now you know as much as me.'

Chapter 21

Nothing real can be threatened

Towering gates parted ahead of them to reveal a white mansion with a four-columned porch and a broad fan of steps rising to the doorway. A world apart from the city of grey prefab blocks, it surpassed Josie's dad's Trafalgar Lodge. She became even tenser. What did the owner of this mansion want with her?

Adam stopped the car and unlocked the doors. 'Okay, come with me.'

Glancing over her shoulder, she noticed the gates had closed again. Giant hedgerows enclosed the grounds. Josie's legs felt shaky as she followed Adam up the steps.

A bearded man in a waistcoat opened the door and eyed Josie like an aging doorman at an upmarket club. He exchanged a few words with Adam in Polish, then beckoned her in.

Josie gazed around the hallway at the giant mirror, at the grandfather clock with its loud swinging pendulum, at the uncommonly high ceiling, the wide staircase, the striking framed photograph of the earth viewed from space. She heard the door shut and saw Adam had gone, leaving her on her own with the man.

'May I take your coat, madam?' he said.

Being addressed as "madam" set Josie more at ease and she let him help her out of it.

He disappeared for a moment into a side room and returned minus her coat. 'I will take you to Mr Kogut.'

He led her along a corridor, the chequered marble floor squeaking beneath her shoes. Stunning space photographs hung on the walls: galaxies and nebulae and a close-up of Saturn's rings. Josie almost bumped into the man when he stopped suddenly by a high panelled door. He knocked on it, then stepped aside and gestured for Josie to go through.

A man of about fifty, plump-faced, with spectacles, sat behind a desk. He rose to greet her, his paunch protruding above the desktop. 'Welcome, Miss Davenport. My name is Arkadiusz Kogut. It is my pleasure to meet you.'

Josie took a few paces forward, her feet sinking in the carpet, but stopped shy of Kogut. 'How do you know who I am?'

'Did Adam not explain?'

Trying hard to hide her nervousness, she shook her head.

'Your father contacted me. He heard you'd come to Poland and he asked my help to find you.'

'You know my dad?' A rush of energy surged through her. 'Can I to talk to him?'

'Of course.' Kogut turned the telephone on his desk so it faced her, then lowered himself into his high-backed chair.

Josie had no idea if her dad was still in the States or what number to call him on. Before she could ask, Kogut produced a sleek electronic organiser from the inside pocket of his made-to-measure suit – *Armani*, she guessed. He moved the phone again, tapped in a number for her, then passed her the receiver.

Her pulse quickened. 'Dad?'

'Josie, Princess! Where are you?'

A tide of relief swept over her. 'In Warsaw. I...'

'I've asked someone to find you, a man called Kogut...'

'I'm with him. I'm at his house.'

'You are?' Josie's dad breathed out and the line crackled. 'Good old Arkadiusz, I knew I could count on him. He'll look after you until I get there.'

'You're coming to Poland?'

'You're my daughter, of course I'm coming. I'll get the best attorney and bring him with me. Whatever's happened, we'll sort it out.' He paused. He sounded short of breath. 'Josie, what did happen? Tell me, so I can help you.'

Josie didn't want to talk with Kogut listening in. 'I'm not

alone.'

'I will leave you in private,' Kogut said. 'Come round and sit in my chair.'

After he'd closed the door, Josie held the phone to her face. Her dad was going to help her. For the first time since she'd fled from England she felt a flicker of hope.

In faltering sentences, Josie told her dad as much as she dared... She'd taken the gun with her to frighten Rook. She never intended to use it. But then the kitchen door jerked open, the most terrifying sound she'd ever heard, and she saw someone coming at her with a knife. 'I had to shoot, or he'd have stabbed me. His blood was everywhere. He'd stopped moving and all I could think was, "Please, God, no." If I'd realised he was alive, I'd have rung for an ambulance. Dad, I thought I'd killed him.'

'He's alive, Josie, you didn't kill him.'

'But he'll describe me to the police. Snaz has been arrested.'

'It's okay,' her father said. 'It'll be alright.'

'How? I used my credit card. The police will find me. They'll send me to jail.'

'Princess, listen. Sh, don't start crying on me. You need to be my brave girl.'

'I want you here, Dad.'

'I'm coming. We'll find a way through this. I won't let you down again.'

She must have talked with him for an hour, going over what happened several times. He kept asking questions... Who gave her the gun? Had she known it was loaded? Had it been Snaz's idea to go to Rook's house? His questions became more difficult and finally she couldn't answer them. 'I don't know. I can't remember.' She couldn't bring herself to admit the whole truth, not even to him.

When he ended the call so he could ring his lawyer and make

arrangements to come to her, Josie slumped back in the leather chair. Would the police believe she hadn't meant to hurt the man? She'd gone to Rook's house with a gun, a loaded gun. What had possessed her? A protracted shiver took hold of her body as she recalled sitting on Snaz's bed and watching him load the bullets. 'I can't believe you're making me do this,' he'd said. How crazy, how stupid she'd been. But she wouldn't have fired, she wouldn't have pulled the trigger. The longer she'd aimed the weapon at Rook, the more her hand had shaken. An apology, a softening in his expression, and she would have walked away.

The door opened and Josie looked up startled and saw Kogut peering into the room. 'Ah, so you have finished speaking with your father.' He approached her. 'Your father is a resourceful man, I am sure he will sort things out.'

Did he really believe that, or was he merely saying it to make her feel less bad? Josie wiped her eyes with her fingers. 'How do you know my dad?'

'Oh, he and I have had business dealings.' Kogut had only the slightest of accents. 'How old are you, Josephine? May I call you by your first name?'

'I'm twenty-three.'

He hovered near the desk and she stood up, aware she was sitting in his chair.

'What sort of host am I? Forgive me, I have not offered you a drink. What would you like? Coffee? Tea? Or there is herbal: camomile is supposed to be calming.'

'I'm fine,' she said, noticing the time on the wall clock. 'Pete will be worried where I am.'

'Pete?' Kogut inquired. 'Your boyfriend?'

'Yes,' she said. 'Kind of.'

'Is he aware of...your situation?'

'No. He'll think something's happened to me. Can someone take me back to where I'm staying?'

'Is that wise? Why not call Pete and tell him you are okay? I think it would be better if you stay here. Safer, I mean.'

Josie hesitated. Even though Kogut knew her dad, he still gave her the creeps. 'What would I tell Pete? I can't not go back.'

Through the large round lenses of his glasses Kogut continued to survey her. She was used to men looking at her, but not directly into her eyes, as though attempting to read her mind. 'I cannot believe it is true,' he said.

'What's not true?'

'That you shot someone.'

Josie shuddered. She hadn't been certain how much her father had told him.

'Surely the police will grasp it makes no sense.'

To escape his examination, she went to the window. The floor-length velvet curtains were drawn and she groped among their pleats to find where they met. Beyond the terrace, a lawn stretched to an ivy-covered wall ribbed with a metal guard. A magpie swooped from a tree and joined another on the grass. Josie watched them and sensed Kogut watching her. Summoning courage, turning to face him, she saw he'd returned to his seat behind the desk. 'I don't want to sound ungrateful,' she said, 'but I really need to get back. If Pete's worried, he might call the police.'

Kogut made a steeple with his hands. 'Why not tell him you met a friend of your father? It would not be a lie. If it makes you more comfortable, your boyfriend is welcome to stay here too. Fancy him being Adam's cousin! I can send Adam to fetch him here. There is plenty of space for an extra guest.'

'I don't want Pete to find out. If he comes here – if he sees this place – he'll suspect something. He already does. And what about my things: my car, my clothes?'

'Where have you left your car?' Kogut asked.

'Outside the flat.'

'Where Adam's parents live? The police will be looking for it. I doubt they are searching as hard as I was, but it would be wise to hide it somewhere off the roads. If you give me the keys, I will arrange for someone to move it.'

Josie recognised it made sense to move her car. She reached into her bag and found a spare set of keys.

'What a small world it is,' Kogut said when she came over and handed them to him. 'I had twenty people searching Warsaw for you and all along you were staying with Adam's family.'

'So is Adam going to drive me back?'

Kogut sniffed. 'I thought you had agreed to stay here? It is what your father expects.'

Josie held firm. 'I told you, I have to go back. Pete won't want to move out of his aunt's place. If I say I want to stay somewhere else, he'll be insulted.'

He remained silent a while. 'Did your father say when he is coming here?'

'The day after tomorrow, he thinks. He's still in Boston.'

'Okay, we will compromise. Here is what we will do. Waldemar will drive you to Ursynow, to the flat. Adam will go too, and collect your car. Speak to your boyfriend and explain that I am a family friend and have invited you to stay with me. Or perhaps you can think of another story...except do not mention that Adam works for me, and do not give anyone my name.

'Then, when you've spoken to him, telephone me and I will collect you. On your own, or with your boyfriend, it is up to you. Tomorrow at the latest. It is not safe for you to remain there and risk being arrested before your father comes.'

Josie nodded.

'Here is my card with my number.'

'Thanks,' she said.

'Wait,' he said. 'I'd better give you his number too.' With a gold pen he wrote a telephone number on the reverse of the card. He picked up his phone, spoke in Polish into the receiver and Josie imagined Adam on the other end of the line.

While he talked on the phone, she gazed around the study. On one side, bookshelves rose from floor to lofty oak-beamed ceiling and she made out titles in English and French, as well as Polish. Framed calligraphy hung on the other wall. She read it: "Nothing real can be threatened." And another next to it: "Nothing unreal exists."

'We all make mistakes,' Kogut said, startling her. 'It does not change who we are.'

Josie didn't understand what he meant, but gave a nod.

'May I ask you a question? I hope you will not think it rude.'

'What question?' Josie expected it to be about her shooting Rook's son.

'What kind of man is Pete?'

Josie stared at him.

'You cannot keep him from hearing the accusations against you or from finding out what happened. It is going to be a difficult time for you, but for him also. I wonder if he has the strength to support you.'

Josie's head dropped at the thought of Pete discovering what she'd done.

'If Pete loves you, he will stand by you,' Kogut said. 'Then again, perhaps the question is, "do you want to involve him?"'

Chapter 22

The shoes she wore to church

The policeman led Snaz into the visitor's room and Grace rose to her feet. 'Simon, what's happened?' Her hair was dishevelled and her chestnut-coloured forehead glazed with sweat. 'Why have they arrested you? How can they make this mistake?'

When the policeman closed the door, leaving them alone, Grace held out both her arms. Snaz felt limp in her embrace.

'The detective I spoke to says you're involved in the murder I've heard about on the news. Speak to me, Simon. How can they think you had anything to do with it?'

What to say? All through his childhood and teenage years Grace had done her best by him, always putting him first. She'd believed in him, probably the one person who had done. It would crush her to discover the truth.

'They are victimising you with this false and malicious accusation.' Snaz heard the anguish in her voice. 'It must be mistaken identity. I'm going to the chief officer of the station to make a complaint about wrongful arrest.' She had on the shoes she wore to church, the ones with the white and navy buckles. 'Look at me, Simon. Why don't you look at me?'

The movement of lifting his head to meet her eyes was the hardest thing he'd ever had to do. 'Don't make a complaint,' he said. 'I am involved.'

Her lips curled in a grimace. 'No, not you.'

Her faith in him filled Snaz with shame.

Her eyes shrank from him and she made the sign of the cross.

Snaz might have fallen to his knees and begged her forgiveness, or beat on the door so the policeman would take him back to his cell, take him away forever. But he simply stood there, helpless to comfort the broken woman who'd tried for more than twenty years to teach him right from wrong.

With one hand clutching her wounded breast, Grace slumped onto a chair.

In the excruciating silence, Snaz grew aware of her breathing, each intake more strained than the last. When she fumbled in her coat for her inhaler and gasped with it to her mouth, dread rose in him. 'Grace, should I get you help?'

She waved him away and finally her wheezing subsided. 'What have you done?' she managed to say between toiling breaths.

'I'm sorry.' A pathetic thing to say, but pathetic was how he felt.

'Tell me why?' Another silence followed before some unwarranted hope lifted her face. 'Are you protecting someone? Is that it?'

'We didn't intend to use the gun. Josie asked me to get her a weapon so she could frighten Curtis Rook, but nothing else should have happened.'

Grace jolted. 'Josephine Davenport is involved?'

'I didn't want to help her, but she said she'd leave me.'

'That Jezebel is responsible!'

'Dean ran at her. She fired in self-defence.'

Grace covered her mouth. '*She* shot that young boy? Oh, Lord, he was only sixteen.'

'He had a knife. He would have killed her…'

His aunt didn't let him finish. 'What about the man? Did she shoot him too?'

Snaz stalled, aware the truth would destroy her. 'He'd seen her shoot his son,' he began.

'I knew it!' Grace said before he could say more. 'The Devil sent her. Tell the truth, Simon, and the police will let you go. Why do you protect her, when she has killed?'

'I'm not protecting her. I've told them she did it.'

'Oh, Simon, didn't I warn you about her?'

Snaz bowed his head. He could smell the jasmine scent of his aunt's perfume which he'd bought for her last birthday. All the love she'd shown him: the money for his college fees, the pep talks on Sunday afternoons when he'd come home late the previous night, or had too much to drink, God knows how many prayers... It hadn't been enough.

'If Josephine shot that man, why are the police charging *you*?'

'I got the gun for Josie. I was there.'

Snaz recognized in his aunt the white-eyed expression of horror he'd seen on Rook's face. Again her breath became laboured. 'You were there when she murdered him?'

He wished more than anything he could deny it.

'And you didn't stop her?' She twisted her neck away.

'I didn't expect her to shoot. We only planned to frighten him.'

Her body writhed. 'Please, no.'

'Josie lied to me, Grace. I never meant to hurt anyone.' He reached out to console her, but with a wave of her forearm she blocked his hand.

She drew on the inhaler. Never had she appeared so old or frail. 'Go,' she said. A single word that made him shrivel inside.

He retreated towards the door, part of him wishing he had the gun with him so he could turn it on himself.

'Tell me, Lord,' she pleaded out loud, 'what did I do wrong?'

'Nothing.' Snaz looked at her, but found her gaze fixed on the wall.

'I brought you up and you break the gravest Commandment.' She clasped her chest. 'Of course I've done something wrong, if you give that woman a gun to use to kill someone. And his boy, a sixteen-year-old child. Josephine Davenport is a murderer *with your help*. You have helped her to do this evil thing.' Grace wrung her hands together and then held them still as if in prayer.

Her distress pained him. If anyone else had caused her such grief, he wouldn't have stood for it, he wouldn't have let them.

But he alone was responsible.

No, he couldn't face her any more. Let him end up in the Hell they spoke of at her church, it wouldn't be worse than this. 'Goodbye, Mum,' he said, startling himself when he called her that, but she'd been more of a mum than his own.

In that instant she came to embrace him and kissed his forehead. 'Simon, you must pray. We both need to pray so He has mercy. Forgive him, Father, for he knew not what he did. Oh why did you do it? Tell me why?' She shook him like a child.

'I thought if I helped her, she'd love me.'

'She has used you. Always she has been using you. I recognised it the first time I saw her, winking her eyelashes like the harlot she is. I could tell she only had love for herself. Why were you so blind?'

'If I knew she'd wanted to kill him, I promise I wouldn't have helped. I wouldn't have got the gun.'

Grace pulled away, her eyes enlarged with fear, and Snaz wondered what he'd said. He feared he'd given himself away.

'Did you have the weapon in my house?'

'No,' he answered.

'When you visited me, did you bring it?'

'On my life, never. I kept it all the time at my flat.'

Uncertain, she observed him until at last she seized his hands. 'You were my little sister's baby. You would not have done these things, but Satan had hold of you and tempted you with that girl. I will always stand by you, even if you were the one…' She shuddered. 'But you have said it was not you. Only, tell me again and let God be your witness.'

Snaz's head sagged onto her shoulder. He knew what question was coming.

'Did you kill the man?'

'No, I swear I didn't.' It had become automatic, one more lie on top of all the rest.

Chapter 23

Mysterious friend

Greg ignored the ringing telephone. Captivated by the weather forecast or perhaps by the busty blonde weathergirl, he continued to stare at the TV.

'Will someone answer it?' Josie pressed Pete, anxious it might be her dad finally returning her call.

Pete shrugged and Josie was on the verge of answering herself, never mind what they thought, when Dorota came scurrying from the kitchen, wiping her hands on a dishcloth. For some inexplicable reason, she smoothed her thinning hair before picking up the phone.

She started conversing in Polish and Josie, disappointed, turned back to the television. The forecast predicted snow.

It startled Josie when Dorota, with a quizzical look, held out the phone to her.

She sprang from her seat, her pulse racing. Dad must have got her messages at last.

'Dad,' she said, 'why didn't you ring me sooner?' She had to be careful what she said: Pete and Dorota were listening, and even Greg had diverted his gaze from the TV.

'Josephine, it is me, Arkadiusz Kogut.'

She closed her eyes, deflated.

'Adam gave me this phone number. Have you heard about your father?'

'He hasn't called me. I keep ringing him, I must have tried five times since last night, but all I get is his voicemail.'

'You have not heard?' He paused. 'Josephine, he has had a stroke.'

A chasm opened and engulfed her.

'I will not lie to you, his condition is very serious. He is at the best hospital in Boston. The doctors are doing all they can for him.'

A stroke. Her dad. But she'd spoken to him yesterday and he'd sounded... No, he hadn't sounded fine. And Kogut was saying... *a stroke.* But her dad had promised to help her. What would happen to her if...? *If he died?*

'Gather your belongings,' Kogut said. 'I will come for you right away. Tell your boyfriend I am a friend of the family. Tell him I have arranged a seat for you on a plane, so you can fly to be with your father. Wait for me outside the flat. Josephine, do you hear me? Are you still there?'

She became aware of Pete standing next to her. 'Darling, what's up? Is everything okay?'

Pete prised the receiver from her limp hand. 'Who's there?' he said. 'Hello?'

Josie left him, staggered to the bedroom and made an effort to haul her suitcase onto the bed, but she couldn't muster the strength to lift it. She stood over it, her mind galloping. *Very serious. Doctors are doing all they can.* People don't use that phrase if someone's going to recover. *Think, Josie, think. Belongings. What do I need?* She grabbed a T-shirt, underwear. Her money was in her handbag. She caught sight of her travel jewellery box and took it. What else? Make-up bag. Change of clothes. She had a sense of déjà vu as she seized her black skirt. She tipped out the still-to-be-wrapped Christmas presents from Pete's carrier bag and stuffed it with the items she'd collected.

Pete came up beside her. 'Darling, I'm sorry.'

She stared at him.

'The man on the phone told me about your dad.'

'I have to go,' she said. 'I have to see him.'

'Of course.'

'I need to pack.'

'When are you leaving? Tomorrow? Not tonight! How will you get to England? You can't *drive* in this state, surely.'

She shook her head.

'Okay, well do you want us to go to the airport and check if there are any spare seats on the late flight?'

'Someone's picking me up – the man you spoke to. He's a friend of the family. He's arranged it already.'

'When?'

'He said he's coming now.'

'Are you serious? I better get packed too.'

Josie clutched her make-up bag to her chest. She'd decided not to involve Pete. But how to tell him? Say it. Be direct. 'I'm going on my own.'

His eyes widened. 'Don't you want me to come with you?'

Josie would have preferred to slip away when he wasn't around, so she didn't have to explain. 'He's only booked one seat on the plane.'

'He? Who is this mysterious friend?'

'One of Dad's business contacts who lives in Warsaw.'

'Well, do you want me to get myself on another flight tomorrow?' Pete must have grasped the answer from her expression, because his eyes dropped and he looked away.

'I'm not going to London. Dad's in America, so I'm going straight there. It'd do no good if you came with me. What could you do?'

'Be there. Be with you.' He held her captive with his stare.

'Don't,' she said.

'Don't what?'

'Make it even harder. I have to do this on my own.'

* * *

Three silhouettes loitered in the dusk by the frame of the broken swing. Josie sensed they were watching her. The one who'd been perched on the back of the bench rose and stepped down off the seat. She glimpsed a spark as he lit a cigarette.

She walked a few paces to stand under a street light. How much longer before Kogut arrived?

An approaching car flashed its headlights as it negotiated the craters in the road, but when it came nearer it turned out to be one of those baby things, far too small to be his. She curled her toes inside her shoes, stamped her feet to warm them. The biting wind blew ripples in the puddles on the ground.

All the bad things she'd wished upon her dad and now, when she needed him, he was in hospital, maybe unconscious. He might die.

Laughter somewhere, a mocking kind of laugh. Josie stole a glance at the youths and saw only two of them by the swing. Then she registered the other one, the tallest, striding towards her. A gust blew his hood off and he pulled it back on over his head. She looked about, hoping to see other people, but there was no one else. Instinctively she held on to the key in her pocket – something sharp.

The youth approached with a swagger. *He's going to pull a knife,* Josie thought. Instead of running, she braced herself. *Let him do it. Let this all be over.* But a few metres away, he stopped. Josie heard the creak of the apartment lobby door and, looking round, saw Pete.

In the distance, the laughter again.

Pete came up to her. 'You left without a proper goodbye. Why didn't you wait for me?'

She glanced back and forth between him and the one in the hooded tracksuit, who had crouched and was tying his laces.

'You didn't say goodbye to Greg and Dorota.'

Her would-be assailant had vanished, but he must be hiding somewhere near.

'It's freezing out here. Come back and wait inside the flat.' Pete's breath rose like smoke from a pyre. 'Josie, why are you blanking me out?'

'God must hate me.'

'What?' Pete took a step nearer. 'I didn't hear you. Say it again.'

'I can't take any more of this.'

'More of what?'

'Have you ever felt like you're being taunted?'

'Who's taunting you? Josie, I love you.'

'You wouldn't,' she said. 'You wouldn't love me if you had any idea.'

'Whatever it is, whatever's making you hurt – and I don't just mean your dad's stroke – I want to help you through it.'

'I'm not good enough. You shouldn't have taken me back.'

'When you left me, it was your pain that made you say those things. All the hurt and resentment you're carrying around with you. Josie, I don't know what happened to make you not trust people, but I do know one thing. I care about you. I love you. But...' He breathed out. 'If you don't feel the same way about me, I still want to be your friend.'

She wanted to fall into his arms when he said that, or part of her did. But the puddle between them was like an ocean. And then the door to the apartment block opened again and a man came out with an Alsatian straining at its leash. The youth in the hood walked past – just a boy, Josie realised. And a car pulled up, a Mercedes. The rear door opened and she saw Kogut inside. 'I'd like that too,' she said to Pete. 'To be your friend.'

Pete stepped forward, treading in the puddle, and she let her head rest for a moment against his cheek.

'Take care,' he said to her.

'You take care too.' She picked up her bag and felt unsteady as she walked the few steps to the car.

Kogut acknowledged her when she sat next to him. 'That man is Pete?' he asked.

The car pulled away and she swivelled round to look out of the rear window. Perhaps she should have told Pete everything, asked him to come with her. Maybe he would have stood by her.

Her heart beat faster and it crossed her mind to tell Kogut's driver to stop and turn back. No, it wouldn't be fair on Pete.

'I would not have put you together,' Kogut said.

Josie watched Pete growing smaller, and wondered if she would ever see him again.

Chapter 24

After the fall

Light encroached above the curtains, enough to make out the hands of the carriage clock on the bedside table. Josie struggled to lean up in bed, still feeling knocked out from the tablets Kogut had given her to help her sleep. For a terrifying moment it crossed her mind she might have had sex with him. She still had her knickers on under her nightshirt, but it alarmed her, what could have happened and still might. Men like Kogut weren't kind for no reason.

She tried to reassure herself that he wouldn't try anything when her dad might get better. But if Dad didn't recover, she'd be reliant on Kogut's help. Then she'd have no choice but to give him whatever he wanted in return.

Josie felt giddy as she got out of the double bed. The clock said twenty past nine. It couldn't be so late, surely, but when she checked her watch it showed the same time. She began getting dressed; got halfway through doing up her blouse before realising one side was lower than the other, and she'd missed out a button. What had been in those sleeping pills? In future, she'd stick to taking just one.

When she noticed the phone on the dressing table, Josie thought of calling her brother, but she feared the news would be bad. Instead of going to the phone, she parted the velvet curtains and wiped an arc in the condensation on the windowpane. A drop of melt water fell from the roof and punctured the fresh coat of snow on the ledge. How sombre the world looked in white.

Josie stared for a while at the garden. No, she couldn't take not knowing. She had to make the call.

The phone rang eight times before her sister-in-law answered. 'Hello? Nathan, is it you?'

'Clara, it's Josie.'

'Oh.' There followed an awkward pause. The two of them had never hit it off. 'Have you heard about your father?'

Josie braced herself. 'I know he's had a stroke.'

'He's in intensive care.'

She closed her eyes in relief. Still alive.

'His condition's very serious. Nathan's gone with your mother—' Clara corrected herself: 'He's gone with Beatrice to Boston. They're with him at the hospital.'

'He's going to live though?'

'I...I think you should see him.'

Josie sat back on the bed, sensing what Clara meant. 'He's not going to make it, is he?'

Clara didn't reply.

'I want to see him,' Josie said. 'But...' How to explain her situation?

'Josie, I had two detectives here yesterday.' Clara's voice fell to a whisper. 'A man has been murdered. It's absurd, but for some bizarre reason, they... I don't know how to say this... They appear to think you might be involved.'

Josie took a while to recover. 'Me?' she feigned surprise.

'They've arrested your boyfriend and they have it in their heads you're somehow involved as well. I told them they must be mistaken.' Clara paused. 'You're not involved, are you?'

'I must talk to Nathan,' Josie said.

'Nathan's in America,' Clara replied.

'Can you give me his mobile number? I don't have it. Wait, I need something to write with.' Josie dropped the phone onto the bed and scanned the room, but couldn't spot a pen. She rummaged in her handbag...all she could find were cosmetics. She opened the drawers of the dressing table: both completely empty. Flustered, she went back to her handbag, grabbed a mascara pen – it was a choice between that or a lipstick – and plucked the last tissue from the packet to write on.

Clara read out the number: '07761…'

Josie could barely hold the crayon. 'You're going too fast. Say it again.'

'I wonder if,' Clara said, 'before you call Nathan, maybe I ought to speak to him first.'

'Why?'

'I think it would be better. I'll give you the number for the hospital. The nurses are very helpful, and if you tell them you're Joseph's daughter…'

Josie didn't let her finish. 'I don't want to talk to some nurse. Nathan's my brother and I want to speak to him.'

'I'm sorry. He told me last night he doesn't want to talk to you.'

'What?'

'Josie, please. He's taking Dad's stroke very badly…'

'He isn't your dad, he's mine!'

'He thinks it's connected to this wretched drama with you and your boyfriend and the police.'

Josie felt a swooning sensation. 'Are you saying…? Did Dad have the stroke because of me?'

'When people are distressed, they say things they don't mean. Let me talk to him again,' Clara said. 'It's night-time in Boston, but I'm calling him when it's morning there. He might have calmed down. He probably regrets what he said. Let me give you the number for the ward.'

Powerless to argue, Josie found herself scribbling the number Clara read out.

'When the police ask where you are, what should I tell them?' Clara asked.

'Don't say anything.'

'Josie, isn't it better for you speak to them and clear up this whole business? I mean, even if your boyfriend did have a part in it... It's nonsense, isn't it, the idea *you* could be involved?'

'Of course it's nonsense. But please don't tell the police where I am.'

Josie gathered herself, took a few laboured breaths, before ringing the hospital. She had to wait ages before someone answered and then they put her on hold, made her listen to vaguely familiar classical music which was serene and gentle and made her want to cry. A knock on the door startled her. When it came again, louder, she hung up the phone in alarm. Kogut! She moved away from the bed – better to go out to him than have him come into the bedroom – but the door opened before she reached it.

To her relief it wasn't Kogut, but a woman, middle-aged and trim. 'Hello,' the woman stopped in the doorway. 'I am Yvonna,' she said with a timid smile. 'Forgive please my not-so-good English. Arkadiusz asks me to check if you awake and if you are feeling okay?'

Josie nodded.

'Are you ready to have breakfast? What do you like for me to prepare?'

'Are you... Are you Kogut's wife?'

'Mr Kogut? Me with Arkadiusz?' The woman gave an embarrassed chuckle. 'No, my husband is Waldemar. You have meet him yesterday when you first come here. Waldemar and me, we together are looking after this house.'

Josie followed Yvonna down the staircase. Feeling giddy, she had to concentrate on every step. As she entered the dining room, Kogut acknowledged her. He wiped the crumbs from his mouth with a napkin. 'How did you sleep? Join me, please.'

Josie sat opposite him. The oblong table could have seated a dozen people, but only two places were set.

'Would you like an English breakfast?' Kogut said.

'Could I have a black coffee? I don't eat breakfast.'

He said something in Polish to Yvonna, who nodded and then left the room. 'No wonder you are thin as a stray cat. At least have some cereal. You must eat to keep your strength up.' He stretched across the table to offer her the frosted cornflakes, but she shook her head.

His veneer of a smile faded and he reached into his pocket for his mobile phone. 'You must want to speak to your family, to find if there's any more news.'

'I've spoken to my sister-in-law. I used the phone in my room.'

'Oh, right. How is your father?'

She twisted her feet together. 'Clara thinks he's going to die.'

Kogut opened his mouth but checked himself.

Josie wondered what he'd intended to say. 'My brother blames me,' she said.

'How can he blame you?'

'He says Dad's stroke is my fault.'

'But that is ridiculous.'

'He's right. It can't be a coincidence. Dad hears what happened and the same day he has a stroke.'

'A man who works the hours he did is tempting fate. He chain-smoked too.'

Josie's eyes fell to the place mat in front of her. 'He's always been healthy. He's only sixty-four.'

Before long Yvonna returned with a tray and set a croissant, pistachio-sprinkled yoghurt and a glass of orange juice in front of Josie. 'Fresh, squashed today,' she said. 'Coffee is coming one minute.'

'Do have the yoghurt at least,' Kogut urged when Yvonna had gone.

Josie picked up the silver spoon and tasted a saccharine mouthful, sieving the nuts on her tongue.

Kogut helped himself to more cereal from the box. He ate it dry, without milk. After a few spoonfuls he seemed to grow aware of the sound of his crunching, chewed more slowly, and then stopped. 'Whatever happens, I will help you,' he said.

'But I don't know you.'

'Your father did. Does.'

She let him wallow a moment in his slip. 'How did you meet my dad?'

'I told you, through business. Your father was one of the first from the West to recognise the opportunities in Poland after the fall.'

'I didn't kill Rook,' Josie said, looking straight into Kogut's eyes.

'To think so is absurd. If you tell me what happened, I can speak to a lawyer.'

She bit her lip, afraid to say more.

'I don't doubt for a second you are innocent, but what do I say to the lawyer? If I'm to help you, I need to know what happened.'

'I wanted to frighten Curtis Rook.'

'Why? Had he harmed you?'

'If it wasn't for him, my mum would still be alive.'

'But your mother is Beatrice?' Kogut asked, confused.

'No, she's not.'

'You are adopted?' His eyes widened. 'Joseph is not your natural father?'

'He is. I was born before he got married. But it doesn't matter. What matters is I didn't kill Rook. And I only shot his son because he attacked me.' She felt breathless, still uncertain if she should be telling him these things.

'You did shoot the younger man?'

'I had to, or he'd have killed me.'

Kogut's expression was impossible to read. 'Why did Aziz murder Curtis Rook? That wasn't self-defence?'

'Snaz panicked. We thought I'd killed Dean.'

'He had no other motive besides Rook being a witness? No reason of his own for wanting to kill this Rook?'

'No.'

'But he went there with a weapon?'

'We had the gun to frighten Rook. I dropped it before I ran from the house. Snaz must have picked it up.'

Kogut's mobile buzzed on the table, but he switched it off. 'They can wait. Besides Aziz, had you told anyone else you planned to frighten Curtis Rook?'

'No,' Josie said, but then she remembered. 'I did speak to Erin, Mum's friend who told me about Rook.'

'Go on,' he encouraged.

'Rook used my mum. He turned her into...' Josie couldn't bring herself to say the word *prostitute*. 'Mum wouldn't have been murdered if it hadn't been for him.'

'What exactly did you say to this friend?'

'I asked her what she'd do, if she had a chance to pay Rook back. She said she hoped one day he'd feel the same fear my mum must have felt.'

Kogut stroked a tuft of grey hair above his ear. 'May I ask a question? It's one the police are bound to ask.'

She waited.

'They will wonder why the gun was loaded, if you didn't plan to use it, except to give Rook a scare.'

Josie took hold of the napkin and wiped her mouth to buy time. 'I was frightened,' she stammered. 'He could have turned violent'. She realised how lame it sounded, how inadequate an explanation. To her relief, she heard footsteps in the hallway, Yvonna coming with the coffee. But Kogut was right: the police would ask the same question. And she realised she'd need to have a convincing reply.

Chapter 25

Every poisonous kiss

'I wasn't wearing gloves!' Snaz said the moment DCI Mercer entered the interview room. 'I'd have worn gloves if I'd planned to shoot Rook.'

'Wait for the tapes.' Mercer fumbled in his pocket and raised his handkerchief to his nose in time to catch a sneeze. 'Cheers, Dan,' he said to DS Turvey, who was loading cassettes in the machine. 'You've given me your blasted flu.'

The detectives sat opposite Snaz. 'Interview resumes eighteenth December, sixteen-thirty-two. Present are DCI Mercer, DS Turvey, Simon Aziz and Mr Francis, representing the suspect.' Mercer fixed his glare on Snaz and repeated the caution. '… Anything you say may be used as evidence, do you understand?'

Snaz nodded.

The DCI laid his watch on the table. 'What did you want to tell us?'

'I didn't have gloves on. Search for my fingerprints and you'll find them on the doorbell. Josie had gloves, but I didn't. If I wanted to kill Rook, wouldn't I have worn gloves?'

Mercer showed no reaction.

Snaz continued, 'If I meant to shoot him, I'd have gone to his house on my own. Why would I take Josie with me? I could've killed Rook without her. But she needed me there to get inside the house.'

Mercer sniffed. 'You may not have intended to kill Curtis Rook, but things didn't go to plan, did they? Josie shot Dean and you thought she'd killed him.'

'We both thought she had.'

'What did you do next?'

'Me? Nothing. Josie picked up the gun and shot Rook. He was

kneeling by his son and she…' Mercer's wide-eyed expression made Snaz break off.

'Josie picked up the gun?' the DCI asked.

'Yes.'

'So you *do* recall her dropping it? Yesterday you told us she'd kept hold of it all along.'

Snaz cursed his mistake. 'She might have dropped it.'

'Well, she must have, if you remember her picking it up?'

'It happened so fast.'

Mercer leaned forward. 'That's interesting. How long would you say it was between the two shootings?'

Confused, Snaz turned to his solicitor.

The DCI carried on. 'Josie shoots Dean unintentionally. In horror, she drops the weapon. Then she composes herself and, before either you or Curtis Rook react, she picks it up again and shoots Curtis in the chest?' Mercer spoke in a tone which made it sound like the most implausible story he'd ever heard.

'It's what happened,' Snaz said.

'Was there no interval between the two shootings? Did Josie shoot Curtis right away?'

'Almost.'

'So no more than, what, ten or fifteen seconds?'

'Where is this leading?' Snaz's solicitor said.

The detective eyed Snaz for a long time before replying. 'A witness heard a single gunshot.'

A fountain of terror rose in Snaz again. 'What witness?' Mercer had a twisted smile on his face and Snaz sensed he somehow knew everything and only needed proof. One slip, one wrong answer, and the detective would nail him.

The solicitor came to his rescue. 'DCI Mercer, my client has co-operated fully and it sounds to me you have nothing concrete to refute what he's said. How much longer are you going to keep him here without bringing a charge?'

'You want me to charge him?' Mercer glanced at DS Turvey,

then faced Snaz square on. 'Here's your starter for ten *years*. Simon Aziz, I'm charging you under Section 16A of the Firearms Act: possession of a firearm with intent to cause fear of violence. Now let me make something clear. We're going to find Josie and when we arrest her, the time for deals will be up. Whichever of you pulled the trigger will go to the court charged with murder, thank you and goodnight. Think about it, but don't take too long.' With a sudden movement, he grabbed his watch from the table. 'Your time is running out.'

* * *

'Okay, head up for the camera.' The custody officer's barked order startled Snaz and he blinked at the flash.

How close he'd come to admitting he'd shot Rook. Mercer's eyes had fixed on him. Seconds longer and he'd have cracked. But suddenly the other detective had sneezed, and Mercer suspended the interview.

Snaz felt the weight of his unsaid confession. He could still call back the detectives and admit the truth. Mercer had hinted he'd be willing to do a deal. No, he mustn't let himself be intimidated. The witness might only have heard one shot, but no one could have seen Josie outside the house. If someone *had* seen her after she'd run out, Mercer would have charged him with murder and he wouldn't be getting bail.

'We're done here, quit daydreaming,' said the policeman. 'Come with me.'

Snaz walked slowly so the custody officer had to wait. When he'd asked in his cell for toilet paper, the pig had given him two sheets.

A blonde WPC catwalked towards them, handcuffs jingling against her skirt. 'You on for the Christmas drink-up, Samo?'

'Wouldn't miss it for the world.'

Snaz felt a weight lifted off him when they went through the swing doors and didn't turn down the corridor which led to the cells. But he knew they'd arrest him again. This was nothing more than a stay of execution. Josie's dad would hire some hot-shot defence lawyer who'd tell her what to say so the police believed her story. It wouldn't even surprise him if she got away with shooting Dean.

He'd kill her if that happened, even if he had to wait twenty years for the chance. The thought of how she'd used him made him rigid with rage. Snaz understood her scheme: shoot Rook and pin the murder on him. *Devious, manipulative bitch.* She must have planned to set him up when she begged him to get her a gun. Perhaps she'd begun plotting from the day she found out he knew Rook.

Two years ago, when Grace had her lumpectomy and Snaz dreaded her cancer might come back, Josie had promised she'd be there for him and he'd held her and let himself cry in her arms. He wanted to hurt himself for being so stupid, for believing she loved him. Every time they'd had sex, each wet-lipped smile, every poisonous kiss. It had all been nothing but an act.

The policeman led him into a room which looked like a small laboratory. It reeked of disinfectant and everything in it was white. Snaz watched a skinny man with glasses lever on plastic gloves.

'Open your mouth wide,' the man instructed him. 'I'm going to take a buccal swab. The quicker we get it over with, the sooner you'll be able to leave.'

Snaz unclenched his jaws. The man rubbed a cotton-wool pad against the inside of his cheek, dropped the sample into a test tube, and then prepared another swab. 'Once more, nice and wide for me. This time on the other side.'

Snaz felt dirty and for the rest of his life he'd never feel clean.

The pig Samo led him to the booking area, where he saw his solicitor waiting for him. 'Simon Aziz,' the pig announced him to the policeman at the desk. 'Don't worry,' he sneered at Snaz, 'We'll save a cell for you.'

Snaz wanted to smash the bastard. He'd be able to make him buckle with a single well-placed punch. He felt a hand on his shoulder. 'Steady,' his solicitor said.

Snaz clenched his fists against the side of his legs. They'd keep him locked up if he reacted and he'd lose any chance to get away. Francis had warned him to expect five to eight years, or as many as ten, if he got unlucky with the judge, simply for getting Josie the weapon. His anger shifted back to her. She must be laughing at him, thinking she'd got away with it. He'd jump bail, go to Poland, and if he found her shacked up with Henderson, he'd beat their heads together and see which of their skulls cracked first.

The other PC held up a see-through bag and Snaz recognised his wallet and keys inside it. Then he set a sheet of paper in front of Snaz. 'Sign here to confirm you understand the charge.'

Snaz began reading but, desperate to get out the door, gave up after the first two sentences and just signed it.

The cop took the page and handed him another form. 'This sets out your bail conditions. First, you report to this police station daily. Second, you live and sleep at 19A Edencourt Manor—'

'But that's my aunt's place, not mine.'

'Your aunt Mrs Grace Freedman, that's correct.' The sergeant continued, 'Third, you surrender your passport. We already have it here.'

His stomach churned and he looked from his solicitor to the policeman and back again. If they kept his passport, how would he escape?

'If you wish to vary any of the conditions of bail you may appeal, stating your reasons,' the policeman said.

'I want to appeal,' Snaz jumped in.

The officer glanced at the wall clock. 'The next session of the magistrates' court isn't 'til tomorrow. If you don't accept the terms of bail you'll be remanded in custody overnight.'

His solicitor intervened. 'The conditions are reasonable, Simon. I'd suggest you agree to them.' He picked up the pen and offered it to him and Snaz's last drop of hope drained away.

Chapter 26

Something you will regret

Sunlight bathed the lawn, tips of grass poking through the snow, but the patio remained in the shade. Josie shivered as she smoked her cigarette.

'Say a prayer for your father,' Kogut had said.

She'd felt like kicking him when he'd told her that. Every night she used to pray as a child, praying for her mum – or the woman she thought was her mum – to love her, and for her dad to spend time with her, even occasionally, instead of always being away. Her prayers never got answered and by the time she went away to boarding school she'd given up. God didn't exist or, if He did, He obviously didn't care about her.

Make my dad get better. Get me through this and keep me out of prison, she said in her head. She had little hope. She'd shot a sixteen-year-old. If God hadn't listened to her before, He would hardly start to now.

Taking another draw on her cigarette, Josie winced when she noticed the colour of her hand, a deathly shade of violet. Every time she wanted to smoke it meant having to stand outside and freeze. Forget Kogut and his stupid house rules. Next time she'd go upstairs and smoke in her bathroom.

She held the cigarette in her other hand and buried the frozen one deep inside her coat pocket, wishing she had a pair of warm gloves. She wondered what Snaz had done with the ones she'd worn that night and stupidly left in his car. The police probably had them, another piece of evidence against her.

To keep herself from turning into an ice sculpture, she marched to the furthest corner of the terrace, stamping her feet in the crisp snow.

Why, just when she needed him, did her dad have a stroke?

In her heart, she knew the answer. Nathan was right: it would be her fault if he died.

Josie remembered Nathan's wedding reception, the last time she'd seen her dad. She'd taken Snaz along with her and asked him to keep her in check. She didn't wish to ruin the day for her brother, but part of her had wanted to make a scene.

Dad waited until Snaz went to the bathroom before coming up to her. 'Princess, darling.' He caught her off guard as she helped herself to another punch from the bar. 'How are you?'

'I came here for Nat. Doesn't mean we have to talk.'

'How long have you been with Simon? It must be, what, four years you've been together?'

'What do you care?'

'Of course I care. I want you to be happy. You know, when you first started seeing him, I thought you might be doing it to get at me. I didn't think it would last.'

'Another thing you got wrong.'

'Do you love him?'

'I enjoy having sex with him,' she said, loud so that everyone nearby would hear. It gave her pleasure to see him cringe.

'Let's go outside the tent. Why do you cheapen yourself? Spite me if you want to, but you're better than that.'

'You always worry what people think. Maybe it's time they found out how you abandoned Mum and me.'

She did go outside, only to get away from him, but he followed her. 'If you... If you do love Simon and you want to marry him, you'd have my blessing.'

'Oh, your blessing! Like I need that!'

'I want to make it up to you, Josie. Let me be a proper father.'

What, like twenty years too late? 'Thanks, but no thanks. Stay out of my life.'

She shuddered at remembering what she'd said. Even immediately afterwards, walking away from him, she'd felt small. She'd known she'd gone too far.

Josie finished her cigarette and threw the stub behind a giant terracotta pot. She wanted to smoke another, but not enough to let her hand freeze. Ahead of her, the path continued through a long trellis covered with ivy. Curious where it led, she walked on through it and emerged opposite the garage block. Josie spotted her Mini parked outside – or it looked like her Mini – but it had a Polish registration plate. She took a couple of steps nearer. No, she recognised the sticker in the rear windscreen. Definitely hers.

Dad had bought her the car as a birthday present. He'd wanted to go to the showroom with her and help her choose one, but she'd told him she'd rather go with one of her girlfriends, thanks, so could he send her a cheque? How she wished she'd spent that day with him. *Too late now,* she thought. Her breath rose in the icy air.

But maybe it wasn't too late to say sorry and tell him she hadn't meant what she'd said. An idea flashed in her mind to fly to America, and her heart started to race. She could go to Boston to be with him. There must be flights from Warsaw. In a second she convinced herself that being with her dad was all that mattered. She retraced her steps in the snow, hurrying to tell Kogut. He'd be able to arrange her ticket. Perhaps she could still fly out today.

As fast as she could in her high-heeled calf boots, Josie scurried back through the tunnel of ivy and across the snow-covered patio. Slipping on ice, she flung out her arms to somehow keep her balance. She took care over the final few steps.

She slid open the heavy patio door, ready to tell Kogut what she'd decided, but when she got to the study she found it empty. Kogut's newspaper lay folded on his desk, neatly as though he'd yet to read it, and their coffee cups had gone. He'd mentioned a meeting in Warsaw he needed to go to. Anxious in case he'd left already, Josie rushed through the gallery into the hall. 'Oh,' she squeaked, when she turned a corner and came face to face with

Waldemar. 'I'm looking for Ko... For Arkadiusz.'

'Mr Kogut is preparing to go out.' Waldemar stared over her shoulder, his frown growing more pronounced. 'May I take your boots, madam?'

Josie saw she'd left a dripping trail of muck across the otherwise pristine marble floor.

'I'm sorry,' she said, plonking herself on the bottom stair, struggling out of her boots. 'I have to talk to him. Is he upstairs?' When he nodded, she raced up the steps two at a time.

Josie hesitated on the landing. The long corridor had four doors on either side of it, all of them closed. Which room was Kogut's? She approached the door opposite her bedroom, knocked on it, and getting no response, turned the handle and peered inside. Sheets and curtains covered everything: a three-piece suite, a piano, redundant tables and chairs. A dulled oil painting, a nondescript landscape, leaned against cardboard boxes by the wall. She sneezed as she withdrew and shut the door.

She rapped on the next door along, heard Kogut's voice and went in without thinking. Naked apart from Y-fronts, he stood in front of her. A cross of dark hair ran down his bulging belly and across his flabby chest. 'Josephine!' he called after her, grabbing his dressing gown off the bed as she backed away, 'I'm... Give me a minute.'

She could feel herself blushing. *Why don't I think before doing things?* He'd get the wrong idea. She couldn't make up her mind if to stay in the hall, or wait downstairs, or go and hide in her room until he came back from his meeting. In the end she went to her room, but left the door open and sat on the end of her bed, clutching a pillow. When she heard him she thrust the pillow aside and shot up, getting to the door at the same time as him.

He'd put on a crisp shirt and pressed trousers, and he held a jacket in his hand. 'What is it? Is something the matter?'

'I want to go to the States to see my dad.' When he didn't

reply, she added, 'I can't let him die without seeing him.'

'But you cannot go to America.'

Josie's heart stopped, and then resumed pumping doubly fast to catch up. 'What do you mean, I can't go?'

'If you leave Warsaw the police will arrest you. The risk is too great.'

'But I have to be with him. He's dying. Can't you do something?'

'You might be able to get out of Poland, but the police would stop you when you arrived in Boston, if not at the airport then at the hospital for sure.'

'I don't care. At least I'll have seen him. I want to go.'

'Josephine, you must not rush into a decision like this. You could go to prison for ten years.'

Ten years? His warning sent her reeling.

Kogut reached out a hand to touch her, but changed his mind. 'We can talk in the evening. I cannot get out of this meeting, but we can talk when I return. I'm sorry, I have to leave or I will be late.'

He headed downstairs and she followed him. 'What about my dad? If I don't go today, he might die.'

Kogut ignored her. She watched in disbelief as he put on his jacket and Waldemar helped him into a coat. He was simply going to leave.

'You promised you'd help me,' she said from the stairs.

'I promised, and I will. But if the police arrest you at the airport, what then? Think, Josephine, do you want to spend the rest of your youth in jail? Your father is unconscious. He would not recognise you. I will be back in three hours. If you are still determined to go when I return, I will make arrangements. But reconsider, please. Do not do something you will regret.' Kogut paused briefly by the mirror to straighten his hat, and then went outside, Waldemar following after him.

The front door closed behind them with a thud and Josie

heard the key turn in the lock. *Something you will regret.* His parting words echoed in her mind.

Abandoned in the cavernous hallway, she felt completely alone. She thought of her dad when she'd walked away from him that day at Nathan's wedding reception, and understood how he must have felt. Sinking on her haunches, she sat at the bottom of the stairs.

Chapter 27

Deliver him

Snaz walked out of the police station and breathed freely for the first time in three days. Fresh air. Daylight. Somehow he had to stay out of prison. He'd do whatever it took.

Right now, he wanted to get away from the nick as fast as possible, but Grace remained by the doorway, frowning at the blanket grey sky.

'Do you want me to fetch the car?' Snaz asked, but she shook her head. After putting her hat and gloves on, she ventured down the ramp.

Snaz marched ahead, unable to walk at his aunt's dawdling pace. How tempting to disappear in the crowd of shoppers and pretend he didn't hear her calling for him to wait. He wanted to vanish and leave everything behind. He side-stepped to avoid a leggy woman strutting towards him in his path, but she moved the same way. She stepped around him and laughed. Snaz felt giddy as he watched her pale-blue umbrella bobbing above the sea of heads.

Grace caught up with him. 'Don't rush off. You know I can't hurry with my asthma. Is this our bus stop? Check when the next one is due.'

'We don't have to take the bus. Wait for me here and I'll get the car.'

'No,' she said.

'Then come with me. It's not much further. I'm parked in the next road.'

'Did you buy that car with your own money, or was it paid for by *her*?' His aunt sought cover under the bus-stop shelter and a woman wearing glasses moved her shopping bag to make room on the red plastic seat. A teenage kid shifted along to the end of the bench without looking up from his phone. Snaz consulted the timetable, the keys for the BMW in his hand. Checking the time, he realised Josie had given him his watch too. He remembered feeling embarrassed to accept it: he knew nothing about watches, but enough to tell this one hadn't come from the *Argos* catalogue. She'd said if he didn't take it she'd be offended: 'I like buying you presents. Don't be so proud, Snaz. Besides, it's my dad's money and it's not like he's short. You can show you love me in other ways.' Now he understood better what she'd meant. She must already have been hatching her plan.

'You've missed the 82,' said the woman in glasses.

'There's no bus for ages,' Snaz told Grace. 'And it'll only take us to the roundabout, so we'll have to walk the rest of the way in the rain. If you let me drive, we'll be at your place before the bus turns up.'

She shook her inhaler. 'I can live with getting wet. There could be a plague of locusts and I still wouldn't get in that harlot's car.'

The boy started up from his phone. The woman stared at Grace too and her bulging bag slipped in her lap, a tube of toothpaste falling onto the pavement. *Let her pick it up herself,* Snaz thought. He'd had enough of helping people. From now on he'd look after himself.

'I need to stop by my flat to get some clothes,' he said. 'If you won't come with me in the car, I'll go there on my own and meet you back at yours'.'

'Don't you dare.' The force in his aunt's voice startled him. 'I gave the officer my word you would stay with me. I am not letting you out of my sight.'

'I want to get some things to wear.'

'You have enough clothes at my flat. Everything you need is with me.'

The boy snickered at him. If Grace hadn't been there, Snaz would have landed a fist in his mouth. He gripped his car keys tighter and kicked the kerb with his heel.

The traffic inched forward, a van belching fumes. At this rate it'd be half an hour before the bus got there. Across the street, women walked weighed down with shopping bags, while men raised their brollies to look and let them pass. A young girl in a yellow mac skipped in the rain, beaming her sunshine, but she didn't look Snaz's way.

The girl went into a pet shop with her dad. 'My fish!' Snaz suddenly remembered. 'They'll die if I don't feed them. I have to go to my flat.'

His aunt's eyes narrowed into slits and she gave him a fiery look. 'A man is dead.' She crossed herself. 'How can you worry about fish?'

* * *

Grace made Snaz sit by the window and squashed up beside him, trapping him in. Throughout the bus journey, he didn't dare to glance at her, except when she gave him a tissue to wipe his nose.

He leaned his head against the glass. He must have dozed off, but when the bus juddered to a halt, he jolted upright and looked through the grime-caked window. To his shock, he recognised the road he'd taken back from Rook's house to Josie's flat.

When the bus doors opened, Snaz saw the vandalised shelter where he'd stopped the car, the dustbin into which he'd throw up. He remembered his throat burning from the vomit, and his body shaking as he sat back in the car. He'd wanted Josie to reach over and hold him, but her hands remained clasped in her lap. So cold, she'd sounded. 'Just drive and get me home.' She wouldn't even let him come up to her flat. 'I'll phone you,' she'd promised. Three whole days he'd waited for her to call.

* * *

By the time the bus reached their stop and they'd walked to his aunt's flat, Snaz had started to shiver. Grace unlocked the front door and let him in first and he stepped over the Christmas cards lying on the mat. She closed the door, then immediately wrapped her arms round him, squeezing him tight the way he wished Josie had done.

'Why, Simon? Why?' Finally she loosened her embrace and let him breathe.

What could he say? He picked up the two white envelopes and offered them to her.

'Leave them on the table with the rest,' she said.

He noticed a small stack of cards. 'Aren't you going to open them?' he asked.

'Later. Go run a bath and clean yourself. You'll find fresh clothes in your wardrobe, all ironed. I'll prepare an omelette with bacon.'

'I didn't want to hurt anyone. I didn't think it would end with him being killed.'

'I know you didn't. All of this is down to that Jezebel. God sees the truth.'

* * *

Snaz found a pair of brown corduroy trousers Grace had bought him a few months ago. He snapped off the price tag, clambered into them, and tucked in his shirt. Feeling dizzy, sapped of strength, he sat on his bed to put on a navy V-neck jumper. *Money,* he thought. He'd need money to get away. His account was overdrawn though and he'd reached the limit on both of his cards.

Tomorrow, after he'd reported to the police station, he'd meet his mate Dave, give him the keys to the BMW and ask him to sell it. It must be worth four or five grand, but he'd take half that. If he could get a flight to Guyana, he could fix up cars there, or anything. He wouldn't care what work he did, as long as he stayed out of prison.

Grace interrupted his fantasy. 'Simon,' she called. 'Dinner is on the table. Come while it's hot.'

Snaz smacked the bedding in frustration. Even if he did raise the cash, he couldn't go anywhere without his passport.

While he'd been in the bath, Grace had opened all her Christmas cards and put them on the mantelpiece and the windowsill. A large one with a nativity scene had pride of place above the TV. Snaz checked who'd sent it, wondering if perhaps it could be from his mum, but it was signed *with blessings from Norman and Lucille.*

His aunt bustled in from the kitchen, wiping her hands on a white and red dishcloth which Snaz took at first sight for a rag stained with blood. 'You are right, Simon, this year more than ever we should celebrate His birth. After dinner, you can bring the tree from the garage.' She added after a pause, 'Whatever happens we will handle this together.'

They sat opposite one another at the table and his aunt joined her hands in prayer. 'Dear Lord, bless this food and bless us. We pray for the man who died, and for his son. May the boy live, Lord, and recover from his wounds.' She paused, bowed her head. 'And we pray for Simon. Deliver him safely, Lord.'

When she'd finished, Snaz echoed her "amen". 'Grace, can I ask you something? You know the Ten Commandments?'

'Exodus chapter twenty.'

'Won't there be times when you have to break them?'

'What do you mean? They are God's word.'

'But aren't there exceptions? What about in the war, when the Allies killed the Nazis? Sometimes you don't have any choice.'

'Why do you ask these questions? It is not you, but that evil woman, who has killed.'

Snaz fell silent.

'Simon, God has forgiven you. Do not concern yourself with her.'

Chapter 28

Murderer

Snaz lay in his bed, waiting. His aunt had switched off the light in her bedroom half an hour ago, but he wanted to be sure she'd fallen asleep. One more time, he went over his plan in his head. He tried to remember more details from the documentary he'd watched about illegal immigrants stowing away in lorries to get into the UK. Customs checked the trucks entering the country, but did they also check them when they left? He didn't think so. Why would they bother to? He convinced himself it had to be worth a go.

He'd take a sleeping bag and some water and food, drive to a service station on the M20 and find a big lorry, a foreign one. He wondered how much he'd have to pay a truck driver to smuggle him across the Channel. Three hundred? Five? What if the driver demanded more?

Another idea flashed in his mind: perhaps he could find a Polish lorry to take him all the way to Warsaw. He imagined Josie's face when he tracked her down.

The central-heating system had gone quiet. Surely Grace would be asleep by now. Snaz slipped out of bed and tiptoed in his socks to the wardrobe, aware that his aunt slept with her bedroom door open. Millimetre by millimetre he opened the cupboard door, cringing when the hinges creaked. He wrestled a black training top on over his T-shirt, then perched on the end of the bed to put on his tracksuit bottoms.

Stepping into the corridor, Snaz could hear his aunt's rhythmic breathing which threatened every so often to break into a snore. Outside, a cat gave a protracted yowl, as if on purpose to wake her. He froze for a moment before venturing down the stairs.

Arms outstretched, Snaz felt his way to the kitchen, where the moon's eerie glow shone through the window. He crouched by the cupboard under the sink, located the torch, then returned with it to the living room and shone it around to find Grace's sewing basket. He remembered she kept money in it. Once, in his teens, he'd pinched ten pounds from it and then, feeling guilty, returned it before she found out. Now though he had no alternative. He sat with the wicker basket on his lap and promised himself he'd make it up to Grace one day.

He slipped his hand into the pouch inside the sewing box expecting to find an envelope. But there was nothing, not a single banknote. He spotted a folded share certificate, but a fat lot of use to him that would be: to pay a lorry driver, he needed cash. He rummaged around in the main compartment of the box. A needle stabbed his finger and he jerked his hand away, cursing under his breath.

What to do now? He'd reached his overdraft limit and payday wasn't for another week. His eyes fell on his aunt's handbag on the table by the armchair. Perhaps she had cash in her purse.

The sound of a car stopping outside made Snaz sit up. Thinking it might be the police, he shot up to go to the window and the basket went flying, its contents tipping all over the floor. He swore aloud this time and then stood in bated silence in case he'd woken Grace. When he heard nothing from upstairs, he peered through the gap between the curtains. No police car, only a red Renault Clio. Breathing again, he slunk to the floor and, shining the torch to distinguish the buttons and reels of thread from the pattern of the carpet, he gathered everything up. Josie had reduced him to stealing from his own aunt. No, he wouldn't stoop so low. Taking Grace's savings would have been bad enough, but he wasn't going to steal from her purse.

Hurrying, listening out for any noise from upstairs, he stashed all her sewing kit back in the basket, arranged things as neatly as he could. If he left and never saw his aunt again, he didn't want her knowing he'd been ready to steal from her.

One thing, though, he did want to take with him. Remembering it, he went straight to the sideboard, found the photo album in the bottom drawer and began flipping through it until familiar faces caught his eye. He saw Grace as a girl, with her younger sister in a pushchair and clutching a black baby doll. Snaz didn't like to look at photos of his mum.

He turned several pages in one go, passing over the rest of the black and white pictures, and arrived at a blurred print of himself posed as Rambo, with his red school tie around his forehead. He turned another page and saw one of Grace and him together, feeding the geese in the park.

On the next-to-last page, he found what he was searching for: his favourite picture of his aunt, the first one he'd taken with the camera she'd bought him as a prize for passing his GCSEs. In the picture, a proud smile lifted her cheeks. With care, Snaz slid the print out from its pocket.

Searching in the drawer for an envelope to protect the photo from getting creased, his hand alighted on Grace's building society passbook. His pulse quickened when he saw it bulging with cash: ten-pound notes, twenties... There had to be at least five hundred quid. If he took a hundred or two she might not even miss it.

His finger still stung from the needle prick. Raising it to his lips, Snaz became aware again of Grace's photo in his hand. No, this time he'd do the right thing by her. Closing the passbook with all the money still inside, he put it back in the drawer. He'd get cash some other way, would steal it if necessary, but not from Grace.

Snaz arranged his aunt's copies of *Every Day with Jesus* so the drawer would close, pausing when he heard a sound outside. He listened but heard nothing more. His mind must be playing tricks. He pushed the drawer shut, was standing up, when CRASH! – right behind him – shattering glass. Someone shooting at the window! He dropped to the floor, scrambled for the torch. Shards of glass across the carpet. A brick in the middle of the room. Tyres screeched and a car sped off, and then the light came on upstairs. From the landing, Grace screamed his name.

* * *

When the doorbell rang, Snaz hid himself in the kitchen. Out of sight, he listened to his aunt talking with the cop. 'Who would do this?' he heard Grace sob. 'Tell me who?'

Snaz had no doubt about who'd thrown the brick. For the last three seasons, he'd gone with Matt Rook to each home match. From the stand, they'd celebrated every goal together, shrieked in relief at last-ditch tackles, yelled with one voice at each missed chance. He hadn't shot a stranger. He'd killed his own mate's dad.

Murderer. Matt's message taped to the brick had only one word, but that word said it all.

Slumped at the table, head in his hands, Snaz understood regret.

What had possessed him to get Josie a gun and let her talk him in to loading it? When he couldn't persuade her to drop her mad plan, he should have gone to the police.

'If you love me, you'll help me,' she'd said to him.

'If *you* loved *me*, you wouldn't ask me to,' he'd wanted to reply, but he hadn't dared.

He couldn't change what he'd done, but he could do the decent thing and confess. Never mind the consequences, he should go into the living room and admit to the cop, *I'm the one who shot Rook.*

Snaz stared in the direction of the doorway, and a slow shiver passed through his body. The living room felt like another country. The beads in the kitchen doorway might as well have been metal bars.

If he owned up, he'd go to prison for life, while Josie,

scheming bitch, would still be free. It couldn't be right for him to take the punishment, not when she'd used him. If she loved him, it might be different. He could cope with a twenty-year stretch, if he knew she'd be waiting for him at the end of it. His mind clutched at the flimsiest of straws. Seeing her, holding her hands across a visiting-room table, would help him to get through each week.

But Josie didn't love him. She'd left him and shacked up with Pete. It made him sick.

The door beads rattled and his aunt and the cop emerged through them. 'Hello, Simon.'

Snaz flinched at the sight of the PC who'd tricked him with the question about Henry's goal.

'Do you know who did this?' The cop had the brick with him in a see-through plastic bag. He wore the same self-satisfied smirk as when he'd come to Snaz's flat.

'Answer the policeman,' Grace prompted.

Snaz had the feeling that if he didn't own up now, he'd never be able to. Except how could he admit to killing someone with Grace here in the room? It would rip her apart if she knew the truth. He shook his head. 'I didn't kill Rook,' he said for his aunt's sake. 'I didn't do it. It wasn't me.'

Grace flung her arms around him, and then railed against the cop. 'See how you made him suffer, keeping him in a cell, treating him as though he killed that man. He is innocent, look at him. We have told you who is responsible for the murder. Why don't you find her? Why do you persecute my boy?'

The cop continued to stare at him. Snaz could take it no longer and turned away, only to see the man's face reflected in the window.

'Without any leads, there's not a lot we can do,' the cop at last said to Grace. 'Perhaps tomorrow, if your nephew has any ideas about who threw the brick, he can get in touch with us.'

'Are you going? What about the window?' His aunt's voice

became muffled as she followed the man into the front room.

'You'll need to contact a glazier to get the pane replaced.'

'Oh, I thought... Can't you do that for me?'

'No, madam. You'll have to call a glazier.'

'Can you recommend somebody?'

'They're listed in the phonebook.'

Snaz heard the front door close, and then the clatter of the chain. *An eye for an eye and a tooth for a tooth.* How could he leave Grace alone? What if Matt came after her?

Chapter 29

Words in her dream

Shafts of sunlight streaked across the room towards the vase of lilac. The scent of the flowers reached Josie in her bed.

She felt oddly calm, her body less tense, even relaxed. Words from a dream lingered in her mind: *It's okay. It'll be alright.*

She tried to recall the dream, but could only remember scattered images... Watching a stream, a gently flowing river. Standing on a bridge, Adam there too. Adam kissing her. *Some chance of that!* And those words: *It's okay. It'll be alright.*

The carriage clock on the bedside table showed a quarter past nine. She remembered taking sleeping pills, double the stated dose. With effort, she moved her legs, sat upright and stretched her arms. Through the window she surveyed the silent garden, its lawn like an enormous green and white flag, half of it still beneath a blanket of snow. On the patio too the snow remained, except where footprints had hastened the thaw.

Josie put on clean clothes and made her way downstairs. After trying in the dining room first, she found Kogut in his study, seated at his desk. This morning he didn't greet her with a smile and from his grave expression, Josie knew.

'Don't.' She stopped him before he could say it. Until she heard the words, her dad was still alive.

'I'm so sorry,' he said.

She shook her head and when he said, 'He died in the night, he wouldn't have felt any pain,' she fled back to her room. Kogut came after her, but she grabbed her coat, pushed past him in the doorway and ran downstairs again, and then out the front door and across the snow-covered lawn.

Josie sat in her car, watched as drops of melt water fell with hypnotic regularity from the rafters of the garage onto the bonnet. Dripppsssplash. Dripppsssplash.

Her dad had bought her this Mini. She'd taken his cheque and put the birthday card aside, hardly glancing at the message. Maybe he'd signed it, 'with love'. She'd give the fifteen thousand pounds now to have the card back.

Dad had only been sixty-four. If she'd thought it possible he might die so suddenly, she would have made up with him, seized the olive branch he always held out. But she wanted to punish him for abandoning Mum and her, and it suited her to have him think he had to buy her love. One day she'd be ready to forgive him, but she kept putting it off, and now that conversation, that making up, that hug she so desperately wanted, would never take place.

Josie pulled her handkerchief from her pocket. No, she'd cried enough. She wasn't going to cry any more.

She thought about the funeral and what she'd wear to it. She'd lay a single white rose on Dad's coffin and everyone would stare at her and whisper among themselves: "She's to blame for his stroke... Well, her mum *was* a prostitute. Is it any wonder she turned out bad?"

Before long, Josie spied Kogut in the rearview mirror, an ungainly figure lumbering towards her through the snow. He opened the passenger-side door and she smelled his musky after-shave as he sat beside her. 'I searched all over the house for you. Then I noticed your tracks across the lawn.' He recovered his breath. 'Josephine...'

She cut him off. 'I wanted to see him. I wanted to make things up with him, but you didn't let me go.' She said it to make him feel bad, to make him feel her pain.

Another drop of water splashed on the bonnet. She clutched her handkerchief in her fist. In the corner of her eyes, she noticed Kogut join his hands together in his lap, as if in prayer. For a long time, they sat in silence.

'Aren't you going to say anything?' she asked.

'If I can do something, if I can help in any way.'

'What can you do? You can't bring him back.'

'I am here for you,' he said. Then he added, 'It is okay to cry.'

'I'm not crying.' She resorted to her handkerchief, blowing her nose and wiping the corners of her eyes. 'When did you last see my dad?' she asked, trying at least to sound strong.

'When I went to London in September I met him at his club.'

Her resentment grew. This stranger, this foreigner she hadn't heard of until a few days ago, had seen her father more recently than she had. How could it be right?

'He showed me the photograph of you he carried in his wallet,' Kogut said.

Josie faced him. 'Is that true? He carried my photo?'

Kogut nodded. 'When your father rang and told me you were in Poland, it struck me how worried he sounded. I could tell how much he loved you. I promised him I would find you and look after you until he...for as long as you needed my help.'

She felt Kogut's hand on her shoulder and wished it was her dad's.

Then she remembered again those words in her dream. *It's okay, Princess. It'll be alright.* Her dad had said those words to her! It had been his voice in the dream. He did love her. And he wanted her to know.

Chapter 30

Against the wall

Josie sat on her bed, toying with the mobile phone Kogut had given her, scrolling through its menus and functions. 'If you want to speak to anyone, it is safer to use this instead of the landline,' he'd told her. 'Much harder for the police to trace the call.'

She had two phone calls to make, but dreaded both of them. If she rang her sister-in-law to ask about arrangements for Dad's funeral, Clara might tell her Nathan didn't want her there. She decided to ring Erin first.

She had Erin's husband's business card wedged as a bookmark in the self-help paperback in her handbag. She keyed in the number, but forgot to add the dialling code for England and had to start again. After half a dozen rings, when Josie began to doubt if anyone would pick up, one of Erin's daughters answered with a cutesy hello.

Josie couldn't tell if it was Lucy or Sam. 'Is your mum there?'

'She's in the bathroom. I'll get her.'

Josie heard a clack as the girl placed the receiver on the table. She imagined the chaotic scene in the hallway: the girls' toys and gym kits lying on the floor like modern art, Tyler's fishing gear and his spirit level in the corner, their demented poodle bounding around... 'Mummy!' the girl screeched up the stairs. 'There's a woman for you.'

Josie paced the room, still unsure whether to confide in Erin. She heard her voice in the background: 'Who is it?'

'I dunno, she didn't say.'

'Hello,' said Erin into the phone.

'It's Josie.'

'Oh, Josie, love! Didn't you get my messages?'

'No, I...'

'Have you heard about Curtis Rook? I couldn't believe it when I saw the news.'

'Erin...' Josie tried in vain to get a word in.

'Tyler and me had the telly on, and Rook's picture flashes up and they show all these coppers and – what are they called, in the white overalls? – forensics people, swarming about outside his house. I said to Tyler, "I know that man." It's horrible to say it, but he had it coming, didn't he? But what about his son? They tried to kill him too.'

Josie's pulse quickened while she waited for the woman's torrent to end. 'They didn't try to kill his son. *They* didn't realise his son was in the house.'

'You reckon?'

'I know who did it,' Josie said.

'You know? Who?'

Her heart started hammering. Her stomach felt suddenly loose. 'Snaz.'

Erin took an age to respond. '*Your* Snaz? No, that's silly, he can't have had anything to do with it. I saw him the other day in *Tesco*. What on earth makes you think...?'

'Erin, I was with him.'

Silence on the other end of the line. Josie had the feeling she'd made a huge mistake. She overheard Erin saying to her daughter, 'Samantha, go to your room.'

Josie's hand trembled as she gripped the phone and reminded herself why she'd told Erin. The police already knew she'd shot Dean. She *wanted* Erin to go to them and tell them what had happened, so they wouldn't believe Snaz's lies about her shooting Rook too.

'Your boyfriend murdered Rook! And you were there!'

'Listen, please just listen,' Josie begged. 'I only wanted to scare Rook. But his son ran at me with a bread knife. Two more seconds and I'd be dead. I had to shoot him.'

'You? You shot that boy?'

'Boy? He was a head taller than me. He had a knife.'

Erin said something away from the phone that Josie couldn't make out.

'We never meant to kill Rook, only frighten him.'

'Why even do that?'

'Why do you think? You told me how Mum died. If you hadn't told me… If you hadn't interfered…'

'I might have said some things about Rook, but that isn't the same as…'

'I didn't kill him,' Josie cut in.

'No, your boyfriend did.' Erin made it sound like it made no difference.

'I didn't ask him to. I ran from the house and he… He could have followed me. He *should've* followed me. But he picked up the gun.'

After a while, when Erin didn't respond, Josie said, 'He's told the police I shot Rook.'

'Hand yourself in,' Erin said.

Josie reeled. She slid onto her haunches against the wall. 'You're supposed to be on my side.'

'Which is why I'm saying to you, if Snaz has lied to the cops, you need to tell them the truth.'

Josie heard a knock on the bedroom door. Kogut. Before she could decide whether to hang up or ask him to go away, he came into the room. She watched him place a tray with a cup of piping coffee and a croissant on the dressing table, moving an empty mug to make more space. On the phone, Erin kept on yapping. 'Will you help me?' Josie interrupted her.

'What do you expect me to do?'

'Tell the police I didn't kill Rook; I wanted to frighten him, but that's all.'

'I have to talk to Tyler first,' Erin replied.

'Why? It has nothing to do with your husband. I'm asking you for help.'

'The way your boyfriend stared at me in the supermarket... I didn't like it.'

'Oh Erin, are you serious? What do you think he's going to do?'

'Have you spoken to your dad?' Erin said. 'I'm sure he can help you.'

'He's dead,' said Josie. 'He had a stroke.'

'Bloomin' heck. Why didn't you tell me?'

'It only happened yesterday.'

Erin didn't say any more. No wonder: Erin hated her dad and encouraged her to hate him too.

'I'm going to his funeral. And when I do, the police will arrest me. I'll go to prison unless you talk to them and make them understand.'

Kogut gave up the pretence of not listening and came closer.

'So are you going to help me?' Josie asked Erin one more time.

'I'm not sure what I can do.'

Josie raised her head in frustration and her eyes met Kogut's. 'All you have to do is come with me to the police. You know me, Erin. Tell them I couldn't have murdered Rook. Do it for my mum's sake!'

Erin stayed silent, and Josie crumpled Tyler's business card in her fist. She'd said all she could say to persuade Erin. It didn't help to have Kogut standing over her, listening in.

'I have to think this through,' Erin said.

'Well if you have to *think* about it, don't bother.' Josie slammed down the phone.

'Who were you speaking to?' Kogut asked.

'A friend of my mum.'

'Of your natural mother?'

Josie nodded. '*Some friend.*'

'Would you like her – is it a woman? – would you like her to visit you here?'

'What's the point? Besides, I'm going back for the funeral.

When is it, have you heard?'

Kogut glanced at the windowsill, a collared dove perched there. 'They have not fixed the date yet. It is unlikely to be until the New Year. Your father's body is still in the States. Josephine, we should talk. Shall we go downstairs?'

'I'm fine here,' she said.

Kogut looked around the room. Her quilt and blanket lay scrumpled across the bed. He brought the dainty stool from by the dressing table nearer and eased himself down onto it, as if uncertain whether it would support his weight. 'I have talked to a lawyer in England. He is retired, but he used to be a highly respected defence barrister, one of the best.'

Josie glanced up. 'Will he defend me?'

Kogut nudged his large glasses higher up on his nose. 'Even with all his experience, he is doubtful he could keep you from going to prison for a very long time.'

'But Dean attacked me,' she cried.

'His assessment is ten to twelve years.'

'Twelve *years*?'

'The police are convinced you are guilty. They have released Simon Aziz.'

Josie stared at Kogut, incredulous. 'Released him! But *he* murdered Rook.'

'You had a loaded firearm. You did shoot Rook's son. And while Aziz gave himself up, you fled abroad.' Kogut leaned back and the stool creaked.

'You think I deserve to be punished, don't you?' she asked. 'You all do. I shot someone. I deserve to go to jail.'

He stood, went to fetch her coffee and offered it to her, a consolation. 'Josephine, please do not give up. I am determined to keep you out of prison.'

'How, when even your lawyer doesn't give me a hope?'

'There is another way. Say you did not return to England?'

'I can't stay here all my life.'

Kogut said nothing.

'Even if I don't go back for the funeral, the police will find me. They know I'm in Poland.'

'The police will never find you. Take your coffee and I will explain.'

Josie accepted the cup.

'It is true that the police are searching for you in Warsaw. Our task is to trick them into thinking you are no longer here.'

'How?' The cup felt warm in her hands. She sipped the coffee. It tasted strong and peaty, the way she liked it.

'Some details have still to be sorted, but give me one more day and the plan will be perfect,' Kogut said. 'I will need to take your car.'

'My car?'

'The plan is to transport it out of Poland. We will take it in a truck, through Slovakia and Hungary and on to Brasov. My contact there is an excellent man. He is arranging everything: staff at a motel will say you spent a night there, a garage attendant will swear he remembers your face. All for dollars.' Kogut rubbed his fingers together and appeared to be pleased with himself. 'I must also take your credit card.'

'You want money from me?'

'Josephine, no.' He frowned. 'The card is for my drivers to use, to create a trail, so the police can trace your journey. We need evidence to show you headed for the Black Sea.'

'So the police will look for me there?'

'Better, Josephine. They will stop looking for you altogether.'

Josie put the cup down on the carpet and sat up. 'Why? How come?'

'There will be an accident in the mountains south of Brasov. The passes are treacherous at this time of year. When your car is found burned out in a ravine, it will be quite plausible that you lost control and skidded off the road.'

'But...' Her excitement crashed into fear. 'I won't be in the car? Will I?'

'Good heavens, of course not.' Kogut seized her hand. 'You will still be here. You will be living in your new home, with me.'

Chapter 31

Hope

Snaz reached the police station early, but the cop at the counter made him wait for twenty minutes to sign his name on a sheet. Then, as soon as he'd signed the paper, they let him go. He'd expected another interrogation from Mercer. His hope grew that perhaps they did believe his story.

He moved along the street, feeling unsteady on his feet as though he'd had too much to drink. He passed the chemist and what used to be a record shop, but had become another *Starbucks*. People stepped out of his way. When a siren blared close behind him he thought the police had realised their mistake, until he noticed an ambulance stuck in traffic at the lights.

A store's Christmas jingles taunted him as he walked by. Everyone else appeared happy.

'*Big Issue*, sir?' Even the homeless man had a smile on his face.

Snaz turned into the side road where he'd left his car, treading a crooked course around rubbish bags heaped on the pavement. A cat had clawed a hole in one and had its head buried in a takeaway box, but it bolted off when he approached. Stone lions guarded one of the houses. Next door, an old Austin Maxi with its bumper hanging loose rusted on the overgrown lawn.

At last, Snaz saw his BMW. Someone had lodged two fliers under its windscreen wipers. Damp from the rain, they tore as he peeled them from the glass. He sat in the car, opened the glove box and retrieved his mobile phone.

You have four new messages. First new message, received on Monday at 11:37 am:

'Yo Snaz, it's Dave. Where you been, man? What's goin' on?

Two pigs came round on Saturday and asked me where you were last Wednesday night. I said you were with me, watching the game. I dunno what kind of shit you're in, but Walrus is after you and all… Says if you don't show your bony arse here at half eight tomorrow, he'll have your P45 ready on his desk. And he says you better have a good excuse for why you ain't rung in… Like, tell him you got laryn-wotsit – whatever that thing's called where you lose your voice.

'Say, catch this. I got four numbers in the lottery on Saturday. When I get the cash, I'm going to book a flight to New York. You wanna come? Hang out, maybe catch some baseball? Wait up, Walrus alert. Text me and let me know what's goin' on.'

If Dave had won money, maybe he could loan him some… Then Snaz remembered, without his passport, he was trapped.

Second new message, received on Monday at 7:29 pm:

'Hello Simon, err, Snaz. This is Bel from the hospital radio. I realise it's a big favour to ask, and you're probably doing something else, but if you could spare a couple of hours on Boxing Day, it'd be a massive help. You've got my number – give me a ring if you can. Thanks. Oh – and happy Christmas. I would've sent a card, but I decided not to do them this year and use the money to get little presents for the kids on the ward. Bye, then. Hope you can do it. Thanks for helping in the past.'

As Snaz waited for the next message, he noticed a fight about to kick off across the road. A scrawny guy wearing glasses seized a man by the scruff of his jacket and started marching him backwards. The other man had an extra twenty kilos on him, at least. Any second, he'd land a punch on the flyweight and break his nose. A girl came scampering from one of the houses and tried to keep them apart.

'…Seventy-five poxy quid!' Dave T again. 'For four numbers! And I had the bonus ball too, but they say it don't count unless you have five. That ain't right. I should've won at least a couple of grand. They rob you, man: ten quid I give them every week and I've been doin' it for five years...'

Snaz stopped listening. The small bloke had lost it. He flailed his arms in the air while the other man simply took it. Snaz looked on as he rasped a scar in the paintwork of a souped-up Corsa, before the blonde rushed up and prised the key from his hand. An ancient woman set down her shopping bag to watch.

'...I'm not with Pete any more...' Snaz became aware of Josie's voice on the phone. 'The stuff about me and him being back together: I only let him think that so he'd let me stay with his family while I figured out what to do.

'I'm sorry if you think I used you. When I ran from the house, you could have followed me. I never asked you to kill Rook. You chose to shoot him and you can't shift the blame onto me.

'There's something you should know. When I went outside and you were still in Rook's house, a man saw me. He spoke to me, right by your car. That's why I had to leave England – in case he described me to the police.

'Maybe he's not spoken to them yet. But he heard the gunshot and he saw me outside the house, so he knows I couldn't have shot Rook.' She paused. 'I won't spend time in prison for a murder I didn't commit.'

Numbed, Snaz sat with the phone in his lap. Could she be lying, wanting to spook him so he cracked?

If anyone had seen Josie, they'd have gone to the cops by now, surely. He wouldn't have been granted bail. If a witness had really seen her, the police would have charged him with murder and not only with getting the gun. She must be making it up.

He listened to her message again from the beginning. 'Snaz, we need to talk. I'm coming back to England. My dad died and I'm going to his funeral. I'm ready to tell the police the truth.' Her voice sounded cold and unfeeling, like she was reading the words from a script.

As Snaz listened it dawned on him that it didn't matter whether anyone had seen Josie. With her family's money, she could bribe someone to say whatever she wanted them to. He heard her threat again: 'I won't spend time in prison for a murder I didn't commit.'

Chapter 32

Who we are

Josie sat at the dressing table in her bedroom. She'd put on so much make-up in an attempt to bring some life to her face that it made her look like a tragic clown. She couldn't understand why Kogut insisted on taking her out. If he wanted to go for dinner with his friends, fine, but he didn't have to drag her along with him. Christmas or not, she wanted to be on her own.

Before long, she heard him knock on her bedroom door. 'Are you ready?' he said from the corridor. 'It is time to go.'

'Arkadiusz,' she called him by his name for the first time, uncertain if she'd got the pronunciation right.

The door opened a little and he peered around it. He'd changed into a dinner jacket and bow tie. He looked at her like a critic would a painting. She had always felt self-conscious wearing white.

'Maybe I shouldn't go,' she said. 'I'm not feeling up to meeting anyone. You go, if you like. I'll be okay here by myself.'

He shook his head. 'It is Christmas evening, *Wigilia*. There is no way I can leave you on your own. Besides, Helena and Roman are expecting us. They have prepared a meal for us both. The company will do you good.'

'But you want me to stay in Poland,' Josie said. 'What if the people we're visiting tell the police I'm staying with you?'

'They will not tell.'

'How can you be sure?'

'Because they are my friends.'

'Well, what if someone else sees me?'

'You will be out of the car for less than a minute. Still, I will find a scarf for you to wear on your head. I'm sure Yvonna won't mind if you borrow one of hers.' He laid his hand on her arm.

'Josephine, I promise you, I would do nothing to put your safety at risk.'

Josie followed Kogut down the steps to his black Mercedes. He carried two large bags in one hand and a magnum of wine in the other. 'Would you hold this for me while I drive please?' He gave her the bottle and she glanced at the label, but couldn't read it in the dark.

'What's in those?' she asked, as he placed the bags in the boot.

'Christmas presents. The rest are already in here.' He opened the passenger door for her, then walked around the front of the car.

When he sat beside her, Josie drew down the hem of her skirt to cover her knees. The iron gates parted ahead of them and they turned onto a tree-lined road. Through gaps in the row of tall evergreens, Josie spied townhouses and villas, though she saw none as impressive as Kogut's. 'Who are these people we're going to meet?' she asked.

'My friends Helena and Roman, and Ola, their daughter.'

'They don't know what I've done, do they? You can't make me see them if they know.'

'Of course not. I explained your situation to them only in general terms.'

'But they might find out? They might read about me in the papers, or see the news?'

'Then I will tell them you are innocent. You *are* innocent,' he added. 'Try to relax. An evening out will do you good.'

At the end of the long tarmacked lane, they came to a barrier. Kogut lowered the window and stretched out his arm, but couldn't quite reach the reader on the post to swipe his pass. He had to undo his seatbelt and get out of the car.

She noticed, stuck to the steering wheel, a laminated card with the word PAMIETAM written on it in a large bold font. She'd seen the same word in a frame on Kogut's desk, and also on the mirror in the hall.

Kogut waited at the junction for a gap in the traffic. A couple of times Josie would have pulled out if she'd been driving, but Kogut hesitated.

'What does *pamietam* mean?' she asked him.

He corrected her pronunciation. '*Pum-ien-tam*. In English, it would be "I remember". It is to remind me of who I am.'

'You forget, do you?' she said, perplexed.

'Sometimes. We all forget who we are.'

After driving in the dark for ten minutes, they came to a village. Kogut stopped alongside a parked car and put the gearbox into reverse. He began backing into the space but then, shaking his head, drove forward again. Reversing once more, he started turning the wheel out again too soon. He gave up manoeuvring backwards and forwards and switched off the engine with the car still half a metre from the kerb.

'Don't worry about the presents, I will come back for them later, after dinner,' he said as they got out the car. 'You can give me the wine.'

They walked to a modern apartment block, much smarter than the one Pete's family lived in. Josie asked Kogut, 'What did you mean before, when you said we forget who we are?'

He stopped. 'Look at the sky.'

She stared where he pointed, away from the town. One by one, specks of light appeared. The longer she watched, the more stars she could see.

'There are over a hundred billion stars in the galaxy, and a hundred billion galaxies beyond our own. The light from some of them takes thousands of years to reach us, millions even.' He breathed in deeply and finally exhaled. 'Seventy years we live for, eighty if we are lucky. And after that, do we simply die? It would be illogical if we were nothing but flesh and bone. We *have* a body. We *have* a mind. But what we *are* is Spirit. Divine, eternal

Spirit. Me, you...your father. Spirit never dies.'

Josie continued to stare at the heavens until a woman dressed in a trouser suit opened the door. She embraced Kogut, kissing him on one cheek, then on the other, then a third time for good measure. She looked slightly older than him – about sixty, Josie reckoned – but she still had blonde shoulder-length hair. From her familiarity with Kogut, she wondered if they might be related, brother and sister perhaps, though she had much lighter hair than he did, and pastel-blue eyes. Josie was comparing their faces in search of a common feature when the lady turned to her and, with overdone enthusiasm, seized hold of both her hands. 'Josephine, how wonderful that you are visiting with us for Christmas. I'm Helena. Please excuse that my English is not so good. Come inside, come with me. It's cold out here. You look pale.'

A man emerged from the kitchen. 'My partner Roman,' the woman introduced him, taking Josie's coat. A slender man, almost bald, he wore an apron over his turtleneck sweater and khaki corduroy trousers. He greeted Josie with a warm smile and a slight bow of his head.

'I do love your scarf,' Helena said as Josie untied it and took it off. 'What a beautiful colour it is. How you say this colour in English?'

Josie had to think. 'Teal.'

Passing Josie's coat to Roman, Helena led her into the lounge, where a girl in her late teens sat curled on a sofa. The girl didn't acknowledge them. 'Aleksandra?' Helena lifted the headphones from her daughter's ears. 'Aleksandra, don't you hear me with your music on? Our guests are here. Say hello to Josephine from England.'

The girl rose and held out a hand, not quite in the right direction, and her mother had to guide her to where Josie stood. 'Hello, Josephine. Call me Ola.' Her manicured nails were painted a subdued shade of pink. 'Are you well?'

'Fine,' Josie said, out of habit feigning a smile.

'Your hand feels cold. Is it snowing?' Ola asked.

'No, it's a clear night.'

'So, Arkadiusz has finally found himself a girlfriend?'

'Aleksandra!' Her mother affected shock.

'What?' replied Ola. 'It's about time, don't you think? Where is Arkadiusz anyway?'

'Here I am.' Kogut continued in Polish to the blind girl, and Josie wondered what he'd said that caused her to giggle.

Feeling her way back to the sofa, Ola beckoned Kogut to sit next to her.

Josie remained standing in the middle of the room.

'Please.' Helena gestured to an armchair by the window. 'Dinner be ready in five minutes. Roman is heating *bigos*. Tell me, what do you think of our decoration?'

Josie glanced at the diminutive Christmas tree on the table beside the bookcase, as understated as the rest of the room.

'No, not tree. I mean the *szopka* – the crib.'

On the glass-topped coffee table stood a wooden manger with carved, painted figures: a cow and a donkey; shepherds bowed and kings kneeling before the baby. Joseph had an arm missing and Mary looked too big, far too large for the poor scraggy donkey to have carried her.

'We bought in Zakopane when we went there for holiday. I know, it's very traditional and I'm sure in real world birth of Jesus takes place nothing like this. But it's again a nice story, don't you think so: the new life with the new promise? I stopped go to church long time ago, but I miss it at this time of year.'

* * *

Josie felt shy to ask for a glass of water, so the sour taste of the vinegar-drenched herrings lingered in her mouth. The others spoke in English, trying to include her in the conversation, but their efforts only made her feel more left out. She hadn't heard of the writers they talked about, never mind read their books.

If anything, Kogut sounded the most enthusiastic: 'We create our own experience,' he declared to nods from Helena. 'What you think, you become.' Their hostess agreed with everything he said, interrupting only when she didn't understand the meaning of a word. Ola also appeared to be a convert, coming up with clever answers when Kogut turned devil's advocate to challenge her in jest.

Josie found herself warming to Roman more than to the women. He said very little and she assumed all their new-age talk must be above his head too. But when the conversation turned to people dying in Malawi because they had no clean water, he chimed in as animated as the rest. Josie could only nod: they all knew far more about it than she did.

She finished her herrings before any of the others, and the next course – steaming-hot sauerkraut with wild mushrooms – too. No doubt they considered her ignorant. She didn't understand why Kogut had brought her here, unless he took pleasure in showing her up.

Her mind kept returning to what he'd said outside. *We are Spirit.* What did he mean? She stared at him, the dancing flame of the candle between them, and she felt a growing urge to confront him. *We're all Spirit?* Well if he really believed that, why did he live in a mansion and have people to cook and clean for him, and Adam to drive his Merc? Or perhaps he'd set up the whole evening, but why would he? Not to get her into bed with him, surely, when he could have chosen a hundred more obvious ways.

Josie waited for a break in the conversation, but she couldn't get a word in while Ola offered her solutions to the world's problems. She spoke like a proper little oracle, like the world's leaders simply had to follow her suggestions and everything would be sorted. Josie couldn't help but smile when Ola spilled some greasy cabbage from her fork onto her plush velvet dress.

When Roman brought the carp from the kitchen and set a plate in front of her, Josie recalled the live fish in the bath at Pete's family's flat: the ripples it made in the water, the languid movement of its fins. Pete and his family would be having their meal too, an empty space at the table where a week ago she'd sat.

Josie had hoped Pete might change her and show her another way to live. She'd allowed herself to get close to him because a part of her did want to change. Instead she'd ended up hurting him twice now. She'd been kidding herself, to imagine a relationship with someone so different could ever have worked.

Helena borrowed her daughter's plate to cut the meaty fish into small, bite-size chunks for her. The emeralds in Ola's earrings looked real. Weren't they wasted, on a girl who couldn't see?

'You are not eating,' observed Kogut.

'I'm not hungry,' Josie said. 'I've had enough.'

'You've been very quiet, Josephine.' Ola spoke to her for the first time since they'd sat at the table. 'Tell us about yourself.'

The invitation jolted Josie. 'Like what?'

'Do you study?'

'No. I went to drama school, but I left it after a year.'

'So do you work?' Ola pressed.

'I do some modelling.'

'Oh, really? What kind?'

'Magazines. *Fashion* magazines.'

'What colour is your hair?'

'Blonde.'

'Oh, but it's much darker than yours is, Ola,' said the girl's mother, returning her plate. '*Bardzo ostry —*'

'Vivid,' Roman translated.

'Almost halfway towards red.'

Josie realised, if she did stay in Poland, she'd have to dye her hair to avoid being recognised. Maybe black would suit her.

'... Josephine is very beautiful.' Helena interrupted her thoughts. 'Don't you think so, Arkadiusz?'

Kogut took a long moment to reply, until Josie looked at him. 'Yes, she is. Very.'

Ola struggled to capture an obstinate piece of fish on her fork. 'But of course, it's what's on the inside that counts.'

Chapter 33

The gift

'Hurry up,' Grace said when Snaz came downstairs. She'd already opened the front door. She liked to be early wherever she went, but especially for church.

'It's not even quarter past yet. We'll be the first ones there.'

'You know I can't rush with my asthma.' She bustled him out of the way so she could lock the door, then scurried off across the courtyard, leaving him trailing behind. She only slowed as they neared the church. Snaz noticed the new extension, its roof tiles glazed with frost. At Easter, the last time he'd sat through a service – *celebration*, they called it – they hadn't even started work on it. Pastor Norman had still been cadging for funds.

'Did you bring any money with you?' Grace asked. When he shook his head, she reached into her handbag and extracted her purse, handed him a crisp five-pound note. 'For the offering,' she said.

Grace hesitated when she saw the pastor in the foyer, talking with a woman dressed as though for Ascot, and with a man in a waistcoat, whose jarring voice Snaz recognised. A couple of years ago, he'd heard him give a sermon about Judgement Day and Hell.

Grace hovered, trying to attract the pastor's attention, but he barely acknowledged her. Neither the man nor the woman moved to make room for her in their circle.

To Snaz's relief, his aunt gave up and helped herself to a programme and a copy of the newsletter from the table. 'We'll speak to him afterwards,' she said, loud enough so the pastor would hear.

She waddled to the front of the empty chapel and set her

overcoat on a chair in the centre of the very first row.

'Do we have to sit at the front?' Snaz asked.

'We need to leave space for people who come in late. Now shush and let me pray.' She borrowed a cushion from the next seat and lowered herself onto her knees.

The grey plastic chairs were identical to the ones in the police-station waiting room. Snaz sat with his arms folded. On the stage, a dreadlocked young woman practiced her flute, while a carrot-haired boy with freckles tuned his guitar. Behind the preacher's lectern, a gigantic pine cross reached towards the roof, and a garish tapestry of Christ overlooked the musicians: arms outstretched, He stood amid the clouds. Snaz always felt uncomfortable here, and tried to avoid visiting his aunt on Sunday mornings. Her life revolved around church, and he'd never had the heart to tell her how he felt.

The woman with the flute smiled at him. He looked away from her, picked up the newsletter from Grace's chair, but after scanning a couple of lines he put it down again. 'I'm going to the loo,' he told his aunt.

Standing at the washbasin, rubbing his hands under the cold water, Snaz felt a hand on his shoulder. Startled, he spun round.

Pastor Norman looked high on drugs. His mane of hair stood on end. 'Simon, how wonderful that you've joined us today. It's been a while. I'm glad you've come.'

Snaz shook the water from his hands. The pastor stood between him and the towel dispenser.

'Your aunt told me you're in trouble. Is there anything I can do?'

'She's told you? What's she said?'

'That you're in trouble with the law. That it's serious this time. She's concerned. We all are.'

'All?'

'The elders. We've been praying for you. If you want to talk to someone about it, someone apart from your aunt, maybe I can help?'

'I'm all right, thanks.' Snaz dried his hands on his jumper and began to back away.

'That's what I like to see: a young man eager to get to the service.' The pastor added, as Snaz bumped into somebody in the doorway, 'You know where to find me if you change your mind.'

The chapel was teeming when Snaz returned, buzzing with chit-chat and with young children running around. He nearly stamped on a toy racing car that came hurtling down the aisle.

He might well have shouted at Grace if he hadn't found her engrossed in conversation with some people in the row behind. He couldn't believe she'd told Norman, him of all people. Now the whole church probably knew. He looked around, uncertain if people were talking about him.

The service began with the Calypso carol, the one he'd liked at school. Singing was the last thing Snaz felt like doing. Grace raised her arms skyward and lifted her voice above the rest.

After the carol, the flautist read from the Gospels, and then Pastor Norman strutted like a cockerel from his stool to the lectern in the centre of the stage. He cast his eyes around the hall. 'Come in, Dorcas.' He beckoned to a woman by the door. 'There is a seat there on the right.' A line of people shuffled along to make room for her.

'It always amazes me,' Norman began, 'when I hear people claim there is no interest any more in Christianity, as if the gospel could pass its sell-by date or lose its appeal. No interest? Well let them come here and observe for themselves!' People laughed. 'Here we are, on this very special day, and our chapel is bursting to the rafters. And all of us are here for one reason: to celebrate the birth of God's Son.'

Again, he surveyed his audience. 'Hands up all of you children who opened your Christmas presents this morning.' The young child who'd come in late with his family and sat next to Snaz shot up his hand.

The pastor came over, crouched in front of the boy and Snaz observed the hairs sprouting from his ears. 'What gift did you receive, Tommy?'

'A PlayStation,' the boy replied into Norman's microphone.

Snaz shifted in his seat.

'Really? You must invite me round to try it out... And what about your little sister?' He turned to the girl next along in the row. 'What did your mummy and daddy get for you?'

'Not mummy and daddy... Father Christmas!' said the girl.

All around Snaz, people erupted in laughter.

'Oh, how daft of me!' The preacher held up his hands. 'Yes, of course I meant Father Christmas. What gift did you receive from him?'

'A new bicycle.'

'Oh, very nice!' Norman exclaimed. 'Would anyone else like to tell me about their favourite present?'

'I got a racing car!' shrieked a boy from the back. Probably the car Snaz nearly crushed underfoot.

'Now that's more like it!'

To Snaz's relief, Norman went away to speak with the boy.

'You have it with you? May I see?'

The curly-haired child showed him his toy.

'Shall I let you into a secret? I wanted one of these myself, but Lucille – I mean Father Christmas – gave me socks.'

Even Grace chuckled this time.

'You know,' said Norman, returning to the platform with a bound, 'we often receive gifts at Christmas that we don't really need – whether it's a bicycle or a model car or another pair of socks. But there's one gift that's different, because it's one all of us need. I mean the gift of forgiveness, the gift of Jesus Christ, who was born on this day some two thousand years ago.

'Now, this gift is for every one of us...for every man, woman and child.' He pointed three times into his audience. 'But let me explain something to you, because it's very important, particularly when there are people here today who don't come to church every week and who maybe have yet to turn to Christ.'

Snaz felt certain the pastor meant him.

'Let's suppose your father sends you a gift. Imagine a present wrapped in shiny silver paper and tied at the top with a bow. But let's say that when you're given the gift you don't open it. Instead, you put it away in your wardrobe, or in the garage, or in the cupboard under the stairs. The gift has been given to you, but it won't be of any benefit until you choose to accept it.

'We were created in the image of God, but all of us have fallen short. Who among us can claim, at all times, to have served God with all our heart and loved our neighbour as our self? In that sense, we are all sinners. And in the exact measure we sow, so also must we reap. What we do unto others, we receive back. This is an inescapable law of the universe. The Lord is just.

'But the good news is that this is not the whole story. Our Father in Heaven has given us a gift. His gift of salvation can wipe our slate clean and save us from punishment for our sins. Still we need to accept that gift. How? First, we must have faith. But it's not enough only to pray with fine words and to *say* we believe. If our faith is genuine, it leads us to a second thing.' Eyes wide, he stared straight at Snaz. 'We become changed. No matter what the cost, we follow the true path shown us by the Lord. Otherwise the gift is like that unwrapped present in the garage: you will never benefit from it, you will never receive forgiveness. And one day, you will pay the price.'

Chapter 34

A new life

Josie stepped outside her bedroom. She hadn't been imagining the sound: a whirring noise like a washing machine. But it couldn't be the washing machine, because that was downstairs. Josie tiptoed along the corridor and when she came to the room at the end she saw Kogut pounding on a treadmill with his back to her, scurrying to keep up with the pace.

His shorts exposed pale legs, blubber more than muscle. His blue T-shirt had damp patches under the arms.

She backed away, but a floorboard creaked and he glanced over his shoulder in time to spot her.

'Josephine,' he said, his face like a glacé cherry. 'Don't go.' He hit the emergency-stop button on the machine, grabbed his towel to mop the sweat from his forehead. 'The price I pay for last night's meal.' He got down off the treadmill and collapsed into the only chair in the room, a large wicker one better suited to outdoors. 'How did you sleep? I hope I did not wake you.'

'I had a nightmare,' Josie said. She'd dreamed of being lost on her own in a forest with howling wolves closing in. 'I couldn't sleep afterwards.'

'You are anxious. Of course you are.' Kogut caught his breath. 'But remember, we have a plan. Tomorrow we put it in action. Some people will come here to take your car.'

The room had weight machines and an exercise bike besides the treadmill. Josie stood by the bike and grasped its handlebar. 'I've been thinking about your plan. What if it doesn't work? You can fake a car crash, but the police won't believe I'm dead. Not if they don't find my body.'

'Ah, but they will find a body. My contact Ovidiu – an excellent man – will borrow one from a morgue. The car will be burnt, don't forget. All we need to convince people is a lock of your hair.'

A queasy feeling welled inside her. 'How can you borrow a body?'

Kogut rubbed his fingers together, as if to say: "Money talks".

'That's not what I meant. It isn't right.'

He took a gulp from his water bottle. 'Why? No one will be harmed. The person is dead. The body is only a shell.'

She went to the window and tried to lift it to let in some air, but found it locked. Facing Kogut again, she said, 'Wouldn't it be better if I handed myself in? I could tell the police the truth. Why are you shaking your head?'

'If you tell the truth, no one will believe you. The police are convinced you killed Rook and a jury will think the same. Rook's son will testify against you. He will say you were the one who he saw with the gun.'

'But I dropped it. I ran from the house. Why hasn't that man gone to the police?'

'Which man?'

'The one who saw me outside Rook's house.'

Kogut sat forward. 'Someone saw you there? Who?'

'A man walking his dog.' An idea flashed in her mind. 'We could offer a reward so he comes forward. If he saw me outside while Snaz was still in the house, it proves I didn't kill Rook.'

'Not necessarily. He could have seen you before you went in.'

'Don't you understand? He came as close to me as you are now. I'd hardly kill someone *after* that, would I, knowing I'd been seen?'

'Even if this witness testifies and they find Aziz guilty of the murder, it will not stop them sending you to prison too.' Kogut paused when he noticed her flinch. 'I do not want you going to jail. Not for *any* length of time.'

'But don't you...' Josie's throat ran dry. She began again, 'Don't you think I deserve to?'

'If you had not shot Rook's son, you would very likely be dead.'

In her mind, she's back in Rook's living room, aiming the gun. Rook has spotted her hand shaking and his expression changes. The fear leaves his eyes. Now it's her who's more afraid. She hears a clunk, someone behind her. She turns and sees a man with a knife.

'You are not a bad person,' Kogut said. 'You are not a danger to anyone else.'

'I shouldn't have gone there. I shouldn't have taken a gun.'

'Do you regret it?'

Josie nodded.

'You would not do the same thing again?'

'No.'

'Well then, if you have learned your lesson, what would it achieve to shut you in prison?'

Josie watched Kogut drain the last of the water from his bottle. She'd shot someone. Did he think she could simply move on?

'All this exercise has given me an appetite,' he said. 'I tell you what, why don't you make us both breakfast? I will have a shower and then join you downstairs.'

Josie stood in the middle of the kitchen, daunted by the size of it, uncertain where to begin. At home in England, she rarely ate breakfast: maybe a yoghurt or a small piece of fruit while waiting for her coffee. She couldn't remember preparing breakfast for someone else.

She searched in three cupboards before spotting the wooden breadbin on the worktop. The one remaining croissant felt hard. Maybe Kogut wouldn't notice? Josie hesitated, but decided to use the wholemeal loaf instead.

She opened the top drawer, saw the bread knife and froze. A blade of that size would have cut straight through her. Kogut was right, she realised. She'd had no choice but to shoot.

Recovering, she cut the bread, dropped two slices into the toaster, then filled the kettle from the tap. In the fridge, she found eggs and smoked bacon medallions. She cracked open the eggs on a frying pan, added pungent-smelling mushrooms and a ripe tomato which spilled its juice when she quartered it, and then stood ready with a fish-slice to flip the sizzling bacon. Doing normal everyday things helped her escape from her thoughts.

Hearing footsteps, she jumped. Kogut already? 'That's quick,' she said. Her words hung in the air when she turned and saw Adam scowling at her.

It took her a moment to summon courage to break the silence. 'Happy Christmas, Adam.'

'Is it?'

'I didn't expect... I thought you'd be with your family. Or with your girlfriend. Is Kogut...? Is Arkadiusz making you work?'

'He needs someone here while Yvonna and Waldemar away on holiday,' he said. 'Not that it is your business.'

'Do we have to be enemies? I'm making breakfast for Arkadiusz.' She used Kogut's first name on purpose. 'Would you like me to make you some too?'

'No thanks.' Then he said, 'It's burning,' and she smelled the bacon frying to a crisp. She scrambled to flip it over... *Come on, blasted thing.* She struggled to turn the last stubborn piece. When she looked back again, Adam had gone.

Kogut smiled when Josie set the plate in front of him. 'I could get used to this,' he said. 'Yvonna will come back from Krakow and find herself out of a job.'

Dressed in a casual sweater and check shirt, he appeared more approachable than he did in his suit. Josie fetched her own breakfast, a smaller portion, and sat opposite him. 'I saw Adam just now.'

'Oh?'

'I'm worried he'll go to the police.'

Kogut stopped with his fork poised in front of his mouth. 'What did he say?'

'Nothing. But he doesn't like me.'

'Do you not think so? Well, whether he likes you or not, he will not inform on you. I have spoken to him, and Yvonna has too. He listens to her.'

'What did you say to him – about me?'

Kogut resumed eating. She watched him chew on the over-crisp bacon. It took him an eternity to swallow what he had in his mouth. 'I said you are in trouble; that the police wrongly suspect you. I also told him your father died. Adam understands about grief.'

'Does he?'

'He lost his girlfriend – in a real car crash. A drunken driver.'

'Adam's girlfriend's dead?' Josie thought of the mousy girl in the photograph she'd seen back at the flat. It made sense now why Marcin had got the idea she'd been involved in a hit-and-run. 'When did she die?'

'Three years ago or thereabouts. Afterwards Adam abandoned his studies and lost his job. That is why Yvonna asked me if I could find work for him. His girlfriend was Yvonna's niece. Excuse me.' He got up from the table and went to fetch some honey, which he proceeded to spread on the toast. 'You are right though, we will need to tell him the whole truth when he realises you are staying here for good... Eat up, before your food goes cold.'

Josie couldn't eat her bacon – she'd been careful to give Kogut the less-badly burned pieces. After tasting the eggs and the mushrooms – somehow she'd even managed to make a mess of those – she put down her knife and fork. Adam already looked on her with contempt. It'd be even worse when he knew all the details. Every time they passed one another he'd be thinking, *She shot someone. Does she feel no guilt? She ought to be in prison.*

Kogut changed the subject. 'Thank you for coming with me to meet my friends last night. I promise you, they will not tell anyone about you staying with me. What did you think of Ola?'

Josie thought hard to find something nice she could say about the blind girl. Kogut obviously liked her, so she didn't want to be rude. 'Her English is good... *You* get on well with her. She likes you.'

'Do you think so?'

'The pair of you were laughing like... I don't know... You seemed really natural together.'

'I have an idea,' he announced. 'Since you are going to be living here, you should learn to speak Polish. Why don't I ask Ola to teach you? She would be good company for you, someone nearer your age. What do you say?'

Ola would love that, Josie thought: being the teacher, getting snooty when she didn't pick things up straight away. 'I was rubbish at languages at school.'

'Come on, you are intelligent. With Ola's help, in three months you will have learned enough to get by. Come next Christmas, people will mistake you for a native *Polka*.' He had a broad grin. 'I will arrange a new identity for you and a passport so you can travel, though I do not think it will ever be safe for you in England. Imagine,' he said, beaming, 'you have the chance to start a new life.'

Chapter 35

Adam

Josie stood by the sash window in her bedroom warming her legs against the noisy rattling radiator and watching snowflakes swirling in the wind, ducking and diving like flies. This time last year she'd been looking forward to going skiing. Now she found herself a prisoner, unable to even go out to the nearest shop to buy cigarettes. She felt a sharp craving for one and wondered whether Kogut would go and buy her a packet if she asked him? He'd already told her he didn't want her to smoke in his house, and that she ought to give up.

She jolted when she spotted Adam outside, marching across the terrace, armed with a spade.

Her heart did a canter, like it did each time she saw him. She knew Adam could inform on her, that he'd love to just for the satisfaction it'd give him, and then all of Kogut's scheming wouldn't help her a jot. It disturbed her that he thought she'd killed someone, or that she'd intended to shoot Rook's son. Adam was Pete's cousin and her sole link with the outside world and her former life. She wanted him to like her, and it hurt when he met her every attempt to start a conversation with stony silence or a cutting remark.

She'd put her foot in it yesterday by asking him why he wasn't spending Christmas with his girlfriend. But how could she have known his girlfriend had died?

Maybe that was why she felt a connection with him: he'd lost someone, like she had. He understood how it hurt. But whatever the reason, Adam was the only person here who she felt able to relate to.

Kogut himself, Josie couldn't figure out. One moment he'd come over all virtuous and spiritual, or would shut himself away in his study to meditate for an hour, like at the moment. The next thing though, he'd speak about stealing someone's body from a morgue as if it was a perfectly reasonable thing to do. If he had genuine motives for helping her, surely he wouldn't stoop to a plan like that? He might be biding his time, waiting until after Dad's funeral, but she expected him to make his move on her sooner or later. Each night as she lay in bed trying to sleep, she dreaded a knock on her door. Merely the thought of sex with him made her recoil: his cold flabby body pressing against her. But if she needed his help, what choice would she have?

Kogut's servant Waldemar gave her the creeps too: always frowning, his eyebrows merged together, making her feel guilty without saying a word. Yvonna appeared pleasant enough, but Josie struggled to think of anything she had in common with her – and if Kogut did come on to her, Yvonna would be of no help. As for the girl Ola, who Kogut wanted her to make friends with – his affection for her *did* seem genuine – what a Pollyanna! Josie couldn't comprehend how anyone, least of all a blind girl, could be so happy, so upbeat.

No, she didn't feel comfortable with any of them, and she couldn't see things improving. If she was going to live here for any length of time, the only way it might be bearable would be if she had Adam on her side.

* * *

Josie wrapped herself in the plush sheepskin coat Kogut had given her for Christmas. It had an Italian label and judging by its touch, must have cost a fortune. She hadn't liked to accept a gift from him, but rather wear it than freeze. Checking herself in the mirror, she immediately felt discouraged. Her face had aged ten years in the last two weeks. Perhaps if she put on some make-up? She told herself that would do more harm than good: *I'm going to explain myself to Adam, not to chat him up.*

She slipped out the back door and made her way across the patio, careful not to spill the mug of coffee she took with her. At first she tried to walk in the footprints Adam had made, but she couldn't match his long strides. She followed his tracks around the side of the building, placing her hand over the mug to shield it from the snow, and thought of what to say to him. *I brought you a coffee to warm you up.* She wondered whether he'd even take it. And if he did, then what?

If she told him everything, he might still blame her. But he already thought the worst. Her heart, her legs, her whole body were quaking. The truth. She had to tell him the truth.

Josie turned the corner and saw Adam by the front door, talking with two men. Something about them – their look, their demeanour – she knew that they were police. And Adam was talking to them. Telling them about her.

She backed away, out of sight around the corner, uncertain whether they'd spotted her. She didn't think so – they hadn't looked her way. But they'd search the whole house and...

Kogut! Her only chance. She started running and – 'Arrghh!' – boiling coffee scalded her hand. The mug smashed on the patio but she kept on running, trying to think where to find Kogut. His study. Try his study. She tore through the kitchen, slipping and sliding on the floor, dodging the table and chairs. Along the corridor she slowed to a stagger, aware of the sound her boots were making, aware of voices in the entrance hall ahead. Adam and the police, coming this way. She froze, trapped. Then darted for the nearest door. The police were going to the study. Adam had told them she was here.

Chapter 36

Waiting for you

The sergeant slid a form across the counter. 'Sign at the bottom,' he said.

Snaz gripped the biro and scrawled something he barely recognised as his own signature.

'Okay, that's all.'

'You mean I can go?'

'Report here again on Wednesday at the same time.'

Snaz pushed the front door but it wouldn't budge, and he thought the cop had played a cruel joke on him. Then he noticed the sign saying "pull". He emerged into the damp dreary day, his relief giving way almost immediately to the thought the police could arrest him any time they wanted to. Even if they didn't do him for murder but only for possession of a firearm, he'd still go to prison for five years.

Across the road, the branches of an ivy-smothered oak tree creaked in the gusting wind. Snaz noticed a solitary leaf on one branch somehow clinging on.

Lowering his head, he tramped to his car. When he sat inside it, turned the key in the ignition, the engine choked and thought twice before spluttering into life. The battery needed replacing – another thing to do. Not today though, he had too much else to worry about, like how to handle his aunt. He pulled out and as he drove he began dreading the conversation he'd have with her. "How did it go at the station?" she'd ask. "Have they arrested Josie yet? Why didn't you listen when I told you to stay away from her?"

Lying in bed in the dark, the pastor's words running through his mind, he'd resolved to admit to Grace that he'd shot Rook. Now though, the idea struck him as mad. If he told his aunt, she'd make him confess to the police when they obviously had no evidence against him. Why should he take the blame for murder and let Josie get away with using him? He'd killed Rook to protect her. What did she expect him to do after she'd shot Dean? Let Rook go to the police, or come after them both? All he'd done was down to Josie. He was a victim too.

Suddenly Snaz noticed a red car in his mirror pull out to overtake him. What were they playing at, overtaking here with the parked cars on the other side of the road? Before he could speed up, the car had already cut in front of him. Snaz swore out loud at the driver. He checked the speedo: he was doing thirty-five himself. And the red car was fifty metres in front of him – he saw it shoot past a zebra crossing without stopping for a woman with a pushchair waiting by the kerb. *Idiot*, Snaz thought, slowing so the woman could cross. What if she'd stepped out?

Snaz watched the child in the pushchair, the mum with her hair blowing in the wind. And then it dawned on him. He'd held a gun to his own friend's dad and pulled the trigger. What right did he have to judge anyone else?

At Muswell Hill Broadway he did a U-turn and found a place to stop the car; switched off his mobile phone so Grace wouldn't be able to hassle him. Then he trekked to the shops, found an off-licence and spent most of the cash in his wallet on a four-pack of *Stella* and two bottles of the strongest cheap wine he could find.

It must have been over a year since Snaz last took the lift up to his second-floor flat. He usually sprinted up the stairs two at a time, but today he didn't have the energy to walk up them. He wondered if he might be coming down with the flu bug everyone was talking about, but he had no other symptoms, no cough or sore throat. Only his strength had drained away.

He stooped to pick the post from his doormat: a credit-card statement, three copies of the menu from *The Happy Garden* Chinese takeaway and a solitary Christmas card. He ripped open the glitter-dusted envelope, and when he saw the soppy photo of a puppy in a Santa Claus hat, he guessed right away who'd sent it. "Dear Simon, Happy Christmas!" She'd written *Happy Christmas*, even though the printed message said the same thing. "Have a fantastic New Year. Love, Marie." And after her name, she'd added three crosses, like she used to on the valentine cards she'd sent him at school.

Snaz put on the door-chain and then, leaving the card on the table along with the menus, slumped on the couch with his cans of beer. If he'd stayed with Marie, he'd be living a normal life, quiet and anonymous. Maybe he'd even have kids.

But how could he have stayed with Marie after meeting Josie, when what he felt for Josie was a thousand times more intense? Marie bored him, had done since he'd known her at school, whereas Josie made him come alive.

He could still picture Josie the night he first met her, in a club in Camden Town. The way she looked, innocent but with a smouldering sexuality at the same time...he couldn't work out if she was twenty, or only sixteen. He'd wanted to go up to her, but something – maybe an intuition – kept him away.

All night though he kept stealing glances at her, until once when he looked at the table where she'd been sitting, she wasn't there, and he saw the bloke who'd been coming on to her drop something into her drink.

Snaz could have done nothing. If he'd done nothing, he wouldn't have ended up walking Josie to a taxi. She wouldn't have given him her phone number. He'd never have seen her again.

Snaz cracked open his fourth can of lager. Maybe if he drank himself comatose, he'd be able to sleep and not lie awake thinking of Rook as he had every night since that first one. When his phone rang he started but made no effort to get up from the couch. He did wonder who might be calling him on his landline, until he remembered he'd switched off his mobile. No doubt it'd be his aunt checking up on him, fussing as usual, wondering where he'd got to. He ignored the phone, and after six rings it diverted to voicemail. But then, a few seconds later, it rang again. 'Who the...?' he cursed. Surely if it'd been Grace, she'd have left a message. But who else could it be if not her? Snaz's eyes came to rest on Josie's portrait, staring back at him from the wall.

Putting the can down, stumbling to his feet, he lurched to the table to grab the phone. 'Hello?' Quiet on the other end of the line. After a while he said, 'Go to hell then,' and slammed down the receiver.

As he slumped back on the couch, a thought struck him: what if it *had* been Josie? He convinced himself it must have been, and by hanging up on her he'd lost his one chance to talk. She was the one person he *could* talk to about what had happened, the thing they'd done together, the thing he *had* to talk about to someone to stay sane.

When the phone rang again, he rushed to answer it. The caller said nothing, but this time Snaz could hear breathing. 'Josie? Is it you?'

The voice – familiar yet so unexpected – sent a chill through his body. 'Do you remember me, murderer? Do you remember your mate Matt? I'm outside by your car, waiting for you. Are you going to come down here or are you going to make me come up?'

Chapter 37

Flames

Josie pinched her nose and managed to stifle her sneeze. She felt a second one coming. Her ribcage convulsed as she fought to keep from making a sound. This was what she'd come to: hiding behind musty curtains, one eye on the window, in case the police walked by outside. Her hand throbbed from the scald, screaming out to her to run it under cold water, but she didn't dare move. They could be in the next room.

For five minutes, maybe longer, she stayed rooted to the spot. Apart from her breathing, she couldn't hear a sound. Peering out from behind the curtains, she saw her wet footprints on the carpet, a bold exclamation mark pointing right to her, and realised the uselessness of trying to hide. If the police came in the room, that was it for her. What did she mean, *if*? They knew she was in the house. They weren't going to leave without her.

Any second they'd come in through that door, slap handcuffs on her and take her away in their car. Her mind grew dizzy with thoughts of interrogations, court, prison at the end of it. If it had to happen, she wanted it to be over. She didn't understand why they were taking so long to come to the room.

Josie blew cold air onto her hand. They might search every room in the house before they came in here. She tore off her coat – too hot now – and threw it onto a chair. She felt tempted to put an end to this torture of waiting and give herself up. Perhaps she should have done that right at the start, and not run away. She took a step towards the door, but another thought made her stop. Kogut might be talking to them, attempting to bribe them. He might try, if it was only these two policemen who knew she was staying in his house.

The longer they didn't come to the room, the more she

believed it possible. But a bribe would simply extend this limbo she was in. Every morning she woke scared it'd be the day when they tracked her down. Wouldn't she be better off caught?

She expected the door to open, but it still made her jump. It wasn't the police, but Adam. To her surprise, he was on his own.

'What are you doing in here? Mr Kogut wants to see you in his study,' he said.

'The police are with him, aren't they? Thanks for grassing me up.'

He stared at her. 'What you talk about? What police?'

'I saw you speaking to them.'

'When?'

'Just now.'

'Those two men now? They weren't police.'

She met his eyes. 'Is it fun for you to toy with me like this?'

He took a step nearer and his expression softened. His voice softened too. 'They've gone. They came to take your car, that's all.'

'My car?'

'Yeah, that crazy plan.'

'The police *don't* know I'm here? You haven't told them?'

'Why would I tell them? That's not for me to do.' Before she could say anything, he said, 'It is a crazy plan though, to pretend you're dead.'

'But Kogut says it's the only way.'

He snorted. 'You could give yourself up.'

'I can't. It's too late for that. Snaz has gone to the police and lied to them. He's told them I shot Rook. They won't believe me if I tell them the truth.'

'What is the truth?'

'I'm not a murderer. I shot Rook's son to defend myself. If I hadn't, he would have killed me.' She covered her face with her hands, the way she'd done then. 'When I saw the blood and he wasn't moving, I kept thinking *move, please, move*. But he didn't.

He just lay there, and I... I panicked... I dropped the gun and ran.' Josie wiped her eyes. 'I thought Snaz would follow me. At that moment, I wasn't conscious of anything except that I had to get out, away from there. But Snaz didn't come after me. He picked up the gun and he... *Stupid, stupid man.* He wanted to protect me.'

What she wouldn't have given for Adam to take a step closer, to reach out and put his arms around her, or at least tell her he understood. She waited for his reaction, her heart thumping against her ribcage.

'You're not even sorry.'

For a moment the beating stopped. 'I am.'

He shone his eyes at her. 'If you were sorry, you wouldn't be hiding here. You would go to police and admit what you did.'

'But Rook's son attacked me. He had a knife.'

'You had a *gun*.'

His words cut like a scythe. 'I had it to frighten Rook, not to kill him. Rook used my mum. He forced her to see the man who killed her. Should I have done nothing?'

'Revenge makes you bad as him.'

'Don't say that.' Josie raised her voice, but her words came out more like a cry. 'You don't know how it feels to have your mum taken away from you.'

Adam turned his head towards the fireplace, then back at her. 'The driver who kills my girlfriend is drunk, three times over maximum. Should I get myself pistol like you do and go around to where he lives?' He gave an exaggerated shake of his head.

How could she answer, and yet she felt she had to say something. 'I did think about going back to England and handing myself in. I wanted to be at my dad's funeral...'

'Yes, but you are still here. You are not going back.'

When he moved towards the door, Josie scrambled after him. 'Kogut said I should stay. He said there's no point in me going to prison. I don't deserve to be punished for—'

'No point?' Adam cut her off. 'What about the man who is dead?'

'Snaz is the one who killed him. Why should I go to prison for something I didn't do? Why should I take the blame?'

'Let me ask you one question. If you hadn't gone to this man's house, would he be dead? Would he be shot, if you hadn't gone there with pistol? If it's you who shoots him, or if it's this Snaz, it makes no difference. You and he both are guilty, both the same.'

After Adam left, Josie sat in the armchair and, clutching the cushion to her chest, watched the flames rise silently in the fire. She'd wanted him of all people not to condemn her for what she'd done.

To compare her with Rook wasn't fair. Rook didn't care one bit about her mum's murder. He'd kept on as though nothing had happened, using other women like his property, robbing them of half the money they earned and calling it "protection". Some protection! And the police let him do it. Even her dad did nothing to pay Rook back. Josie swept her hair from her face, grabbed a lock and pulled until it hurt. She'd wanted justice. Nothing more.

Still she felt emptiness inside her, and Adam was telling her it would never go away. Not unless she gave herself up.

But handing herself in could mean she'd spend the next fifteen or twenty years locked in a prison cell. She might be forty-three before she got out. She could barely conceive of herself being forty-three: as old as Erin nearly, or like those baggy women at the gym who struggled to keep up in class. She'd be over halfway to her grave.

Josie got to her feet again and resumed pacing the room. With its antique furniture and chandelier, and fitted bookshelves from floor to ceiling, it might be the drawing room of an Edwardian stately home. The whole house had the same formal air to it: not somewhere to live. How could she be comfortable here? It struck her she'd never feel at ease. She thought of the tall ivy-covered walls enclosing the garden and the iron gates at the end of the drive. It might as well be a prison when she couldn't go anywhere for fear of being discovered. She'd have to go begging to Adam – Adam who hated her – every time she needed a cigarette.

Not for the first time, she wondered about her dad's will. She had the same right to his money as her brother did. If Dad had left her something, she'd be able to hire a good lawyer, one who might be able to convince people she hadn't shot Rook. If she could be certain they wouldn't find her guilty of murder, then she would go back.

Josie stopped by the fireplace, felt its heat against her legs. She needed that dog-walker to come forward and tell the police he'd seen her, *spoken* to her, before he heard the gunshot. He must have heard the shot, it had been so loud. She could picture the man as clearly as she could her own brother. If she returned to London and described him to the police, then surely they'd be able to track him down?

Maybe the best thing would be to go now, in time for Dad's funeral. Kogut had told her over breakfast that they'd set the date for next week. She wondered if they'd bury him in the church graveyard, or if he'd be cremated. And if she did go to the funeral, would the police turn up at the service and arrest her in front of everyone?

Noticing a shadow move against the wall, Josie turned and saw Adam behind her.

'You realise why Kogut is helping you?'

The way Adam looked at her, up and down her body, she understood what he meant.

'Or maybe that doesn't bother you,' he said. 'Maybe to you it's the price worth paying?'

'I'm not who you think I am.' She turned from him and hid her face. Then, when he lingered, she said, 'Go away. Leave me alone.'

'I have one other question. What about Pete?'

Josie wiped her cheeks with the back of her hand. 'Pete knew nothing about what happened.'

'Of course he didn't. He's my cousin. But I ask something different. I ask why you were with him, why did you pretend to be his girlfriend.'

'I didn't pretend.' She'd been attracted by Pete's genuineness, by the fact he valued her not simply for her body, or because her dad had money. She'd hoped some of his steadiness, his peace of mind, might rub off on her and that he might make her a better person. He hadn't, of course. She hadn't wanted to change enough. 'We were friends,' she said.

'You hurt him.'

Josie lashed out. 'I had to leave Pete. I couldn't risk getting him involved.' After a pause, she said, 'If you see him, will you tell him I'm… I never meant to hurt him?'

'Pete has gone back to London.'

'Pete's gone?'

'Yesterday. Marcin said to me, before Pete goes, he throws out all your things.'

At first Josie didn't care about her things, but then she remembered something…something she'd forgotten in her rush to leave the flat. 'But not my mum's locket? He can't have thrown the locket away?'

'Are you worried more about losing your possessions than Pete?' said Adam.

'You don't understand. I don't care about the rest of it, but the locket belonged to my mum. It's the only thing of hers I have. Please, Adam…' Josie would have seized his arm if his body language hadn't warned her to keep away. 'Will you go to the flat for me and look for it? Please will you help me get it back?'

'Tell me something else. When you were with Pete, were you also with this Snaz? Is it Snaz who you really love, or were you using him too?'

Chapter 38

No strength left to fight

From behind the net curtains, Snaz could see Matt pacing in the courtyard below. Matt Rook, the son of the man who he'd killed.

Apart from when Matt smashed his aunt's window with a brick, Snaz had hardly thought about him. They hadn't been close mates. At school, they'd had little in common except supporting the same team. If it hadn't been for Josie encouraging him, Snaz would never have got to know Matt better. Snaz felt his bile rise. That must also have been part of her plan.

Snaz couldn't face Matt, particularly now he'd got himself half drunk. Let Matt come up to the flat. He wouldn't open the door.

He collapsed back on the sofa, reached for his lager, but found the can empty. Crushing it in his hand, he stood it back on the table and it toppled onto the floor. He waited, dreading the doorbell, the inevitable knock. After a few seconds, the tension of waiting became unbearable and he returned to the window but saw Matt hadn't moved.

Snaz wondered if he might be better off facing him. He could tell Matt what he'd told the police: Josie shot Dean and then killed Rook because he'd witnessed it. He could explain that he wouldn't have helped Josie if he'd believed for a second she might use the gun. If he went outside and told Matt straight to his face, he'd be showing he had nothing to hide.

He decided to go down to the courtyard, but as he undid the door chain his legs began to tremble. Who was he kidding? Nothing he could say to Matt would be enough.

Desperate all of a sudden for a piss, Snaz went to the bathroom. Standing over the toilet, he wished he'd left the country like Josie had. He'd give anything to be in some far-off place where no one would find him and where he wouldn't have to see Matt or Grace or anyone else he knew again.

When the knock came, loud and abrupt, Snaz was still in the bathroom. 'Come out, Aziz,' Matt bawled, banging on the door, ringing the bell at the same time, and then adding in a voice no less threatening, 'I only want to talk.'

The door! Snaz remembered he hadn't locked the door and rushed back to the room to grab the key. Where was it? Where'd he left it? He checked his pockets – not there – scanned the cluttered room until he spotted the key on the table with Marie's Christmas card, but before he could seize it, the door handle turned. Matt came in, and he wasn't alone.

Three, four, five of them piled into the room: Mo, wearing shades, and Andy, and a towering black man who Snaz had seen around before but didn't know by name. And at the back of the group he saw Dave – what was *Dave* doing with them? Snaz glanced from one hardened face to the next, and finally at Matt.

Matt looked like a man past caring, a man with nothing left to lose. He approached Snaz and accused him, 'You killed my dad.'

Snaz avoided Matt's eyes and looked beyond him to Dave, but Dave turned away and went to close the door.

'You killed him,' Matt repeated. 'My dad trusted you. *I* trusted you.'

'I...' Snaz broke off, realising nothing he could say would make a difference. From behind someone grabbed him, thrust an arm round his throat, yanking him backwards. He struggled free, but a blow to his face sent him reeling. Before he could recover someone hoisted him up and held him in an arm lock. 'He kicks like a girl,' one of them mocked, but Snaz had no strength left to fight.

They held him in front of Matt.

Pain screamed from Snaz's nose. He scrambled a hand free to hold it and saw blood on his fingers. He flailed his arms, frantic to free himself from the vice-like clasp.

Matt sneered. 'You shot my brother, left him for dead, and then you killed my dad.'

Snaz gagged, unable to breathe.

'What's that? I can't hear you.'

The man who had his arm round Snaz's neck loosened his grip barely enough for Snaz to splutter, 'I didn't. It wasn't me.' He could taste the blood in his mouth.

Snaz saw the punch coming, but couldn't move to avoid it. Matt's fist caught him in the lower stomach and when the black man let go of him he crumpled in pain, fell in agony to the floor. 'That was for my brother,' Matt said.

Snaz was on his knees crawling, trying to make it to the sofa, to clamber upright. He noticed Andy had a knife.

'Admit it,' Matt said. 'Admit you killed my dad.'

Snaz clutched his nose with one hand, his stomach with the other. No sooner had he scrambled to his feet, Matt charged at him and flung him against the cupboard. Another punch smashed into his eye as his head smacked against the wall.

'I know you did it.'

Snaz saw Matt readying to strike once more and raised a hand to protect himself. 'I swear it wasn't me.'

'I don't believe you. If you didn't kill him, who did?'

Blind in one eye, disoriented, Snaz looked around at the walls until he made out Josie's portrait. He pointed at it.

Matt stared awhile at the black and white photograph before snorting, 'What are you saying? Your *girlfriend* killed him?'

Snaz cowered in a corner by the cupboard, hoping to shield himself from more blows. 'Years ago her mum...' He coughed blood. 'Her mum used to work for him. He was meant to protect her...'

Matt raised his fist again. 'I don't want to hear your lies!' Face ablaze, he screeched, 'Get up and fight. If you're innocent, why don't you fight back?' Then to the others, 'Get him up, the murdering bastard!'

Andy and the black man hauled him upright and held him as a punch bag for Matt. Snaz could feel nothing but his eye throbbing, the explosive pain of his nose. He saw the door unguarded, but even if he could break free, he'd never make it downstairs. He looked to Dave, but Dave shook his head and Snaz sensed his only chance to get out alive had gone.

'I hope she was worth it. For your sake, I hope she was worth it,' Matt said. 'When we're done with you, me and Otis here will pay her a visit.' He took the knife from Andy and held the pointed blade in front of Snaz's face. 'Where is she? Tell me where she is.'

Snaz coughed more blood. He focused the one eye he could still see with on the portrait of Josie and for the first time it struck him as vulgar. All this, just to hold her and breathe in her scent. His life, for a fantasy. He saw it now for what it was. He'd given up everything, and not even for love.

Chapter 39

What love requires

When Josie saw the light go on in the corridor she jolted upright in bed. She made out footsteps on the stairs and then in the hallway. They stopped outside her room and she waited, expecting Kogut's knock. After a moment though he continued along the hall.

Josie pulled aside the blanket and got up, seizing the plush white dressing gown Yvonna had given her on her first night, and scrambling it on over her T-shirt. By the time she opened her door, Kogut had reached the end of the corridor. Hearing her, he turned round. 'Josephine, you are still awake then. How is your headache? How are you feeling?'

'Fine. Better.' She'd invented a headache as an excuse for not going out. She hadn't been able to stomach another long evening with Helena and Roman and Ola, and she'd needed time on her own to decide once and for all what to do. 'I need to talk to you,' she said.

'Can it wait until tomorrow? I am very tired.'

'I'm going back to England, to Dad's funeral. Then I'm going to hand myself in.'

'Josephine, why?' Kogut approached her. 'Why throw away your young life?'

'Haven't I done that already? I don't want to be on the run. I want this to be over.'

'But I have explained. The police will stop searching for you once they think you are dead. For a year or two you can stay here, and then…'

'Then, what?'

He attempted a smile. 'Whatever you choose.'

Josie wrapped the dressing gown more tightly around her. 'I

spoke to Adam today.'

'So it is Adam who put these senseless ideas in your head.'

'He told me… He said you're only helping me for one reason.'

'Oh, what reason?'

'Why do you think?' Josie wished she didn't have to spell it out, but Kogut looked at her as though he genuinely didn't understand. 'He said you're helping me because… Because you want a relationship with me,' she whispered.

Kogut's cheeks flushed. 'Adam is letting his own feelings mess with his judgement. I do think you are a beautiful woman. But I am well over twice your age. I respect you. Your friendship is all I seek.'

'What do you mean, "his own feelings"? Adam hates me.'

'Well I cannot think why else he would say such a ridiculous thing.' From Kogut's tone, she could tell she'd offended him.

Embarrassed herself now, Josie asked, 'How can you respect me when I shot someone?'

'You shot him to protect yourself. You feared for your life.'

What he said was true, but Adam's words haunted her all the same. 'Yes, but Rook is dead.'

'Simon Aziz killed Rook.'

'I'm responsible, though.'

'How?' said Kogut.

'I went to his house with a loaded gun.'

'But you did not intend to use the weapon.'

Josie's body shuddered as she imagined being back in Rook's stuffy front room with its nicotine-yellowed walls. 'I couldn't go through with it. I couldn't shoot him.'

'Then why do you blame yourself?'

'Because I came so close to doing it. When we were driving there, I thought to myself, maybe frightening him isn't enough. Afterwards, in the car, when Snaz told me he'd killed Rook, I felt such relief.'

Kogut reached out to her, but instinctively she pulled away

and his outstretched hand dropped by his side.

'I need to fly back to London,' she said. 'Before Dad's funeral. Will you help me?'

Kogut's eyes closed, more than a blink. 'Are you certain this is what you want? You must not rush into a hasty decision without thinking over the consequences. Your father would not have wanted you to go to jail.'

'He says I'll always feel guilty unless I hand myself in.'

'Who does?'

'Adam.'

Kogut exhaled. 'Why do you listen to him? He is like a child. To him, everything is black or white...' Kogut undid the top button of his shirt. 'Let us go downstairs, it is cold here. If you give me a minute, I will come down and we can talk.'

* * *

Josie sat at the kitchen table, her head propped in her hands. She noticed Adam's hat on the radiator, Adam's mug on the draining board by the sink. Why *did* she listen to Adam? Why did it matter to her what he thought?

Kogut appeared in the doorway. Sitting at the adjoining side of the table, he took off his glasses and rubbed his eyes. 'I have been where you are,' he said finally. 'I understand regret.'

'Do you?'

He exhaled. 'Many years ago, I witnessed a killing.'

Suddenly wide-awake, Josie stared at him.

'I have not told anyone this before.' He paused, put his glasses back on. 'It happened during my time in the army. I could have reported the man responsible, the captain. I ought to have done, of course, but I kept quiet. I knew the captain's uncle was an official, someone senior in the government. I put ambition before principle, before people. In every situation I only considered what advantage there might be for me.'

'But you've never killed anyone. Have you?' Something in his solemn expression made her ask.

His gaze dropped to his hands, cupped together on the table. They were smooth, Josie noticed, like a woman's. 'In the past, it did not concern me if anyone got hurt. Money and power mattered.'

Josie stood up, more certain than ever that she couldn't stay here with him; that she had to leave.

The legs of his chair grated against the floor as he shifted to face her. '"Forgive them," Jesus said, "For they know not what they do". I was blind back then. I did not know what I was doing, and neither did you when you went to Curtis Rook's house. When we hurt another person, the truth is we are hurting ourselves – and who in their right mind does that? But today you feel regret, you realise what you did and it repels you. That shows you have grown. If you went to jail, who would benefit? Tell me who would it serve?'

Josie poured herself some water from the tap. She gazed at her reflection in the window and imagined Adam on the other side of the glass, staring back.

'Regret is one thing…' Kogut began again. 'God knows, I have made mistakes, more than most people. And in my personal life as well. I gave my own child up for adoption.'

'You had a child?' Josie met his eyes.

'Two children, both daughters. The younger one, my wife and I gave away.'

'Why?'

'We did not want… No, it is wrong to blame my wife. At the time, I did not want a disabled child. I was not a good man. I was unconscious. Foolish. And I acted in a way that makes me ashamed.' He swallowed. 'But guilt helps no one: neither you nor Rook or his son. Are you listening? Listen, because this is important. You cannot alter the past. What matters is the choice you make in this moment, now.

'You can change – I did – and you do not need to punish yourself. I made my business legitimate and used my money to help others, to help the people I'd wronged. I became their benefactor, their secret benefactor. Surely that is more useful than jail? And the same can be true for you,' he continued. 'If you live the best way you can from this day onwards, that is how to make up for the past.'

He had a soothing, almost hypnotic voice. Josie found herself by the table again, hands wrapped around the back of her chair. 'What made you change?' she asked.

'It is a long story. It is late.'

'Tell me.'

He sighed. 'I suppose I did it for love. My wife and I used to go to church. We were not true believers, it was simply habit, something we did. Then about ten years ago, a new priest took over. He spoke a lot of sense, but at the time I did not like what he said. His teaching had a big effect on my wife though. She decided I was immoral, and for sure she was right. One day she left me, took my other daughter with her. I missed them, and I hoped if I became a better person then she would come back.'

'She didn't come back though?'

Kogut shook his head. 'It took me three years to accept she did not love me. By then, I had read books, I had gone on courses and met new people who inspired me. I found living with kindness – asking what I could give to others, how I could serve them – made me feel so much better inside. For the first time in my life, I began to love myself too.'

'I don't get you,' Josie said. 'One day you're talking about faking an accident, so the police think I'm dead. The next...'

'What?'

'*This*. It might have worked for you, but I don't buy religion.'

'Who said anything about religion? What I am talking about is a way of living. Being authentic,' he added. 'Being true to who you are.'

'Why *do* you want to help me? I'm not used to people being kind to me and not wanting something in return.'

'I see the *real* you, Josephine. I see who you are and who you can be, if you give yourself the chance. Besides, it makes me happy to help you. What else can I say?'

Lifting the mug to her lips, Josie tasted the water. It was Adam's mug, she realised as she drank.

'You have to make this decision yourself,' Kogut said. 'Adam cannot decide for you, and neither should I. I can only advise you, share my own experience.' After a while he added, 'There is a piece of advice I find helpful: "Do what love requires of you."'

Josie nodded as she pondered what he said.

Chapter 40

Spinning a web

Snaz awoke in his bed in Grace's house, aware of a dull pain, pressure in the middle of his face. He reached to touch where it hurt and felt a rough plaster cast over his nose, a thick band of tape stretched across his cheeks. Another plaster covered his left eye.

He remembered blow after blow raining on him, thinking it would never end, and then Matt holding a knife to his throat. Snaz felt his neck, traced a thin scar with his finger where the blade had pressed against his skin.

'Give me one reason why I shouldn't kill you,' Matt had said.

Fear had made Snaz dumb. But even if he could have spoken, he had no reply.

Dave came to his rescue: 'He's not worth doing time for, Matt, scum like him. It's him who should be locked up. Let him rot in prison.'

Matt didn't move. Snaz could feel the blade against his skin. He remembered thinking, *Matt's going to kill me. He hates me so much he'd be prepared to go to jail.*

At last, Matt backed away, but not before spitting in his face. When they did go, Snaz feared they'd come back. He managed to reach his phone and call his aunt for help, but he must have passed out before she got to his flat. He'd come round again in an ambulance on his way to casualty and found Grace sitting next to him, gripping his hand.

The sound of mail being pushed through the letterbox and dropping onto the doormat downstairs startled Snaz and brought him back to the present. A slender beam of sunlight shone through the gap between the curtains. He could make out a pigeon gobbling on the roof. At the corner of the ceiling, he saw a spider spinning a web. Stiff, aching all over, he pulled aside the tangled and twisted bedclothes and sat facing the window. Drawing back the curtains, he saw the long-haired postman on his bike. The tarmac had almost dried after last night's rainstorm and dark stains of oil stood out in the space where Grace's neighbour parked his old car. Two doves flew by the window, screeching, one chasing the other. He noticed the berries on the holly bush, a glorious brilliant red.

When Grace knocked on his bedroom door, Snaz didn't answer, but she came in anyway. 'Oh, you are up, Simon.' For a while she simply stared at his face. 'Shall I make you breakfast? Bacon and sausage and eggs? Are you well enough to come down to eat?'

He nodded, only so she'd leave him alone.

Snaz stared out of the window, seeing familiar sights with fresh eyes. Matt might have killed him. Without Dave's intervention, he'd probably be dead. He began to wonder if perhaps death would've been better. What did he have to look forward to besides prison and nightmares and regret?

When Grace called to him, 'Breakfast is ready,' he hobbled downstairs, each step sending a fresh wave of pain through his body, and sat at the table. Steam rose in his face from the baked beans on his plate.

Grace didn't wait long before she asked the inevitable question: 'Are you going to tell me who did this to you?'

Snaz shook his head.

'Is it the same person who threw the brick? It is, I know. Why do you let him get away with it?'

'Leave it.' He waved her away. 'Please.' He picked up the knife and fork.

He ate slowly, every bite an effort. It made it worse that Grace didn't eat herself, but merely watched him. He grew more and more uncomfortable, worried she might somehow read his mind. For the first time, the prospect of going to prison didn't appear so bad. At least in prison, he'd be alone.

The carriage clock in the sitting room chimed the hour. Ten o'clock.

'You had a phone call this morning,' Grace said. 'From *her*.'

Snaz's knife slipped from his hand and clattered onto the plate, splattering tomato sauce across the pristine white tablecloth. 'From Josie? What did she say?'

'Who cares what she said. It's only lies.'

Snaz thought his aunt might be testing him, watching for his reaction. He busied himself with his food, piled egg and beans on his fork, wanting his aunt to say more but scared to ask her.

Finally she said, 'I told her not to ring again.'

He put down his fork. If Josie had tried to get in touch with him, perhaps she'd had a change of heart. Part of him still couldn't accept she'd used him, that she hadn't cared for him at all. Maybe she wanted to make things right. *Get real*, he told himself. Some chance of that when she'd shacked up with Henderson. She'd planned from the beginning to kill Rook and set him up to take the blame. Anger rose in him, and for a second he regretted not letting on to Matt where to find her. 'There's something I need to tell you about Josie,' he said to his aunt. 'She's going to say I killed Rook.'

'Well it wouldn't surprise me, the devious woman!' Grace sniffed. 'Let her say what she likes. No one will believe her.'

Encouraged, Snaz went on. 'She's going to say someone saw her outside the house.'

Grace looked puzzled.

'... That they saw her outside the house at the same time they heard the gunshot.'

'But they can't have done. It would mean...'

Snaz read the concern on his aunt's face. 'No one saw her. Of course not. She's making it up. But she has money and she'll pay someone to tell the police what she wants him to, so they pin the blame on me. She's admitted on the phone, it's what she's going to do.' He felt the plaster on his nose. 'A real witness would have gone to the police already, wouldn't he?' Snaz asked, forgetting himself for a moment. Every time he opened his mouth he had to watch what he said.

His aunt's silence disturbed him, until she reached across the table and took hold of his guilty hand. 'Look at me, Simon. There will be justice, even if there isn't in this world. Whatever happens, whatever people think, God knows the truth. God will be your judge.'

Chapter 41

No more than our best

As Josie shut the bedroom door behind her, she had a sense that closing it meant no going back. She went to the stairs, flinched when she saw Kogut below in the hall. Part of her had hoped he'd disappeared somewhere so there'd be no one to take her to the airport and she'd miss her flight. Now if she didn't go back to England she could only blame herself.

'So you have your coat on,' Kogut said, sitting to put on his shoes. 'I wondered if I should come and knock on your door. It will take half an hour to drive to the airport. We should go, if you do not want to be late.'

Josie's hand fastened on the smooth wooden banister.

Kogut looked up. 'Josephine, tell me if you are having second thoughts.'

'I saw a TV drama once, set in a women's prison. Half of the inmates carried knives.' Her voice faltered. 'Someone got raped by a warden.' She wanted reassurance, for Kogut to tell her it wouldn't be anything like that in real life. 'I'm scared,' she admitted.

'Then stay here.'

All night she'd lain awake, turning from one side to the other, deciding as many times to stay in Poland as to go. Her mind kept on, *Snaz killed Rook. I didn't ask him to, I didn't make him do it… Why* should *I be punished?* But each time she resolved not to go back, tension grew in her stomach and tightness in her chest. Deep down, she knew she'd left Snaz with no choice.

'You keep saying I should stay here, but how can I? I can't pretend Rook's death is only down to Snaz.'

Kogut stood up, one of his shoelaces still undone. 'If you would stay, I could speak to you about death. I have so much more to say to you. I could teach you things that, if I told you them now, you would think I am mad.' He sighed. 'Oh, Josephine, why do you feel you must do this? If you posed a danger to anyone, then I could see the purpose of keeping you in prison.'

Josie heard a car grind to a halt outside on the gravel drive.

He carried on, pleading with her as though his own freedom depended on it. 'If you have even the slightest doubt, you should not go. You can return to England next week, next month, after you have had time to consider it properly. But how can you have considered it while grieving for your father? If you catch this flight, you are making a decision you will have to live with for years. The police will arrest you, if not when you land then at the funeral...'

'They won't arrest me there?'

'I do not put it past them. Or if they stop you at the airport, they might not let you go to it. Either way, this evening you will be in a cell and it will be too late then to change your mind.'

Josie imagined a dark and windowless room, with no switch to turn on the light. She wanted to be at Dad's funeral, but if it meant spending half a lifetime locked up, sharing a cell with God knows who? And Kogut was telling her the police might not even let her go to the service.

She heard footsteps outside, the driver coming to collect her. She didn't feel ready to make a decision. If she waited a few more days as Kogut suggested, wouldn't it be reasonable? Who could hold it against her if she allowed herself more time?

The door opened, casting sunlight into the hall, and Adam appeared in the entrance. She felt a wave course through her body. Pointing at his watch, he looked at Kogut. And then his eyes fixed on her. 'Do you have any luggage?' he asked.

Josie shook her head.

'It's late,' Adam said. 'We must go.' He wasn't aware of her doubts, her fears. Or maybe he did read her mind, and that was why he pressed her.

Kogut muttered in Polish what sounded like a rebuke.

Adam said no more, but he didn't need to. His looking at her was enough. She walked down the final couple of steps and followed him outside.

He opened the door of the Mercedes for her and for a second she imagined some other life.

'You are doing the right thing,' he said.

His words were a greater comfort than he knew.

But in the car, while she waited for Kogut, the feeling of sickness and faintness came back, like someone had their hands around her throat. Josie wished she'd waited longer in her bedroom. She wondered whether Kogut would have come to fetch her, or if he'd have left it until too late? Even now he took as long as he could, locking the door, but then making out he'd forgotten something and going back inside. He emerged again with gloves on, descended the steps. How many days ago had she watched Adam clear the snow from them? Three? Four? Since she'd been here, she'd lost all track of the days.

Kogut joined her in the back of the car. He grappled with his seatbelt, but Adam didn't wait for him. Already the car was moving, leaving the mansion behind.

Ravens scattered from a roadkill as they emerged from Kogut's driveway onto the private lane. To Josie, the lane seemed shorter that morning. Soon they reached the end of it and Adam opened the window, stretched out his arm to swipe his pass, and the barrier rose.

On the main road, Adam changed gear, sped up past the red-brick church, a deserted playground where the rump of a half-melted snowman kept watch. Josie noticed girls laughing by a kiosk. Women waited at a bus stop, with shopping bags, with children. Around her, she saw people living ordinary lives.

Josie gripped her seatbelt, holding to a lifeline: she might be late, might miss the flight. A traffic light turned to amber, but instead of stopping, Adam floored the gas pedal. At that moment Josie let go. Kogut must have resigned himself too, for she heard his sigh.

In no time they'd joined the dual carriageway. Warsaw's high-rise tower blocks loomed in the distance and around them dark clouds threatened snow.

Kogut reached into his jacket pocket, offered her a folded sheet of paper. 'I have written the contact details for the lawyer,' he said.

She unfolded the page, once, twice, and turned it the right way up. He'd written an unpronounceable name in fountain pen, and beneath it two telephone numbers – a central-London one and a mobile.

'It is a Polish name, but he has lived in England all his life, his degree is from Cambridge. Ring him when you land. Do you have the mobile phone I gave you?'

Josie nodded.

'If the police arrest you, do not say anything until you have spoken to Zwierzynski. I will call him and tell him which flight you are on.'

Josie held the paper to her body. 'I went to Rook's house to frighten him. That's all I wanted to do,' she said.

'I know,' Kogut replied.

But her words weren't intended for him. She felt compelled to explain herself to Adam, to try one last time to get him to understand. If he understood, he might tell her she didn't need to go back. 'I wouldn't have killed Rook. If his son hadn't attacked me, I wouldn't have used the gun... Do I deserve to go to prison? No one ever punished Rook for what happened to my mum.'

Adam glanced at her in the mirror, but said nothing.

'Am I a bad person? Is that what you think?' she asked.

Kogut took hold of her hand. 'No, Josephine. If you are bad, then what does it make me? You are learning, growing, which is as much as any of us can do. We can do no more than our best.'

Too soon, they arrived at the airport. 'You should not be doing this on your own,' Kogut said. 'I should be coming with you, but I hadn't prepared for this. I thought you would not go. I will fly to London tomorrow,' he added.

'You don't have to.'

'I will visit you. I will meet Zwierzynski and go over your case with him.' He paused, then added, 'I will make things right.'

Adam stopped the car right by the terminal entrance and Josie glanced towards the sliding doors as two stewardesses emerged through them, trailing their trolley cases like poodles on leads.

'How will you get from the airport to the funeral service?' Kogut asked.

Josie hadn't considered practicalities.

'I will arrange for someone to meet you,' he said. 'Which terminal do you land in? Don't worry, I will find out. Someone will wait for you in Arrivals. Look for a card with your name on it.'

Adam cleared his throat and Josie held her breath... 'Better to use something else and not her name, Mr Kogut, in case police are there.'

Her heart plummeted and she slumped against the back of the seat. Is that all Adam had to say?

Only later, when the plane rose above the clouds, she considered it differently. Perhaps it was a sign that he cared.

Chapter 42

Death's dark vale

There was no act of God. The aeroplane touched down safely. As it slowed and left the runway, taxied towards the terminal, people began undoing their seatbelts, standing, removing bags from the overhead lockers. Josie remained seated and let everyone else get off first. She imagined a mob of police officers waiting for her, ready to bind her in handcuffs the moment she stepped off the plane. When the last stragglers had gone and she noticed the stewardess watching her, she took a final gulp from her water. She glanced around the cabin and wondered when, if ever, she'd again set foot aboard a plane.

Walking through the terminal, she kept checking over her shoulder. A stern-faced man in a sports jacket followed her onto the moving walkway, holding his phone to his face. She thought he must be a plain-clothes policeman, keeping track of her and making sure she didn't get away. She wondered if to surrender to him, rather than have them seize her – the pack she expected must be waiting at passport control. Less humiliating to go quietly and not have people see. She stopped walking, and as the man approached, her knees became feeble and she had to hold on to the handrail. 'I give myself up,' she prepared herself to say to him, but he continued on past her and she heard him speaking in German. She breathed a silent sigh and clutched her throat.

Josie carried on, lowering her head as she neared Immigration. When she noticed the official in the cubicle scrutinising the passports of people ahead of her, she moved to a different queue.

In Arrivals, Josie scanned the men in suits who were holding up cardboard signs. She spotted one, tall and dapper, with a sign

that read *Pamietam* – I remember – and made straight for him.
'Do you work for Arkadiusz Kogut?' she asked.

'You must be Josephine Davenport. It's my pleasure to meet you,' he said. 'I'm Ryszard Zwierzynski. I'll be representing you.'

'You're the lawyer?'

'Barrister,' he corrected her.

She hesitated before accepting his handshake, unsure whether to trust someone who looked and sounded so slick.

'Everything is taken care of,' he told her. 'I've a driver outside who'll take us to Guildford. The memorial service at the cathedral begins at two, yes? Don't worry, there's plenty of time to get there.' He nevertheless strode at a pace which she struggled to match.

Once they were outside, no one else within earshot, she caught up alongside him. 'I thought they'd arrest me when I showed my passport.' She hadn't quite been able to believe it when the immigration official had handed it back and wished her a good day. For a second, she'd remained rooted to the spot by the booth. 'Will the police be at the funeral?' she asked the lawyer, her voice almost drowned out by a low-flying jet. 'Are they going to arrest me there?'

He waited for the roar to die down. 'I've been in touch with the investigation team and informed them you intend to hand yourself in. They've agreed to let you attend your father's funeral. Detectives will be present there, but no one in uniform. They say they'll be discreet. Afterwards, they'll take you direct from the crematorium to north London, where you'll be charged.'

She flinched. 'What will they charge me with? Please don't say with murder.'

A gaggle of Japanese tourists headed in the opposite direction passed by them.

Ryszard sped up again. 'Let's talk in the car.'

The shiny maroon Jaguar matched the colour of the folded handkerchief in Ryszard's breast pocket. It surprised Josie to see a woman at the wheel – no older than thirty, with pristine catty features and long blonde hair tied in a bun.

As they left the car park, Ryszard rested a slimline briefcase on his lap and took out a leather-bound notebook, which he opened at the first clean page. 'Mr. Kogut has briefed me, but there are a number of things I need to clarify, if I may. I understand if your mind is on your father's funeral, but the police will interview you this afternoon and we do need to prepare ourselves.' He continued with barely a pause, 'Aziz worked for Curtis Rook, right?'

Josie nodded. 'Have you heard how Snaz is?' She'd been thinking about him during the flight. 'I tried to speak to him, but his aunt answered the phone. She said he'd been beaten up and injured.'

'I've no idea and I wouldn't let it concern you.' Ryszard sounded rather curt. 'Tell me, what kind of work did he do for Rook?'

'Rook bought and sold cars. If he needed someone to collect a car from Manchester, Snaz used to take the train up there and drive it back to London for him.'

'These would be stolen cars?'

'I don't think so. Snaz wouldn't have got involved if they'd been stolen.'

Ryszard wrote in an illegible scrawl. 'So had he known Rook for some time?'

Josie didn't understand why all his questions were about Snaz. 'He went to school with Rook's son.'

'Dean?'

'Not Dean, Dean's brother. But Snaz had never met Rook in person, not until later when I…' Josie broke off, looked at the driver.

'Don't worry, you can speak freely. Lydia works for me.'

Ryszard drew a line through what he'd written. 'Whose idea was it to go to Rook's house with a weapon? Aziz procured the weapon, is that correct? Would it have been his idea?'

'No,' Josie said. 'I asked him to get it. He didn't want to, but he did it for me.'

'Could he also have borne a grudge against Rook? Or is it possible Aziz might have stood to benefit in any way from Rook's death? Might he have seen a chance to take over Rook's car business, if he needed money, if he'd established contacts?'

'No, that's ridiculous. If you knew Snaz at all, you wouldn't ask. He only got involved because of me.'

'I'm simply exploring avenues.' Ryszard twirled his fountain pen between his fingers. 'So, on the night of the shootings, Aziz drove you to Rook's house?'

'Yes.'

'And what happened when you arrived there? Please go into as much detail as you can. Details can be extremely important, even if they might not seem significant to you. I don't want any surprises in the interview room later on.'

Josie's throat felt parched.

'Mr Kogut has told me Aziz went into the house alone first,' Ryszard probed.

'We were going in together, but as we crossed the road, he grabbed my arm. He said it'd be safer if he went in on his own, to make sure no one else was there. I waited behind the hedge in the garden until Snaz opened the door.'

'To let you in?'

Josie squirmed, recalling the moment. 'He hesitated when he opened it. He came out and would have shut the door, but I stopped him.' She held her head in both hands, aware that if she hadn't gone up to him, he'd have closed the door and she wouldn't have been able to go in.

'This is something you mustn't mention. As far as anyone else is concerned, Aziz opened the door for you. And perhaps you remember him encouraging you, beckoning you inside?'

Uncomfortable, she shifted in her seat.

'Tell me about the murder weapon. Did you have it when you entered the house?'

'Yes, in my bag.'

Ryszard gazed at the black handbag she cradled in her lap.

'Not this one,' she said, revolted by the thought. She had no intention of ever using the other bag again.

'Okay, so at some point Aziz must have given you the weapon...'

'His name's Snaz. Will you stop calling him Aziz.'

'I beg your pardon. When did Snaz give the weapon to you?'

'When we got to Rook's house. He had the gun in his rucksack in the boot of the car.'

'Now, your defence is that you intended merely to frighten Rook?'

'I didn't plan to shoot him.'

'No, and as far as you were concerned, the weapon wasn't loaded?'

'I...' Josie hesitated. Ryszard didn't want any surprises, he'd said. She had to tell him the truth. 'I asked Snaz to load it. He didn't want to, but I persuaded him. I felt scared. Rook might have had a gun himself in his house.'

Ryszard's tone became firm. 'Not under any circumstances must you admit to what you've just told me. If you don't admit it was your idea to load the weapon, who will know any differently? It will be your word against that of Aziz.'

'But if they ask me, I can't lie.'

'Josie, this is not the time for misguided sentimentality. Aziz has accused you of murder. He is attempting to have you framed for his crime. In this situation there are two outcomes. Either Simon Aziz is convicted of murder, or you are. My task is to avoid the second outcome, and I assure you I will do all I can. But I can't help you unless you help yourself.'

* * *

With each truth-revealing question the lawyer asked her, Josie became more dejected, more persuaded that Rook's death had been her fault. By the time they reached the cathedral, she felt utterly spent. And Ryszard was simply trying to prepare her. He believed her when she swore she hadn't intended to use the gun. How much worse would it be when the police interrogated her, convinced she'd killed Rook and ready to pounce on every little thing she said as proof? She understood that if she admitted she'd got Snaz to load the weapon, they'd jump on that, but she didn't want to lie and make things even worse for Snaz. When the lawyer portrayed it as her versus him, she felt torn inside. Snaz had only gone with her to Rook's house because she'd threatened to go there on her own. More than once he'd tried to persuade her to forget the whole thing.

She checked her watch again, anxious not to be late for the service.

'One more thing,' Ryszard advised her. 'Don't say too much. If they ask you something we haven't been through and you're not sure what response to give, it's better to say nothing. You're grieving for your father. Don't be afraid to play that card.'

'Good luck,' said the woman driver, who until then hadn't spoken. 'You couldn't be in better hands.'

Josie pushed the car door open, knocking it against a people carrier parked too close in the next bay. The afternoon was crisp, almost cloudless. She spotted a Daimler hearse and the black limousine which her brother and stepmum must have ridden in, and felt a fresh rush of nerves, concerned at how they'd react when they saw her. They'd both sounded so hostile when she'd spoken with them on the phone.

'Impressive venue,' said Ryszard, gazing up towards the skyline. 'Fitting, no?'

Josie nodded. Simpler to agree, she thought, though her

father had never been religious – it was one of the few things they did have in common. "Hokum!" he'd declared once at the Christmas dinner table, after Beatrice had read aloud from the Gospels. A cathedral service would have been her idea, Josie had no doubt.

She walked with the lawyer up the steps and through the archway towards the front entrance, where a small group had gathered. To her relief, she didn't recognise any of them. In the lobby, a man offered them each a programme with Dad's portrait on the cover. 'Friends of the family?' He addressed Ryszard.

'Daughter,' Josie seethed.

'Oh, I'm sorry, I didn't realise…' The man's face grew red. 'Nobody informed me,' he tried to extricate himself. 'The first two rows on either side are reserved for family and closest friends…'

Josie's desire to march to the front and claim her rightful place vanished when she passed through the inner doors into the vast main body of the cathedral. Dad's coffin rested on a platform near the altar. Only when she saw it bedecked with wreathes did she realise she hadn't brought flowers; that once again she'd let him down. All of the fight drained out of her and she felt small and insignificant as she walked past the empty rows of seats at the back, conscious of the clack her shoes made on the marble floor. She'd got halfway up the nave when the hushed strains of the requiem began to play. A hundred murmured conversations died down at once and those few mourners still standing found their seats. Josie slipped in behind the last row of guests.

Ryszard, who had been walking ahead of her, did an about turn. 'I saw a few spare chairs further forward,' he said.

Josie shook her head. She couldn't face a confrontation with Beatrice or Nathan, and she was grateful for the forest of grey and balding heads which separated her from them. Who were they all, she wondered, this staid legion of people whom she'd never encountered before? Some must be her father's business contacts, or people who worked for him. Most of them, she suspected, were no more than casual acquaintances, here more for the spectacle than out of any sense of personal loss. And yet many of them would have seen him recently, perhaps days ago at his office, or at the golf club; passed a few words, shared a joke. How she wished she hadn't made herself a stranger in his final months and weeks.

Already the melancholy music was making her eyes well, and the service hadn't properly begun.

A noise not far behind her, a chair's legs scraping against the floor, made her look round. One fleeting glance at the solitary man and she knew he must be a cop. Dressed in a black leather jacket, he hadn't even the decency to wear a tie. He gave her a nod, sending her heart into a spasm. When the service finished and she walked out of the cathedral, he'd follow her like a shadow. And then, when she left the crematorium, he'd be waiting to take her away.

'DCI Mercer,' Ryszard said into her ear. 'Rather unorthodox, from what I gather.'

Josie stole another look over her shoulder. 'He scares me,' she whispered.

'No doubt that's precisely what he's hoping. You stick to the lines we discussed and leave Mercer to me.'

The music faded, and a man in vestments made his way to the pulpit.

In a solemn tone, he read from the Bible a passage which at first bewildered Josie and then made her clench her fists. What relevance did his words have? Dad didn't believe in Heaven. Josie may not have shared much with her dad, but she did know one thing: this wasn't the kind of service he'd have wanted. Her anger grew at Beatrice for not respecting his wishes. If she'd had any say in the arrangements herself, she wouldn't have betrayed him like this.

'… Let us take a few moments in silence as we remember Joseph, each in our own way, and the colour he brought to our lives.' The canon or dean or whoever he was left the pulpit, and with barely a pause the organ started up. One of Dad's sisters in the front row rose to her feet, and soon everyone was standing, even Ryszard, even the shaven-haired cop.

Josie stood too, but the lump in her throat stopped her from singing. Holding the programme in front of her face, she followed the words in her head…

Yea, though I walk in death's dark vale,
Yet will I fear no ill:
For thou art with me, and thy rod
And staff me comfort still.

With each verse she found it harder to hold back her tears.

When the hymn ended and people sat back in the hard wooden chairs, Nathan alone remained standing. Josie watched her half-brother walk towards the lectern, stop by the coffin and lay his hands on its dark wood. He appeared to be about to break down. Feeling protective towards him, her spirits revived and she had an urge to go to his aid. She ought to be up there with him, sharing his burden, sharing this duty. Who else but her among all these people could understand his grief?

When at last he made it to the lectern, Nathan read quickly from his notes, rushing through their dad's childhood, probably scared emotion would get the better of him if he slowed down. Josie had known their dad went to Harvard, but not that he'd been in the high-school football team –she'd never considered him playing any sport except golf – or that he'd edited the student paper in his senior year.

He'd been twenty-seven when his own father had died, also of a stroke, and, the only son among four children, he'd sacrificed the chance to be a correspondent on Wall Street to take over the family business. Nathan read on. 'His global vision for the company and also his fondness for British culture led him to move to London in 1977.'

Josie heard the rustle of paper through the microphone as Nathan turned to the next page of his notes. And then he spoke of how their dad had met Beatrice at a reception at the US Embassy, and of how he'd fallen in love with her immediately. Josie's pulse quickened. What about her own mother? What about *her*, his daughter, didn't she even warrant a mention? She wanted to intervene. As Nathan continued though, she became resigned – had she expected any more? She had her own memories, and no one could take them away from her: Dad comforting her when her pony had to be put down, the dolls he brought back for her from his trips to America, and a few days ago, their last conversation when she'd spoken to him on the phone. He hadn't been angry with her. He hadn't blamed her at all for what she'd done.

She gave up fighting her tears and Ryszard offered her his maroon handkerchief.

She'd never have a chance to make things up with her dad, to make him proud of her. Her life was a catalogue of mistakes.

'Most of all,' Nathan spoke up, jarring her back to the present, 'he was a loving husband to my mother. And a perfect dad to me.' He stalled, and for a second Josie thought he might mention her as an afterthought, but he was merely swallowing his grief. 'He meant everything to Mum and me. And we were everything to him.'

Nathan descended from the podium, returned to the front row of seats, and Beatrice rose to embrace him.

Josie knew then that she couldn't face going to the crematorium, not when they didn't want her there and were happy to pretend she didn't exist.

Something else she had to do would require all of her strength.

Chapter 43

A message

A sudden knock on his bedroom door made Snaz jump. 'Simon,' he heard his aunt say from the corridor, 'are you awake?'

'Yes. Don't come in, I'm getting dressed,' he lied.

'I'm going out. I'm going to Wood Green to look whether *Marks and Spencer* have anything nice in their sale. I'll be back around midday to make you lunch. Will you be all right on your own until then?'

'Fine.' Snaz hauled himself out of bed. 'See you later.' The words slipped out before he could stop himself saying them and for an agonizing moment he stopped in the middle of his room. He couldn't leave it like that. He made for the door, opened it and called after her down the stairs, 'I love you.'

Out of sight, she called back, 'I know you do, Simon. I love you too.'

After she'd shut the front door, Snaz watched from his bedroom window, waited for her to emerge into the courtyard. She waddled across it, her head hidden beneath her woollen hat, her empty shopping bag flapping in the wind. Grace had been the one good thing in his life.

Snaz ate his breakfast, chocolate cornflakes which his aunt kept in the house for when he visited, and finished his final cup of tea. After washing his bowl and cup, he went back upstairs to the bathroom. Out of habit he took the toothpaste tube, but stopped midway through squeezing the paste onto his brush: how pointless, this morning, to be cleaning his teeth. He already had the paste on his brush, so he continued, taking his time for once, brushing in circles the way he'd been taught to. Every few seconds the cold water tap dripped, but he'd never replace its washer now. The new razor, still in its box on the shelf, would never be used.

When he'd finished in the bathroom, Snaz plodded to his bedroom, took his mobile phone from the table and sat on his bed. No new messages. No call from Josie during the night.

Before Josie had spoken to Grace yesterday morning, she'd first tried to reach him on his phone. He'd come close to ringing her back before convincing himself he didn't give a shit about her. At this moment though he wanted to tell her she'd messed up his life. Snaz took a deep breath. It'd been like this when he'd first met her, finding the courage to make the call. Then, he'd feared she'd reject him. Now he hoped she might rescue him: if she knew he was going to kill himself, perhaps she'd take the blame for Rook's death.

After three rings the phone cut to voicemail, not even Josie's own voice. *The person you are trying to reach is not available. Please leave a message after the tone.*

So much for his lingering hope. 'You tried to ring me,' Snaz said, shaking. 'Anyway, I've been thinking this through and I shouldn't have to take the blame. This was your vendetta. I should have gone straight to the police, but I stuck by you. I KILLED MY OWN MATE'S DAD. For you.

'And what do you do? Run off and leave me to take the rap. It's not right! I'm not going to prison.' He held the phone away from his face so she wouldn't hear him sob. He clenched his jaws together, looked at the phone in his hand, the hand he'd used to kill. 'I stuck by you,' he said. 'Remember that when I'm gone.'

Snaz ended the call, gripped his phone for a second then flung it onto his quilt on the bed. He slumped at his desk, the same small desk where as a child he'd done his homework. If he folded back Grace's handwoven tablecloth he'd see the grooves he'd carved years ago with his steel ruler.

He gazed at the blank page of the notepad. People would say

things about him, twist things around, and he wanted Grace to know that when he'd driven Josie to Rook's house the possibility of shooting anyone had never entered his mind. But when Josie shot Dean, dropped the gun and fled...

He should have called the police and told them Josie shot Dean and that none of it – going there, getting a gun – had been his idea. If only he'd rung the police.

At the time though, in his shock, it hadn't occurred to him as an option. Rook had been kneeling next to Dean, and all Snaz could think was, *He saw everything, he's going to come after us.* He'd been scared more for Josie than himself.

If they'd realised Dean wasn't dead, they would have phoned for an ambulance. Dean would have recovered and told the police Josie shot him. Then she'd be the one in trouble. But that wasn't what happened.

Snaz picked up the biro and began to write:

Josie used me.

The pen ran dry and refused to work. He scrawled furious circles in the corner of the page until ink began to flow again:

She swore she only wanted to frighten Rook, to pay him back for her mum's death.

If I hadn't got her a gun, someone else would. When Josie got an idea in her head, she never let it go. She said if I cared about her, I'd help her. I wish I'd had the courage to say no.

She persuaded me that unless we loaded the gun, she wouldn't feel safe going to Rook's house.

'Of course I won't use it,' Snaz remembered her promising. 'You believe me, don't you? It's for self-defence.'

I went as her minder. I told myself, if I could get through that one day, get through that evening, it'd be over and Josie would realise how much I loved her. Maybe then we could be like a normal couple.

I still don't believe she went there meaning to kill Rook. If Dean hadn't attacked her, I don't think she'd have fired the gun. But when she shot Dean, she ran off and left me in the room. Rook was about to lunge for the gun. I kicked it away, then I picked it up.

If she hadn't insisted on going there, if she hadn't made me load the gun, he'd still be alive.

It's not right to blame me for what happened, when all of it was Josie's idea.

Snaz read the note back. He'd written too much. Why should his aunt have to know he'd killed Rook? She didn't deserve the heartache of finding out.

He ripped the page from the pad and started again…

Dear Grace,
Whatever people say, whatever evidence Josie might invent, I didn't murder Curtis Rook. Josie killed him.

No, he didn't want to lie. It would be worse to die and not have told the truth. What if saving himself from Hell depended on it?

He began on yet another page:

Dear Grace,
I love you. Whatever you hear, I didn't mean to do it. I'm sorry for letting you down.

He remembered a line from the Gospels that Pastor Norman had used in one of his sermons: "Whoever would save his life will lose it." Before, those words had made no sense to him, but now Snaz understood what they meant. He hadn't wanted to lose Josie, and as a result he'd lost everything.

Chapter 44

A few small details

Josie took in the plastic mattress on a shelf barely off the floor. *There must be a mistake,* she thought. *They can't treat me like this.* 'There's no pillow,' she protested.

The policewoman sneered and, begging her pardon, inquired, 'Perhaps madam would like a hot water bottle too?' Then the policewoman left and slammed the door behind her.

Alone in the cell, Josie sat on the mattress with her forehead propped against her knees. She felt a tear roll down her face, then another, and soon the trickle of tears became a stream. She cried until her cheeks ached from sobbing.

How humiliated she'd felt when the sergeant made her remove her shoes and she'd had to walk in her bare stockings on the cold hard floor along the corridor to the cell.

Not content with taking her freedom, they'd robbed her of her dignity too by treating her like an animal in a cage. Before, she'd taken for granted the comfort of a proper bed with pillows and a soft quilt to curl up in. Suddenly she found herself denied the most basic things.

Why wasn't there a clock on the wall? Why had they taken her watch? She had no idea how many hours she had to endure until someone came to unlock the door and let her out.

And that stupid fly buzzing around the light was driving her insane.

If she had a hope that in the morning, after the interrogation, she'd be free to leave, or that tomorrow night or in a week or a month she'd be able to go home, stand under a gushing hot shower and wash away the horrible dank smell of this place, sleep in her own bed, she might have drawn strength. But she saw no end in sight, no chance of walking free.

How she hated herself for going to Rook's house with a gun.

Ryszard, her solicitor, had been frank with her: if she repeated to the police what she'd told him, she should expect a fifteen-year sentence. The thought of existing like this for fifteen years… She couldn't. She'd die.

But if she changed a few details in her story, it could alter the whole complexion of the case. She could tell the police it had been Snaz's idea to threaten Rook. She could deny even seeing the weapon until he gave it to her in the car before they went in. No one would know any different if she claimed that. The police might charge her with a lesser crime. And when the case went to court, perhaps a jury *would* believe her instead of Snaz. She was an impressionable young woman from a respectable family: the solicitor's words. She only had to act the part, to change a few small details, as he put it. To incriminate Snaz.

Josie stared at the bare walls, at the heavy door with its locked shutter, at the metal toilet in the corner of the cell, with not a single sheet of loo paper even to dry her swollen eyes. Maybe the lawyer had it right: she owed Snaz nothing, not after he'd lied to the police and told them she'd shot Rook. She might have asked Snaz to get hold of a gun for her, but he'd pulled the trigger. He'd murdered Rook. No way would she let him pin it on her. She'd say whatever she had to, but she wouldn't go to prison for something she didn't do.

* * *

'Josephine Davenport, you do not have to say anything but it may harm your defence if you do not mention when questioned something which you later rely on in court. Anything you do say may be given in evidence…'

Josie listened to the detective. How many times she'd heard those same words in dramas on TV.

'Detective Chief Inspector Mercer,' her solicitor said, 'we are dealing here with a most unfortunate turn of events. Naturally my client intends to co-operate fully. I might add she surrendered of her own volition. But I would ask you to respect the fact that yesterday she attended the funeral of her father. This is a very difficult time for her.'

Mercer chewed over the words. 'You have my sympathy, Josie. I appreciate what it's like to lose parents. It is Josie, isn't it? Or do you prefer Josephine?'

'Josie,' she replied – only her stepmum and Kogut called her Josephine – though she'd passed the point of caring either way.

Ryszard cleared his throat. The dark shadows under his eyes suggested he hadn't slept either. 'In these exceptional circum-stances,' he said, 'I would ask that you admit my client's prepared statement.'

Mercer turned for a second to his colleague. 'Okay, go ahead.'

Ryszard reached over to hand Josie a sheet of paper with typed doubled-spaced writing on it, and gave copies to Mercer and the short-haired female DS. Josie scanned the statement and recognised the wording they'd discussed.

'Whenever you're ready,' Mercer prompted.

Startled, Josie said, 'You want me to read it out loud?'

'Yes, for the benefit of the tapes. Please speak clearly.'

She began, 'I deeply regret my part in what happened.' She glanced across at her lawyer, who nodded to her to carry on. 'I only went to Curtis Rook's house to confront him about my mum's death. I felt, if I could face him and see he regretted using her, and not protecting her, then I'd be able to move on.' She paused, swallowed.

'In the car, outside Rook's house, Snaz took the gun from his rucksack and said I should take it. At first, I'd wanted to threaten Curtis Rook, to make him scared. But on the way to his house, I had second thoughts. I realised how crazy it was to point a gun at someone. It scared me even to touch the thing. Snaz warned me Curtis Rook might turn violent, so I put the gun in my handbag, but I didn't intend to take it out.'

In her edginess she lost her place on the page and it took her a while to find it again. 'Snaz went into the house first. He had some money to give Rook for a car. When Snaz let me in and I saw Rook, straight away I didn't feel safe. I tried to say the things I'd planned to say, about my mum being murdered by one of the clients he'd made her see, but Rook didn't listen to me. He kept coming closer and I felt threatened. I backed away, nearly out into the corridor. I took the gun from my handbag to stop him coming any closer, but I wasn't going to fire it. I didn't even know it was loaded.'

Reading the statement, Josie felt like she was auditioning for a role in a play. Except that the more she read, the less she liked the script, and the less she wanted the role. Aware of her hand trembling, she gripped the page between her fingers and her thumb. It didn't help though, so she put the sheet on the table and continued reading from it. 'I heard a door being opened behind me and saw someone running at me with a bread knife.'

'Rook's son, Dean?' Mercer said.

Josie nodded. '*He'll stab me*, is all I could think. I fired the gun as a reflex. I did it in self-defence.' She added, despite it not being on the page, 'I wouldn't have had time to run'.

As she read on, she imagined herself to be in the house again. 'He lay on the floor, blood all over his shirt. I thought I'd killed him. I panicked. I dropped the gun and I ran from the house.' Josie raised her eyes to meet the detectives', but their expressions gave away nothing. 'I'd shot Dean to defend myself, but I didn't kill Curtis Rook.'

'What happened next?' Mercer asked.

'Next?' She'd reached the end of the writing on the page.

'You said you ran. Where did you run to?'

'Outside, across the road to the car. Somebody saw me – a man with a dog. Hasn't he come forward? I swear a man saw me by the car.'

'Our problem, Josie,' said the female detective, 'is that Simon Aziz has given us a very different account of events.'

'He's lying. I didn't shoot Rook, I swear. How could I have shot him when I was by the car? You have to find the witness. I can describe him to you. Do you want me to describe how he looked?'

DS Orchard shook her head. 'There's no need. We've spoken with the man.'

'You have? Then he's told you he saw me? What did he say?'

The DS didn't reply, but continued, 'You've told us you shot Dean in self-defence.'

'He would have killed me.'

'Is it reasonable to suppose he thought you were going to kill his father, when he saw you threatening him with a firearm?'

'I wasn't threatening him.' Josie recalled Ryszard's advice. 'I had no intention to use the gun.'

'Then why was it loaded?'

She tried to turn the chair to face her lawyer, but found it fixed to the floor. To her relief, Ryszard intervened. 'Detective Sergeant, my client has given her statement. At this juncture, she has nothing further to say.'

'It's a simple question,' Mercer took over. 'I remind you, it may harm your defence if you do not mention when questioned something you later rely on in court. Why was the firearm loaded? Did you intend to use it to murder Curtis Rook?'

'No. I was scared.'

Ryszard came to her aid. 'Detective Chief Inspector, you are trying to confuse my client, who is grieving for her father and under enormous stress. You have her statement. I request this interview be adjourned.'

'Yes, I have the statement.' Mercer waved it like a worthless scrap of paper. His relentless eyes fixed on Josie. 'You've told us Simon Aziz gave you the weapon in the car.'

'He wanted me to take it.'

'And yet when I asked you why the firearm was loaded, you replied it was because you were scared.'

'I didn't say that. That's not what I meant.'

'Whose idea was it to go to Curtis Rook's house on the night of 10 December with a loaded weapon?'

'I've told you. Snaz's.'

'It wasn't your idea to go to Rook's house?' Mercer pressed.

'Yes, but not with a gun.'

'Did you blame Curtis Rook for your mother's death?'

The unexpected question threw her. 'He should have protected her. He took her money, the money she earned, but he didn't protect her from that man.'

'And when you discovered that, how did it make you feel? I mean, if it hadn't been for Curtis Rook, your mum would still be alive today. It must have made you angry?'

'No.'

'It didn't make you angry?'

'How would it make *you* feel?'

'... Did it make you want to kill him?'

'No.'

'Really and truthfully, did the thought never cross your mind?'

'I didn't kill Rook. I didn't go there meaning to shoot him. And it wasn't my idea to take a gun.'

'Then perhaps you can explain to us why you wore gloves?'

The question stunned Josie.

'A witness saw you. I quote: "She was wearing all black, apart from white trimming on her gloves." Why wear gloves, if you didn't have it in your mind to use the firearm to murder Curtis Rook?'

'I advise you not to answer,' Ryszard said to her. 'DCI Mercer, that is pure speculation. It was the middle of December, a cold evening.'

'Fifteen degrees.'

'My client is in the habit of wearing gloves.'

'And are you in the habit of answering questions on your clients' behalf? Josie, how can we help you unless you help yourself by telling us the truth?'

'You have the truth,' Ryszard said. 'I request some time alone with my client. She is in no fit state for this interview to continue.'

'Tell us what really happened,' Mercer persisted.

Ryszard raised his voice above him, 'Josie, I strongly advise you to say no more.'

Chapter 45

An angel

The raw wind buffeted Snaz, making his eyes water as he crossed the courtyard to his car. He had a vague feeling he'd forgotten something. Glancing towards the apartment block, he noticed the skeletal pattern of the long-dead ivy on the wall. His wallet! Snaz stopped himself going back for it. No more excuses. He didn't need money where he was going.

A young boy watched him from the window of the top flat. Snaz looked away and when he checked again moments later the child had gone.

He sat in the car, turned the key in the ignition, but the engine spluttered, then choked and gave a feeble whine. Raising his head to the heavens, Snaz muttered under his breath, 'You're taking the piss!' Turning the key again brought no more than a pathetic death pang groan and he knew he wouldn't get the engine going without a jump-start. 'Why won't you give me a break for once?' He got out the car and slammed the door. His jump-start pack was back at his flat, and if he started asking the neighbours for jump leads it would take too long. He was bloody going to have to walk.

Snaz strode off, casting angry glances over his shoulder at the car – Josie's gift to him – what did he expect? Soon it'd be over and he wouldn't have to put up with stuff like this, with things going wrong. He came across an empty *Diet Coke* can on the pavement and swung his foot at it. 'Bitch!' he spat after it as it clattered in the road.

Before long Snaz was climbing the hill towards the station. A high-speed train thundered by behind the terrace of Victorian houses. He pictured "his" train speeding nearer and imagined standing on the platform and seeing the engine approach, waiting for the moment to launch himself into its path. His body convulsed but he kept on walking. It'd be a split second of pain and then he wouldn't have to suffer any more.

At first Snaz didn't register the car pull up alongside him.

'Can you help me?' a female voice called.

Leave me alone, he thought, but when he looked he saw a girl barely old enough to be driving, dolled up for a party, wearing a spangled black dress which didn't reach her knees.

'I'm trying to find Park Way?'

Snaz stared at her through the passenger-side window she'd opened a quarter of the way down.

'Park Way?' she asked again. 'Can you tell me how to get there?'

She looked so out of place in the big Volvo estate. Snaz guessed she must have borrowed it from her parents. 'Er... yeah,' he said, having to think to remember. 'You're going in the wrong direction. Do a U-turn, take the first left, then go straight until you get to the end of the road. Then if you turn right and follow the road, you'll be in Park Way.'

She nodded, but appeared hopelessly confused.

'Go back the way you came,' he repeated, 'turn left into Holly Park Road, then go right when you come to the end of it. I'm not sure what that road's called, but if you follow it past the school to the end, you'll get to Park Way.'

'Thanks,' said the girl, nodding more convincingly. 'You're an angel.' She smiled, held his gaze for a second, then stalled her car when she tried to pull off.

Her painted lips, deep plum against her pale face, made Snaz think of Josie. When he first met Josie, she'd been innocent too. He wondered if she'd be sorry when she found out he'd killed himself. Probably she wouldn't care at all.

The girl drove away and it didn't surprise Snaz to spot an L-plate on the back of the Volvo. The wind gusted, and he began to walk again with shorter strides than before, aware he was nearing the station. In another five minutes he would be there, descending the stairs to the platform, going to stand where the fast trains passed by. He'd wait on the yellow line. When the train reached the station, he'd close his eyes, take two steps forward and then—

Screeching brakes, the excruciating wail of an animal in pain. The Volvo had stopped in the road. The haunting shriek quietened to an agonised mew and Snaz realised the girl had hit a cat. When he came alongside he saw her at the wheel, her face hidden in her hands. He could see the cat too, under the car, a small tabby, no longer making any sound. He squatted to get a better view, but it didn't move and then an uncanny sensation came over him, like for a split second the temperature fell by ten degrees. He steadied himself on the ground with both hands.

'Is it hurt?'

He heard the girl and, recovering, straightened himself and faced her.

'Did I kill it? Tell me I didn't kill it.'

He nodded.

'It ran from nowhere.'

Her bare arms were shaking like branches of a rose bush, but he didn't know what to say to her. He wanted to tell her, *It's only a cat.*

'It ran out in front of me. I tried to stop. What should I do?'

It had nothing to do with him, Snaz thought, why was she asking him? He should leave her to it and if she had any sense she'd drive away. But she got out of the car and, before he could tell her not to, she crouched down to see the cat herself.

'Oh my God!' she squeaked. 'It's a kitten. I ran over a kitten.'

'You couldn't help it,' he said, and then, 'It's only an animal. It's not like you killed a person.'

The fear in her eyes startled him. For a moment he thought she knew, but how could she? He welcomed the sound of footsteps that made her look away.

'What's goin' on?' a woman rasped, swinging open her garden gate and bearing down on them. Within a couple of seconds she'd bent down, seen the kitten and was crowding the young girl, pointing a finger in her face. 'That's my daughter's cat you killed!'

'I'm sorry. It ran out in front of me.'

'Sorry! You bloody will be.' She had the girl backed against the car.

'Hey!' Snaz found himself intervening.

The woman eyeballed him. 'You her boyfriend?'

'No, I was walking by...'

'Well quit sticking your oar in where it ain't needed.' She rounded on the girl again. 'Bloody learner driver. You shouldn't be drivin' on your own. It's illegal. Your parents know, do they? Give me your address.'

The girl's lips quavered.

'Go easy on her, will you,' Snaz said. 'I saw it happen. No one could've stopped in time. You can see she's upset.'

'She's upset? How's my daughter going to feel when I tell her this stupid girl ran over her kitten?'

The girl stood shivering in her party dress, her face ghostly white, her eyeliner beginning to run.

'You won't give me your address? Right, I'm calling the police. You can explain to them what you were doin' driving on your own.' She got as far as her gate, then did a sudden about turn. 'And don't think of goin' anywhere!' She reached inside the open car door, snatched the keys.

'You can't!' the girl whimpered.

'Watch me!' The woman stormed off.

The girl looked desperate. Her eyes alighted on Snaz. 'Could you... Could you tell her you were in the car with me?'

'I can't.' If the police were coming, he didn't want to hang around.

'Where are you going? She stole my keys!' She pleaded, 'Don't walk away.'

Snaz dug his fingers into his palms. 'You don't need my help. The worst you'll get is a telling off.'

'My dad doesn't know I borrowed his car. He'll ground me for a year if he finds out.'

It's not my problem, Snaz thought. What could he do anyway, even if he wanted to help? As he stepped back onto the pavement, he noticed a truck turning into the road. Just brilliant! No way would it get past the car. Before it even reached them, the driver honked his horn.

'Now what do I do?' cried the girl.

Something inside Snaz told him he ought to help her. He took another two steps away, but his heart thumped harder. No, he *had* to help. This was his chance, once in his life, to do the right thing.

He approached the Volvo again, glanced at the girl, at the truck driver, at the open car door. Then – he didn't have any plan – he stooped down by the tyre and gently lifted the cat in his arms, trying not to look at its wound. Its body still felt warm and it struck him how light it was, like a child's soft toy.

With care, arms stretched out in front of him, he carried the cat up the uneven cobbled path to the woman's front door. She'd left it ajar, and he heard her inside, shouting down the phone: 'She's a learner. She was driving on her own. It's not allowed, is it? I saw her from my window. She must've been doing over forty. It's a residential road... What do you mean, "soon as you can"? How long's that?... This *is* an emergency. I want someone here *now*.' She slammed down the phone.

Snaz saw her striding towards him and braced himself.

She stopped in the doorway, her eyes screaming *get out of my way*.

'Madam.' Snaz took a deep breath. 'I'm sorry about your daughter's cat. But it was an accident – it could have been me driving, or anyone else. Look at the girl: she's seventeen, crying her eyes out. Have a heart.' He held out the animal, a peace offering for the woman to take.

'And what am I supposed to do with it? Ali will be back any moment, and I don't want her seeing it like that.'

'Well, do you want me to take it? Bury it somewhere?'

She stared at him, her mouth open baring yellowed smoker's teeth. 'I thought you were just passing by?'

'I was,' he said. 'I can bury it if you want me to, if you don't want to do it yourself.'

She snorted like a horse. 'You're seriously offering to bury it? You won't throw it in a rubbish bin?'

What did she take him for? He resisted the urge to throw the dead animal in her face. 'If I say I'll bury it, that's what I'll do.' The lorry driver honked again. A queue of cars had formed behind the truck. Snaz said to the woman, 'She's blocking the road. Give me the keys and I'll move the car out the way, okay?'

Snaz wondered what he'd do next if she refused. To his surprise, she thrust out a hand with the car keys. 'Take 'em,' she said. 'What do the police care, anyway, about my little girl's pet?'

Balancing the cat against his jacket, Snaz took the keys in his other hand. 'Thank you,' he said, meeting her eyes again.

And then he was walking down the path, back to the gate. He felt lighter than candyfloss, like an angel with wings.

Chapter 46

How not to suffer

Rain beat against the window, drops merging into rivers as they streamed down the pane. Her watch said two o'clock, but outside it looked like evening. In the street below, all the cars had their lights on. Josie left the window, made her way across the hotel room to the mini-bar. She found no wine left so she filled her glass with scotch.

'That will not solve anything,' Kogut said, peering up from his book.

She took a deliberate swig. Her throat rebelled against the sharp-tasting alcohol, but she forced it down and did her best to stifle the shiver.

Kogut approached her and prised the drink from her hand. 'You were drunk when I got here yesterday evening.'

'And?'

'I heard you being sick in the night.'

'So?'

'Josephine, for goodness' sake, take a look at yourself.' He put his hands on both her shoulders and with unexpected force turned her towards the mirror.

A stranger stared back at her, cheeks colourless and sagging, hair like an old mop. Her eyes sank to the floor.

'Drinking is not the answer.'

'Then tell me what is.'

He sighed, long and deep. 'I can tell you, but are you ready to hear?'

Josie faced him. Could there still be a way out?

'Not while you are in this state. First take a shower. Better yet, have a hot bath. I will call room service and order us a proper dinner. What would you like? What is your favourite meal?'

She scoffed. 'I'm going to prison. A bath and a meal won't change that.'

'No, I'm afraid nothing can alter that now. But they have not charged you with murder. It will only be for two or three years.'

'Only? You say it like it's nothing.' One night at the police station had been too much.

'When you decided to come back to England, I feared it would be worse. You could be in Simon Aziz's position. He will get a life sentence for killing Rook.'

The briny aftertaste of the alcohol lingered in Josie's mouth.

'Going to prison doesn't mean you have to suffer. It need not be the hell you imagine.' Kogut sounded like a doctor telling her she had a terminal illness, but saying he could give her drugs to ease the pain. 'If you resent every moment of the sentence, then yes, it might feel like hell. But if you use the time to go within and discover who you really are, to reflect on how you will live the next fifty years after your release, it could turn out to be a blessing.'

'Prison? A blessing!' She very nearly laughed. 'What do you know?'

'I have been where you are now.'

'What, you've been in prison?' Amazed, she asked, 'What for?'

'Fraud.'

'How long were you inside?'

'For about a year. My boss had been diverting State funds for his own use...'

Josie interrupted him. 'Your boss?'

'Don't get me wrong, I was also guilty, though he had taken more money. When the police found out, one of us had to take the blame.'

'Why you, if he took more? You should have informed on him. I mean, the fraud was his idea, right?'

'It does not matter. I had less to lose.'

'That's all you're going to tell me?'

'My mother had tuberculosis and needed hospital care, more than the State would provide for her. My manager said he would look after her if I took responsibility.'

Josie looked in Kogut's wide-open eyes. She'd found them threatening when she'd first met him, but now they appeared soft. She recognised he had experienced prison. He did know what it was like.

* * *

You'd think in a four-star hotel they'd design it so you could reach the towels from the bath. Dripping water, Josie skittered across the cold tiled floor to retrieve one. She rubbed it over her hair, padded it up and down her body, but the steam made her skin wet again. She took a fresh hand towel, resting a leg on the side of the bath to dry her toes. The last of the water gurgled into the drain and the plughole gave a final belch.

Josie grabbed some of the fresh clothes Ryszard's driver had recovered from her flat for her. She thought of the pack of journalists camped outside it. The ignorant reporter on the news hadn't mentioned the fact Rook's son had a knife and would have stabbed her. She'd shot someone, end of story. No one had any interest in her side.

The blouse Josie put on clung to her still-damp back. She clambered into jeans, brushed her wet hair back and tied it with a clip. She wanted to ask Kogut how he'd coped in prison.

She went through to the living room of their suite and found him still in the armchair, his eyes closed. 'Are you asleep?'

No response. His hands rested on his legs, palms facing skyward.

'Are you sleeping?' she asked again, louder. Loud enough to wake him if he was.

His eyes flickered open. 'I have something for you,' he said, before she could ask her question. 'I would have given it to you yesterday if I hadn't found you drunk.' He pointed to his jacket on the back of one of the dining chairs. 'There is an envelope in the inside pocket.'

She hesitated.

'I do not want to get up,' he said. 'I think I pulled a muscle when I unplugged the TV.'

She went to the jacket, reached into the pocket and her hand alighted on a notebook and a fountain pen.

'No, the other side. That's it,' he said when she found the small envelope. 'Take it. It is yours.'

Josie tore it open and something cold and shiny fell into her hand. 'My locket!' She prised it open with her nail and saw her own yellowed baby photograph inside.

'Do I detect a smile?'

He'd polished it and it glistened like new. And he'd fixed the broken chain. She almost kissed him, but stopped shy. 'How did...? Thank you for getting it back.'

'Adam found it at his parents' flat,' Kogut said. 'It is him you have to thank.'

* * *

Josie ate most of her dinner, leaving only the sprouts. When she finished, she noticed Kogut still had half a plateful of food. He gave her a smile and, taking his time, dissected a small piece of guinea fowl, popped it into his mouth.

She had nothing to do for the whole evening except sit and talk with Kogut. She couldn't go out, not even downstairs to the kiosk for cigarettes, not when people would recognise her from the picture they'd shown on the news. The trial wouldn't begin for another six weeks, but she felt like a prisoner already. She remembered the question she wanted to ask Kogut. 'How did you cope in jail?'

Kogut continued to chew his food, making her wait. 'The truth is I did not cope well. It would have been much easier if I had understood then what I do today.'

'Which is?'

'How not to suffer,' he said. 'We suffer because of our thoughts.'

Josie crossed her legs under the table. More philosophy.

'Who are you, Josephine?'

'What do you mean? You know who I am,' she said.

'Yes, but you do not. You look at yourself in a mirror and that image of yourself is all you see. You perceive yourself as guilty and you think you deserve to be punished.'

'You saw Snaz's photo on the news. He looked so – I don't know how to describe it – hollow, like it wasn't him but only a shell.' She clasped her throat, uncertain whether to share any more. 'I'll be out in three years, but he's going to prison for life, for something he did for me.'

Kogut rested his knife and fork on his plate. 'You did not ask him to shoot Curtis Rook.'

'I made him go with me to Rook's house.'

'How did you make him? He had a choice to go or not.'

'I persuaded him, like I persuaded him to get me the gun. I made him think he had to, if he wanted to be with me. Even in the car on the way there he tried to talk me out of it.'

'Maybe so. But Aziz did not have to shoot Rook.'

'He did it to protect me.' Josie remembered another time he'd stepped in to save her, in a club the first time they'd met. 'Snaz wouldn't be going to prison but for me.' Her words hung in the silence.

'Whatever you have done, whatever mistakes you have made – it does not change who you are,' said Kogut. 'What I'm about to say may not make sense to you now, but one day you will understand.' He wiped his mouth with his napkin. 'Imagine a bad dream. What is the word for this in English?'

'A nightmare.'

'That's it. While you are sleeping, doesn't the nightmare appear to be real?'

Josie nodded. These last nights they'd been so vivid.

'Now, imagine in your nightmare you kill someone. How do you feel when you wake up, and you find yourself in your bed and you realise that you didn't harm them at all?'

'Relieved?'

'Yes, the weight of guilt is lifted from you. You don't feel guilty, do you? You don't punish yourself for things you dreamed?'

'I don't punish myself. Of course not.'

'If the awful thing you thought you did never happened, there is no need for guilt... If it was not real, but only an illusion made up by your sleeping mind.'

'What are you telling me?'

'Remember the moment when Curtis Rook's son ran at you with the knife and you shot him. You thought you had killed him.'

The image would never leave her. This person, this boy, lying in front of her. His shirt turning red. More and more blood.

'It is not real.' He looked around him. 'None of this is real.'

Josie didn't understand.

'You asked me how you can be free of suffering. Only your own forgiveness sets you free. Oh, Josephine, I wish I could give you the experience I'm trying to describe. I wish I could shake you wide awake so you could see.' He gazed at her for a long time, his eyes lit up. When he resumed speaking, he sounded calmer. 'Patience. I must learn to have patience. You *will* see, Josephine. One day, soon, you will wake up.'

Chapter 47

To be at peace

That night, lying alone in bed, Josie tried not to think about the past. 'Going over what happened won't change it,' Kogut had told her. 'Release it. Learn from past experience, but move on.'

He'd made it sound so simple, and no doubt it was for him. But not for her. Josie focused on her breathing like he'd told her, tried to be aware of the air entering and leaving her nose. But it didn't work, or it worked for a few seconds before the thoughts returned like ravens to a carcass... Would she have to share a prison cell? At boarding school, she'd had to sleep in a dorm. She remembered, in her first week there, waking up screaming from a nightmare and the other girls laughing at her. The worst thing would be if she had nowhere private to escape to and always had to be on her guard.

Even before prison, she had the trial to get through and she dreaded that as much: trying to justify what she'd done, only for people to condemn her all the same. Sticking to her story had been hard enough with the police, but inside the courtroom it'd be worse. Snaz's lawyer would cross-examine her. And Snaz would be there himself. What if they put him next to her in the dock? He must have loved her to do what he did. Always her thoughts came back to that.

She'd withered when she first heard the voicemail he'd left on her phone, his words like gravel hurled in her face. "It was your vendetta. I shouldn't have to take the blame."

Josie threw aside the clammy quilt and sat on the edge of the bed, her nails buried in her palms, her body tense and sweaty like in the grip of fever. The days were bearable – she could cope with the days. But each night brought a fresh inquisition.

Reaching for the lamp on the bedside table, groping about for the switch, it crossed her mind to go to Kogut's bedroom. She reached the door before coming to her senses. She craved to be held, but not by him.

She collapsed back onto the bed and sat with her head in her hands, her hair flopping around her. Each night she kept telling herself, 'This is as bad as it gets, it can't get any worse,' and then the following night it did get worse. Part of her felt an urge to pray, but to whom? To the God who'd stolen her mum from her, and now her dad? Still she pleaded: *I can't stand to suffer any more. I want to feel at peace.*

Josie held her locket on the chain around her neck. When Adam had retrieved it for her from his parents' flat, he must have thought she was going to tell the truth. Instead, she'd changed her story and heaped as much blame as possible onto Snaz.

But what was the answer?

There on the table Josie saw the phone. She could call the police and admit to persuading Snaz to load the gun. Except, what would it achieve? They'd double her sentence, but it wouldn't help Snaz. It didn't change the fact he'd killed Rook.

Still Snaz's words haunted her: 'I killed my own mate's dad for you.' He'd shot Rook to save *her* from prison. She knew he hadn't wanted to take her to Rook's house, or to load the gun. The whole plan rubbed against his conscience. She should never have asked him to do those things. But he could have said no.

Who was she kidding? Snaz would never say no to her. No matter how she treated him – seeing other men, ignoring him for days at a time – still he worshipped her. Sometimes she wanted to shake him and tell him to find a girl who could commit to him like he deserved. But at the same time she liked to have him around: someone to depend on, someone she felt safe with. More of a brother to her than Nathan had been. Josie remembered the other time when he'd come to her rescue: years ago, when that man had spiked her drink. She could have been raped. Didn't she owe him, if only for that?

'I stuck by you. Remember that when I'm gone,' he'd ended his message. What if he did kill himself? What else could he have meant?

But the only way to get him off the murder charge would be if she took the blame.

Josie imagined what Adam might say: 'Would Snaz have got the gun if you hadn't pushed him to do it? Did he want to take you to Rook's house, or did you keep pressing him until he caved in? You say you're sorry, but if you were you'd take the blame.'

* * *

When Snaz couldn't sleep, he'd get in his car and go for a drive. One lap around the M25. Josie felt an urge to do that now, or to go somewhere at any rate; to get out of the room, out of the hotel, the four-star prison waiting room and torture chamber rolled into one. She didn't have her car, but she could walk. Walk out of the hotel and keep on walking until someone stopped her or she couldn't carry on.

She dressed in the first warm clothes she found in the wardrobe and wrapped a scarf over her head like the older women in Poland did. Then she grabbed her purse and handbag. Inching the door open, she could hear Kogut snoring in the other bedroom of their suite. She crouched to zip up her boots before slipping out to the corridor.

Josie stepped into the lift, alone with her reflection. Her heavy eyelids shut and she felt a falling sensation. She knew what she wanted more than anything. Only peace.

DING! The shrill bell made her jump as the lift arrived at the ground floor. Josie crossed the lobby, deserted except for a cleaner vacuuming and another stripping the decorations from the Christmas tree. A lone red-faced man sat slouched at the bar.

A bundle of newspapers on the reception-desk counter awaited the new day. It could be her picture plastered all over them. The whole world judged her and no one understood. But worse than that was her own guilt.

The sliding doors parted and Josie stepped outside into the bitter night.

'Taxi, madam?' said the concierge.

She stopped on the carpet by the entrance. In this city of seven million people, she had no home to go to, no one waiting for her with a hug and comforting words. Sure, she could go anywhere. Do anything. And in the morning, when the shops opened, she could be like before and buy any designer outfit from the boutiques. But none of it mattered. None of it could make her happy. *Peace. Belonging. Forgiveness. Those are the only things that matter,* she thought.

'Would madam like a taxi?' the concierge asked again.

She looked at him and connected with his eyes. Those eyes, their expression...somehow familiar, like she'd seen them before. An impulse made her want to say something to him, something more than *yes* or *no, thank you* or *goodnight*. But what to say? 'Yes. A taxi. Please.'

And so she waited, her breath rising in the air. What she wouldn't do to be at peace.

'Cold night, madam.'

She looked at him again, into his eyes. Of course she didn't know him. But she felt, in a way, she did. He was cold, like her. Tired and lonely. Surviving, but no more. Merely coping with an unforgiving world. And his eyes. He could have been Snaz. Or he could have been Adam. Or he could have been *her*.

Peace. Belonging. Forgiveness. She looked in his eyes, and she wished him those things.

'Are you okay, madam?' he asked.

'No,' she said. She'd had enough of lying.

'Can I do anything for you?'

Josie shook her head. 'There's nothing you can do.'

The street was deserted.

'It's late,' he said. 'You might wait forever for a taxi. I'll phone to order you one.'

'No.' She stopped him. 'Don't. Don't worry. I've changed my mind. I'll be okay.'

Chapter 48

Guilty

On Snaz's fourth day in prison, they moved him to a different wing. He drew back when he saw two beds in the cell and realised that he'd have to share it. He'd barely spoken to anyone since he'd arrived. Criminals. Violent men. His strategy was to keep his head down, make it through to the trial and see how long a sentence he'd get. After that, if he did want to end it all, he'd have to figure out how. They had nets in the landings in case anyone jumped.

The lights went out without warning. Half past ten. Snaz turned onto his side and tried to get comfortable. This mattress felt like they'd stuffed it with twigs. He shifted his body away from a spring.

Maybe he could volunteer for a job in the kitchen and smuggle out a knife. The thought of cutting himself made him jolt. The way he'd planned it with the train, it would have been over in an instant. But bleeding to death, slowly...

Snaz turned again. Prison might not be so bad, once he got used to the routine. Yeah, he needed a job, something to keep him busy. Besides, the jury might believe his story. He had no reason for going with a weapon to Rook's house. No reason, except that Josie asked him to. Almost begged him. She had the motive for killing Curtis Rook.

His cell mate, Jon, interrupted his thoughts. 'So what are you in for, mate?'

'I'm awaiting trial.'

'What are you charged with?'

'Murder.'

'Murder?' Snaz heard the mattress creak as the man sat up. 'Did you do it?'

'No.'

'Who was the victim?'

'Some bloke.'

'I'm in for ABH,' Jon said.

Snaz didn't know what the A in ABH stood for, but assumed it must be serious. Not as serious as murder though.

'He had it coming. I'd do it again, too. He deserved it for interfering with my niece.'

'Yes.' Snaz hoped that would be the end of their conversation, but after a bit, Jon piped up again.

'It's visiting day for me tomorrow. My bird's bringing my son. Four, he is. That's the toughest part of being inside. I missed his first day at school. He's learning to ride his bike now and I've got to make do with photos my bird took on her phone.'

'It must be tough for you. How long are you in for?'

'Two years. Reckon I'll be out by summer.' A pause. 'You got a bird outside?'

Snaz sniffed. 'I used to. She's the reason I'm here.'

'Did she do the dirty with that bloke?'

All these questions. Jon might be a plant, working for the police, seeking more evidence to use against him.

'Did the bloke you're charged with killing mess with your bird?'

'No,' said Snaz. 'She killed him.'

'Your girlfriend's the murderer?' He sounded shocked. In the dark, Snaz could make out his silhouette, leaning up in bed. 'Why'd she do it?'

'Revenge. I think she planned it all along.'

'Have they got a strong case against you?'

'I got her the weapon. I was with her when she did it.'

'You're an accessory then? Like when I helped my brother sort out that perv.'

'It's not that simple. Her family's rich. She's hired an expensive lawyer and she's pinning it all on me.'

'She sounds like one bitch. You got a decent brief yourself?'

'Eddie. He took on my case this week. I don't know if he's any good.'

'What kind of name's Eddie for a solicitor?'

'He's someone from my aunt's church.'

'Could count in your favour,' Jon said. 'Your church background. My brief was a total waste of space.'

'I guess it depends on the jury,' Snaz said.

'Yeah, and what mood the judge is in if they find you guilty. Everyone says my sentence is harsh.'

* * *

Grace sat in the far corner of the visiting room, over by the window, at the same table as last time. Snaz walked around the edge of the room. He noticed Jon chatting with his woman and son.

'Simon. My poor Simon!' Grace called out to him above the din of a dozen conversations, making half the room look up.

Snaz cringed. *Keep your voice down!* He didn't want the others to think him soft.

His aunt stood and embraced him, hugging him tight for far too long. Finally she released him from her bear hug. Her smile surprised him. It wasn't the nervous keep-the-faith smile she'd put on last time. Her whole face appeared brighter.

'How are you feeling?' she asked.

'I'm okay.'

'Tell me honestly.'

'Sit down,' he said, taking a seat himself.

'Are you being bullied?'

'You don't have to shout. I'm not being bullied. I keep myself to myself.'

'Are you warm enough? I wanted to bring you a woollen jumper but they told me I couldn't unless you requested it yourself. You need to make a list of everything you want and I'll bring it with me at the weekend.'

At the next table, a woman laughed. Snaz glanced sideways, but her attention was on her partner.

'Simon, I have very good news. Josephine has confessed!'

Confessed?

'She's admitted it. She's going to plead guilty to killing Curtis Rook.'

Snaz's heart thumped. 'Who told you that?' Josie wouldn't take the blame.

'Eddie called this morning when I was getting ready to come here. He thinks they'll drop the charge against you. The murder charge, I mean. They must drop it, mustn't they, if Josephine's owned up?'

'Are you sure you understood right? Has she told the police that she killed Rook? Or only that she shot Dean?'

'Both of them. She's admitted everything. She's pleading diminished responsibility, or something like that.'

Snaz didn't get it. 'Why is she suddenly…?'

Grace's smile broadened. 'I've been meeting with my house group. Pastor Norman has been coming as well. Every night we've been praying for you. Praying that the jury would see through Josephine. But on Tuesday, the spirit moved in Lucile. She said we must pray for Josephine too. Oh, I know what you're thinking. After everything that woman has done, she doesn't deserve our blessing. I had the same reaction. But Lucile, Norman's wife, spoke with a passion. She reminded us of what the Lord said, "Love your enemies". No one is beyond God's love. So we prayed for Josephine and for you and, whatever happens at the trial, that God's will be done. And now she's confessed. Something's been unlocked in her and for once in her life, she's doing the right thing. Say something, Simon. Isn't it wonderful? Justice is going to be done.'

Snaz forced a smile.

Grace must have read his mind. 'I know it doesn't change that Curtis Rook is dead. Nothing can change what happened. Just remember him in your thoughts.'

His aunt reached across the table and took hold of both his hands. 'I had an idea on the underground on my way here. Yes, you'll have to serve a sentence for your part, but Eddie thinks you'll be free in a couple of years. When you get out, why don't we go to Guyana? Not for a holiday. I'm serious, Simon. It'd be a chance to make a fresh start.'

Snaz wondered about it. True, he had nothing to keep him here. No reason to stay in this country and every reason to leave. But even if Josie took the blame, he'd always know the truth. Regardless of the outcome of the trial, wherever he went, his guilt would be there.

Epilogue

As they approached the Quaker Meeting House, Josie went over her story again in her mind. She was Christine's niece from Southampton. She was staying with Christine and Roger for a few weeks as she'd split up with her boyfriend and had come to London to make a fresh start. The part about making a fresh start was true at least.

Josie hoped she'd remember to introduce herself as Denise if anyone spoke to her. She still hadn't got used to her new identity.

'You'll have to go out and meet people some time.' Christine had given her a pep talk over breakfast. 'Just be yourself.' But which self was she supposed to be?

Inside, the Meeting House looked far less formal than she'd been expecting – nothing like a church. Josie saw the chairs set out in a circle around a table, and hung back for a moment. She'd have preferred the anonymity of pews, where she could slip in at the back and not be seen.

On the table stood a vase of daffodils, their petals beginning to unfurl. No sign anywhere of a vicar or priest. She sat next to Christine in the outer row of the circle and tried to work out who might be in charge. Other people came in and, without talking, found a place...a woman with dreadlocks; a man in his seventies wearing frayed jeans. A younger man moved so an ancient woman with a Zimmer frame could have a seat near the door.

Many of the people sat with their eyes closed. Josie closed hers too and concentrated on her breath. She uncrossed her legs, shuffled to get comfortable and let her hands relax, palms facing upwards on her thighs.

Sounds punctured the silence: traffic, Roger's stomach rumbling, a bird chirruping outside.

Once more Josie focused on her breath. In prison, she'd become good at meditating, but today thoughts occupied her mind. Blueberries! Not once in Holloway had she eaten blueberries, and it struck her as the most urgent thing to go to a supermarket and buy some. Blueberries, and cherries too – she missed the colour of cherries as much as their taste.

Only a quarter of an hour gone. Most of the meeting still to sit through. She'd spent so much time in jail simply being, that now she wanted to *do* something, to get on with the rest of her life.

Josie had a technique in meditation for when she couldn't let go of her thoughts: to think of people in her life, and silently wish them well.

First she thought of Christine, who'd started out as her prison visitor but soon became her friend. Every week, without fail, Christine would be there to listen, encourage her, and hold her hand. Christine accepted her without condition; never mind what she'd done. She always gave her such total attention, as though it wasn't only Josie who lived for their half-hour meetings each week.

She gave thanks too for Roger, Christine's partner, who'd helped her to laugh again. 'Josie, that was truly awful,' he'd said when he'd finished the ratatouille she'd prepared for the three of them last night, not a speck of sauce left on his plate. 'That was without a doubt the worst ratatouille I've ever eaten in my life.' She thought of them both: their kindness and generosity, and their love for one another. She wished them many more happy years together.

Next, Josie thought of the wardens in jail, particularly Cooke, who'd treated her like dirt at first but finally put in a good word for her parole.

Then she thought of Snaz, pictured him the first few times they'd gone out together, his smile that had melted her even then. She'd heard that he'd emigrated. Wherever he was, whoever he might be with, she wished him happiness and hoped that one day he'd be able to forgive her.

'Friends...' A man's voice disturbed her meditation. He spoke from the far side of the meeting room. 'I've been reflecting on the words in John's Gospel, "God is love". It doesn't say that God is loving, or only loves us if we do the right things. It states that God *is* love. Love and God are the same. Now, the Bible also says – I don't recall where it comes – we are created in God's image. If that's the case, then our essence – our true identity – must also be love.'

After a few seconds he continued. 'When our lives seem to be without meaning, perhaps it's because we aren't expressing the love that we are. I know from experience that when I hurt someone, when I'm unkind, or sharp, or focused on my own agenda, I feel small. I feel separate and cut off. But I also know that when I warm to people, it warms my heart. When I offer love, I expand and feel more fully alive. When I give of myself, I do receive.' He paused. 'Maybe that's all we need do, Friends. Be ourselves. Let our light shine. Share the love that we are.'

Josie opened her eyes and looked at the man as he sat back down: scruffy, middle-aged and unshaven. And then, in the row behind him, she noticed someone else. Sitting with his head bowed, still with his eyes closed, she recognised Pete. Pete, her ex-boyfriend. Pete, who knew what she'd done.

At the end of the Meeting, everyone shook hands with their neighbours. Christine shook Josie's hand and then Roger did, and then the woman in front of her. Josie leaned back to be out of Pete's sight line. It had been such a long time – she hadn't heard from him since before her arrest. She felt the same anxious tightness she'd felt while waiting to hear the outcome of her parole board. How would Pete react to her? It might be best to slip out without speaking to him. But she wondered how he was doing. And to see him here after so many years – she couldn't not say hello.

After someone had spoken about the charity collection and about a bring-and-share lunch next weekend, people shuffled out into an adjoining room. Roger and Christine stood up. 'Are you coming for a coffee?' Christine asked her.

'In a moment. You go ahead.'

Pete also stayed seated until only the two of them remained in the room.

She acknowledged him with a smile and her tension lifted a little when he smiled back. He got up and came over to her. His hair had begun to thin, and he wore glasses, but otherwise he hadn't changed.

'Hi,' she said to him, standing and holding out a hand.

After a moment he took it, gently to begin with then more firmly. 'Josie, I couldn't believe it when I saw you. I thought you were... How long have you been out?'

'Less than two weeks.'

'Wow. Only? It's been ages since...'

'Eleven years.'

He appeared to be as nervous as her.

'So how are you these days, Pete?'

'I'm well,' he said. 'I'm okay. What about you? What are you doing *here*?'

'I'm staying with Christine and Roger for a month or two. Christine used to visit me in Holloway. She's... We've become friends.'

'Right, I heard she visits people in prison. I didn't realise she'd been visiting you.'

Josie nodded. 'She's remarkable.' What else to say to him? 'So, are you a Quaker then?'

'Yes,' he said. 'You?'

'No, this is my first time at a meeting. I enjoyed it though. I found it very peaceful, or I did until I saw you and then I almost had a heart attack! I still can't get over you being here.'

'Me neither,' he said, appearing to relax. 'You look well.'

'Thanks. You do too. Are you... Are you with someone?'

'Here? Today? No.'

'I mean generally. Are you married?' she asked.

'No. I'm in a relationship. Her name's Nicola.'

'Oh, I'm pleased for you.'

He glanced towards the door and for a moment she thought he wanted to get away from her, but then he said, 'Shall we get a coffee?'

'Sure.'

They went out together and joined the disorganised queue for drinks. Josie spotted Christine chatting with the woman with a walking frame.

'It's good to see you,' Pete said. 'And you're staying with Roger and Christine?'

'Until I find a flat for myself. They live in Highgate,' she added for no reason other than it being all she could think of to say. 'What about your family? Are they all okay?'

'They're fine. All fine. Actually, I'm meeting Adam this afternoon. Do you remember Adam? He's in London.'

'Adam?' Josie felt a quickening inside her. 'What, is he here on holiday?'

'No, he lives here. Works as a tube driver.'

'Adam *lives* in London? How come? Did he marry an English woman?'

'Yes.'

Josie felt her heart sink.

'Married one year, divorced the next. He has a son who he visits once a month, but his ex lives somewhere up north. Bolton, I think.'

'What will it be? Tea? Coffee?' the man serving the drinks asked them.

'Coffee,' Josie said. 'With milk, please.'

'Me too,' said Pete. 'You always used to drink your coffee black.'

She smiled. 'I've changed in a lot of ways.'

They took their cups and went to stand by some bookshelves

in a corner, away from the other people.

'Will you wish him my best?' Josie said.

'Who?'

'Adam,' she said, deflated. She was a fool for even entertaining the thought. Of course Adam wouldn't want to see her. Why on earth would he? He'd probably forgotten they'd ever met.

'Oh, yes, sure. Hey, do you know what's weird?' Pete said. 'The last time I saw him – Adam – he asked if you were still in prison, or if I'd been in touch with you. I said I hadn't seen you since you stayed with me in Poland. Strange coincidence, don't you think...that two weeks later you show up?'

About the Author

Peter M. Parr works part time as a civil servant, which gives him time to indulge his passion for writing. He facilitates workshops to encourage people to reflect on what truly matters. He lives in Hastings, East Sussex, overlooking the sea.

For more of his writing, visit www.thingstoremember.org.uk.

At Roundfire we publish great stories. We lean towards the spiritual and thought-provoking. But whether it's literary or popular, a gentle tale or a pulsating thriller, the connecting theme in all Roundfire fiction titles is that once you pick them up you won't want to put them down.